"A human," it snarled.

"There aren't many of your kind left." It stepped toward him, its sword tracing a figure eight in the air. "You like to play with steel, do you? Perhaps you'll lose your taste for it when you feel it snake through your entrails."

Belatedly, Bill remembered his own sword, and reached for it at his belt. The half-breed's weapon knocked his hand aside with a blow that left his wrist numb. The creature's blade drove forward, but Bill dove aside. He fully expected to feel the slash of steel, but inexplicably the creature staggered and fell.

A red garbed figure stood where the thing had loomed before.

"You saved my life. All our lives."

Bill stared at the figure there. What was it? Not a human being. He took in the other four who were gathering now, having bested their foes. He scarcely noticed the seven creatures lying dead.

"We were stupid to idle in the open," the figure in red went on. "If not for your warning, these orcs might have made their lunch of us."

"You're a cat," Bill said dully. He closed his eyes. When he opened them, the cat still stood there, upright and with all the mannerisms of a man, but with a fine gray fur covering the unclothed parts of its body. And with a face that was distinctly feline.

It responded stiffly, "We are felpurs, not cats."

The League of the Crimson Crescent
A Novel

James E. Reagan

PRIMA PUBLISHING

Dedication

To my wife, Donna, and Billy and Danny

ISBN: 1-55958-671-0
Library of Congress Catalog Card Number: 94-80091
Printed in the United States of America
95 96 97 98 EE 10 9 8 7 6 5 4 3 2 1

Chapter One

Cold. His head hurt. He lifted his hand and realized he was buck naked. He sat up with a start, grabbing his head–which threatened to whirl off into space–with both his hands. He'd never felt so peculiar in his life. Or so totally, entirely naked.

He chanced letting go of his head with one hand long enough to blindly feel around the floor of the cave around him. Nothing. No jeans, no sport shirt, no jacket. No boots, socks, or underwear. Every stitch gone. Even the cave lantern he'd bought this morning.

He wasn't even in the same part of the caverns as when he'd run into that stray stalactite–or whatever it was that had hit him. There wasn't much light here, and no guide, no fellow spelunkers. Some light seeped around the boulder he huddled behind, but that was all.

What had happened? He'd been bringing up the rear of a simple twelve–person private tour of a fairly extensive group of caverns in the Adirondak mountains when suddenly he...what? Bumped his head on a stalactite or something? All he remembered was a plunge into a sudden darkness without limit.

Could he have been waylaid by someone and dragged back here to be robbed and stripped in privacy? Wonderful. Even the state parks weren't off–limits for thugs these days.

He heaved a sigh. Despite being completely in the buff, he had to try to attract somebody's attention. "Hey! Any-

1

body out there?"

His voice echoed back to him. The tour had gone on. Marvelous. He'd have to catch up with it, naked and barefoot. Oh boy, was somebody going to pay for this.

As he lurched to his feet, his head swam, then steadied. The stone floor of the cave wasn't meant for walking barefoot. Wouldn't his grandmother have a fit if she heard about this. She worried if he got wet in the rain, if he missed a meal.

Bill picked his way gingerly around the boulder. His grandparents worried about him way too much. They got worked up if he even took a date to dinner, though he was certainly old enough to already have a wife and family. He worked in New York City, rode in on the train with his grandfather every morning, suited up and equipped with leather briefcase, to take his place behind his desk at the family accounting firm. Every evening he rode back to the suburbs, ate dinner with Grandmother Evans, and spent a few hours with a book or the TV, turning in early enough to repeat the same routine the next day.

If only his parents had lived…things might have been different. *He* might have been different. But every time he tried to do something risky, his grandparents made him swear he wouldn't.

"We lost your parents," Grandmother Evans would say tearfully. "We couldn't bear to lose you, too."

"How about fencing, Billy?" Grandfather Evans had suggested. "Now, that's a good, safe sport. Active enough to keep a young man in shape."

So Bill took up fencing, a sissy occupation for someone his size. It was one of his few extracurricular activities. In time, he began to worry that, under his grandparents' constant devotion, he would become an old bachelor.

He loved his grandparents, he truly did. But he needed some space. This little spelunking jaunt in the Adirondacks had been like a baby's first step toward independence. He'd decided to make small changes, first doing something over which his grandmother would merely tut–tut like a tour of some perfectly safe caverns.

At least, they were supposed to be safe. The brochures hadn't said anything about being knocked out, and waking up naked and bewildered.

Beyond the boulder, he paused to get his bearings. He'd been lying in a side chamber. Here, the main tunnel disappeared to his right into absolute darkness. To his left, it gave a hint of daylight. He turned left.

He saw something next to the wall as he picked his way along. Bending, he took a closer look. Bones. Not little bones either, but the remains of something as large as Bill. They looked fresh, too. He couldn't bring himself to touch them, but he felt pretty sure there were bits of flesh still attached.

He felt his way forward again with sensitive feet, forgetting now to worry about the fact that other sensitive parts of his anatomy were too exposed for comfort. Did grizzly bears live in these mountains? What else would drag something man–size into a cave and eat it raw?

When he stepped into the sunlight, he'd never felt so relieved. *Safe!* he thought.

That's when the creature jumped him. He got a quick impression of something out of a Japanese monster movie. It moved in an upright stride, and sported a head, two legs, two arms, fingered hands, a misshapen face covered with what looked like open sores, and bloodshot eyes. Part of Bill's mind shouted, *Animal!* The other part came to an abrupt stop as he realized the creature wore clothes—crudely fashioned leather garments beneath a voluminous cloak.

The creature tightened an iron–like grip around his throat. Bill saw its mouth move and heard a vile, cooing voice growl, "A tasty morsel here."

The man–creature forced him to the ground, only then releasing one hand from his throat to fumble for a weapon beneath its cloak. Bill tore at the hand still around his throat. He grasped a small finger and snapped it back, breaking it, while the creature slashed his side with some kind of blade. Bill's flailing hands found a sizable rock. Strengthened by fear, he smashed it into the creature's nose.

The thing howled and rolled away, clutching its face. Bill scrambled to his knees and brought the rock down again, this time bashing its skull. It went slack.

Breathing hard, Bill stumbled away from the thing, not daring to take his eyes off it, not daring to believe he'd actually killed it.

He blinked hard. Was he dreaming? Was he really lying in his bed back in New York thrashing in his sleep, having just fought and killed his own pillow? If so, he wanted to wake up now.

He looked around—experiencing something truly awful in that moment. To his surprised horror, he realized he wasn't in New York at all anymore. The terrain before him held nothing in common with the Adirondak mountains.

The knife slash in his side gave him something on which to focus. Though the wound was only skin–deep, he felt himself begin to shiver with shock. He felt nauseous. What was going on? Movie monsters that killed and ate men raw? Strange landscapes? And him naked as a newborn baby?

He again approached the creature–cautiously. He picked up the thing's knife and poked it at the body. Convinced it wouldn't suddenly spring back to life, he searched it, looking for some clue to this bizarre string of events. Under the creature's cloak he found a small leather bag of gold coins. Real gold, such as hadn't been in circulation since way before his time.

The coins weren't American, at any rate. They were stamped with a crowned image. Nonetheless, gold is gold, wherever it's from, wherever you are. You didn't need to be an accountant to know that.

If his confidence didn't exactly rally, at least his practicality did. He stripped the creature, cutting off a good–sized strip of the cloak to wrap around his middle as a bandage. Then, he donned the rest of the leather garments.

"I'm ready for Halloween," he muttered, though nothing about this situation struck him as humorous. His mind raced, trying to figure it out. Maybe he'd just been in the wrong place at the wrong time and was singled out for some weird secret government test: How far can we push a man before his mind bends? How far until it shuts down altogether?

He looked back at the cave. What would happen if he went back in? Would he pass out again and wake up in the Adirondacks? As he stood there, he saw a soft glow that hadn't been there before. He stepped in and shouted, "Hey! Anybody there?"

No answer, but the glow seemed brighter. Warily, he moved deeper into the cavern.

Around the boulder where he'd wakened, he found the

chamber now lit with strange radiance. And he saw something he hadn't seen before: an intricately carved stone altar. Atop it, like something out of a medieval fairy tale, lay an ornate sword. The unearthly light emanated from this magnificent weapon. Bill edged toward it, drawn by some desire he couldn't name. His hand reached for the sword's hilt.

He couldn't explain even to himself how picking up that sword felt right. The hilt fit his hand precisely. By its own glow, he studied the engravings on both the blackened hilt and the tempered blade—fine, spidery writing in some outlandish language. He stretched it out, feeling its weight and balance. In his old fencing days, he'd mostly used foils, but his instructor owned two beautiful antique swords he let his better students try on rare occasions.

He made a sweeping arc, and the movement seemed to bring the sword to life. Bill felt a pulse, a tremble move up into his arm. It seemed to course right through his body, as if it contained some pent up force eager to fuse with him. The sensation felt like solace, like his grandmother's arms after a childhood grief, like words of praise from his grandfather, like what he imagined he'd feel when he finally found his life's mate. Comfort. With a little edge of bliss.

A sheath for the sword lay on the altar. He fastened it to the rough belt he'd taken from the creature but used the blade to light his way back to the cave's entrance. As he stepped into the daylight again, the weapon lost its glow. He sheathed it.

Magic time was over. The creature still lay dead. The not–New–York landscape surrounded him. "I'm at a party and someone's slipped me a hallucinogen," he said softly, though by now he'd stopped hoping he was either hallucinating or dreaming. He was here. Wherever here was and however he'd arrived.

A faint path wound away from the cave's mouth across a stretch of open land. Following it into some woods, he continued for maybe half an hour before coming to a meadow. He heard voices and ducked behind a tree. What now? Somehow, he didn't think he could count on the voices being those of State Forest employees. In fact, he almost hoped it wouldn't be, because he could see the headlines now, "Bill Evans Found in Woods Toting Sword and Knife, Dressed Like a Barbarian." That wouldn't make Grandmother happy, nor would it fit the image of the solid citizen accountant who never missed a day of work, never came in so much as fifteen minutes late. Yet...his hand strayed to his knife all the same.

Five upright, human-shaped figures stood in the meadow, about a hundred feet from him. Something about them struck him as different. For one thing, they wore unusual clothing, all bright yellows and reds. They seemed to be packing up after a lunch break. Hikers? He opened his mouth to call to them but heard a limb snap to his left. He again spun for cover. Eyes sharp, he detected skulking movements within the trees. A yellow fang glinted, and yes, he glimpsed an unquestionably misshapen face. More creatures like the one Bill had killed back at the cave were edging in on the group in the meadow.

The travelers in the meadow didn't notice. To his shame, Bill considered just keeping quiet, just staying safe, under cover. After all, it was none of his business. He didn't even know where he was, and he certainly didn't need to get involved in more trouble.

The image of those bones in the cave surfaced in his mind, along with those cooing words, *A tasty morsel here.*

He stepped from behind the tree. "Watch out! In the woods. They're after you!" He began to trot toward the five.

One of the travelers pulled a sword. Another whipped out a bow and notched an arrow. "Drop your weapon, stranger, or I'll put a bolt through your throat," shouted the female archer.

Bill stopped short, realizing he had his knife in his hand, raised as if to strike. Though he didn't drop the blade, he lowered it. He pointed to the woods. "I'm not the one you have to worry about. There...see those things in the trees?"

An arrow whizzed by his ear, and he dove for the earth. As another arrow buried itself not eight inches from his shoulder, he realized the creatures—not the female traveler—were shooting at him.

He rolled onto his back and saw one of the beasts moving toward him like a blur. He vaulted to his feet, knife in hand, and lifted it just in time to greet his assailant.

The animal—like shriek shocked him as much as the impact of puncturing the creature that slammed up his arm. Bill yanked up hard with his knife. Another scream said he'd reacted correctly. He pulled the knife out and plunged it in again. As the thing fell to the ground, he kicked it for good measure. Then bent and slashed its throat to make sure it didn't attack him or anyone else again.

He'd never killed a thing in his life before today, and now he butchered without a second thought. What the hell was going on? Where was he? What was he becoming?

He scanned the meadow, saw that the group was under attack, and again considered the safety of the trees but only briefly. For whatever good it might do, he headed toward the main brawl.

The five had put their backs together in a circle. The archer, unable to get off her arrows at such close quarters, swung her big bow like a club. The others wielded heavy swords. One, battling two creatures at once, went to his knees and would soon be done for. Bill ran to help him. He drove his knife into the back of an attacker's neck, shoving hard to sever the spinal cord. As the creature fell limp, he tried to stab the second one's neck, but he missed, and the knife slid into the thing's shoulder. It grunted in surprise, twisting on its legs. Its height—and its looks—surprised Bill. It seemed to be some unholy half-breed, part beast, part human. Its manlike eyes glinted cruelly, marking more cunning intelligence than its companions. Regardless, Bill thrust his knife at its belly.

With a simple sweep of its sword, the creature easily knocked Bill's blade aside. He stepped back, frightened by the ease with which the half-breed defended itself.

"A human," it snarled. "There aren't many of your kind left." It stepped toward him, its sword tracing a figure eight in the air. "You like to play with steel, do you? Perhaps you'll lose your taste for it when you feel it snake through your entrails."

Belatedly, Bill remembered his own sword and reached for it at his belt. The half-breed's weapon knocked his hand aside with a blow that left his wrist numb. The creature's blade drove forward, but Bill dove aside. He fully expected to feel the slash of steel, but inexplicably the creature staggered and fell.

A red garbed figure stood where before the thing had loomed.

"You saved my life. All our lives."

Bill stared at the figure. What was it? Not a human being. He took in the other four who were now gathering, having bested their foes. He scarcely noticed the seven creatures lying dead.

"We were stupid to idle in the open," the figure in red went on. "If not for your warning, these orcs might have made their lunch of us."

"You're a cat," Bill said dully. He closed his eyes. When he opened them, the cat still stood there, upright and with all the mannerisms of a man, but with a fine gray fur covering the unclothed parts of its body. And with a face that was distinctly feline.

It responded stiffly, "We are felpurs, not cats. We may owe you our lives, but rudeness does not go unpunished in these parts." The felpur looked at Bill more closely. "From your clothing, however, it would appear that a savage like yourself can hardly be expected to have manners."

"Look, I'm sorry if I offended you. But, well, I'm not having a very good day. My name is Bill Evans, and I started a guided caving tour into the Adirondacks, and well, I'm not sure what happened. Something or somebody knocked me out, I think, and I woke up in a cave not far from here. I was stark naked, and one of those things would have made me a between—meal snack if I hadn't bashed its head with a rock."

He stopped, realizing how crazy he sounded. He wiped his forehead with his wrist. "Okay...let's just say I'm lost. And startled. I've never met a felpur before."

The cat, or felpur, looked disbelieving. The female stepped forward. "He saved our lives, remember Zorth?"

"Quite right." The felpur gravely bowed his head at Bill. Straightening, he said, "I am Zorth Taba–Bethan, and these are my escorts–and my litter sister Quatar." They bowed to Bill. When they straightened, Zorth gestured to the dead creatures and ordered, "Search them."

Bill tried to stay focused. Cats. He wasn't dreaming, wasn't hallucinating. This was real. Whether he understood it or not, it was real.

Zorth was watching him, so he cleared his throat. "You call them orcs?"

"All but that one." He gestured to the half–breed that had nearly impaled Bill on its sword. "That's some kind of abomination, neither orc nor human. It appears to have been the leader of this little band."

"It seemed surprised to see me, said there weren't many of my kind left."

"There aren't many humans left, at least not around here. Few of your species roam free anymore, though the felpur never subscribed to the views of those who would cage all that remain."

"How nice." Bill's sarcasm was lost on the felpur. "And just where is here?"

Disbelief again crossed Zorth's feline face. "You really are lost? Well, considering that we owe you our lives, would you like to travel with us? These woods are dangerous."

Bill agreed. What option did he have?

The female archer, Quatar, brought him two handfuls of gold, silver, and copper coins. "Evidently this bunch has plundered often and well. Here is your share."

Bill stared at the coins. When he didn't take them, she spoke with the exaggerated patience of a kindergarten teacher.

"These orcs plunder many unwary travelers. This is what we found on them. You earned a share. They have no need for it, since they're..."

"Dead. Yes, I understand. I'm lost, not stupid." He took the coins.

She stepped back, ruffled. "If you're coming with us, you might wish to exchange clothes with that one." She pointed to the half–breed's body, dressed in bright clothes similar to that of the felpurs. "Wearing those skins, someone might mistake you for one of those..." Though she didn't finish the thought, her nose wrinkled with aversion.

Bill nodded and turned to the task of undressing another dead creature.

When he came out of the woods dressed like his new allies, Zorth said, "We must move on. If we tarry, more trouble may come looking for us."

Bill asked, "Where are we going?"

"Trillius. Surely even you have heard of Trillius?"

Bill barely shook his head. The less he said the less crazy he would seem.

"It was once a great city," Zorth said sadly. "Since the coming of the current evil times, however, it serves mostly as a distraction, offering gaming halls, sporting events, and pleasure houses of all kinds."

"We're going there to search for our litter brother, Portnal," Quatar said. "He went there two moons ago and hasn't been heard from since."

"Maybe he never made it." Bill motioned to the orcs.

Zorth shook his head. "We heard from one of his party. Portnal and his companions made it to Trillius. But increasingly, people go to Trillius and never again come home.

Portnal went to Trillius to solve this mystery, and now he, too, has been swallowed up by the city."

They traveled for several hours, Bill all the while trying to make sense of this insanity. Finally, the company pitched camp for the night. Sitting around a fire, the felpurs shared their provisions with him. He took a first skeptical taste but found the food palatable.

Zorth brought up the subject foremost in his mind. "So you woke up in a cave, you say?"

Bill nodded. "I was exploring some caverns, like I said, and the next thing I knew I was stark naked in the dark, alone, and not anywhere near..." Should he say "home?" Home wasn't just New York. It was America. Earth. Was he even on his own planet?

Zorth eyed him and at length said, "In Trillius, you will find wise ones far more learned than I. They might help you. After we arrive, I will make inquiries."

Bill felt a little hope resurface.

Zorth said, musedly, "It must be strange, this land where you have no orcs."

"We have men who act like orcs, however, and deserve no better."

Zorth nodded, apparently reassured that no place was perfect.

Lying wrapped in his cloak that night, Bill felt close to tears. In the cool whisper of the wind, he heard the aching truth: He might never again see his beloved grandparents or his familiar world. In novels, sometimes the hero accidentally steps through some hole in the wall of what people think of as reality. If that could really happen, then he could very well be stuck here for the rest of his life.

The next morning, the strange band passed into Trillius, a great walled city that gave every appearance of a festival in progress. Musicians wandered the streets in bright costumes. Jugglers entertained, tossing flaming balls high in weird patterns with mesmerizing speed. Crowds gathered around magicians and soothsayers who offered wondrous secrets and boasted of mysterious herbs to cure myriad conditions.

Zorth said, "Every day is a carnival here."

Bill stared at the entertainment—and the populace—like a country yokel. Finding himself in the company of cat people had been a shock, but now he saw dog people, as well. "Rawulfs," Zorth dismissed them, "Indolent, obnoxious, and ugly."

They weren't ugly to Bill. In fact, he suppressed an impulse to pet one youngster playfully running alongside him. The felpurs hissed at the young rawulf, however, sending it scurrying off to its elders.

An eerie, furry beast, something resembling a tabloid photo of the abominable snowman, passed by. "A mook," Zorth said. A dracon accompanied the beast, chatting gaily. The dracon was a strange, horned, and dragon—like being, able to walk and talk like a human. Zorth warned, "It can breathe acid when angered." He hinted that the mook possessed even more fearsome abilities.

The menagerie included other creatures more human—like in appearance, but everything Bill saw only compounded his realization that he was far, far from home.

Zorth kept testing Bill's story of waking in a completely strange world. "You've never seen elves before? What kind of world has no dwarfs, hobbits, or even gnomes? Next you'll be telling us you've never seen a faerie." At Bill's expression, he shook his head. "You're better than the street entertainers. Stay close. I wouldn't want you to get into trouble."

Bill agreed, but turned as a crowd roared across the street. "Kill him! Kill him! Kill him!" Zorth and his band had stopped in front of an inn called the Prancing Robe. They showed no interest in the chanting crowd. Zorth said, "We're going to get something to eat and drink." Bill couldn't ignore the crowd across the street, however.

"Go ahead," Zorth said. "But don't wander far."

"You're starting to sound like his mother," Quatar said.

Bill crossed to the crowd, jammed together and shouting in unison. Over the head of a group of bearded, cackling gnomes, he saw the spectacle that riveted everyone's attention. Two reptilian creatures were locked in a deadly duel on a makeshift stage, their scaly, sweaty bodies grappling for a single wicked looking sword.

"Cobran is just playing with this one," a dwarf sniffed. "I've seen him slash a throat before the opening bell stops echoing."

"You know how lizardmen are," the dwarf's companion responded. "Sometimes they like to play with their victim before they kill it."

Bill sensed a shift in the fight. Suddenly, one combatant snapped the neck of the other, wrested the blade away, and beheaded its opponent with a fluid killing stroke. The lizard was headless in the blink of an eye.

"Cobran! Cobran! Cobran!" the crowd shouted for attention. "Tomorrow night!" he bellowed. "Cobran battles his latest challenger for Trillius' greatest honor—the championship! For only two silver pieces, you can watch him defend his title. Only one combatant will emerge alive from the ring."

Astonished, Bill turned for the Prancing Robe. Killing for sport! And what he'd just seen was only an outdoor exhibition to drum up business for a bigger fight tomorrow. This Trillius was quite a place. He gripped the hilt of his sword, hoping for a little of that consolation he'd felt yesterday.

The Prancing Robe was a large, three–story building of stone and wood. It reminded Bill of the many Adirondack inns he'd visited with his grandparents over the years. Its rustic charm comforted him in this strange, alien city. Inside, he found Zorth and the others sitting around an oak table, pouring ale into large mugs. A gentle fire flickered in a large open hearth in the center of the room. A pot of stew simmered, giving off a mouth–watering aroma. The felpur waiters hustled about serving the mostly felpur customers, although Bill saw a few elves and Dwarfs sprinkled among the tables.

Zorth and his companions had been joined by others, and as Bill pulled out a seat to join them, one of these strangers bounded to his feet.

"What are you doing?" the felpur snapped. "I know they let just about anyone in this place, but a human? Unchained? Where's your master?" With feline speed, he advanced. "Think you'll sit with us? Scum like you shouldn't be allowed in here. On my estate, a few lashes tend to give your kind the proper attitude, but since I haven't got my whip..." he drew his blade, "I'll have to make do."

Bill automatically drew his own sword. The blade pulsed in his hand as if with a life of its own. It flicked forward, batting the felpur's blade aside. Steel rang as his old fencing moves came back to him. His sword clanged with the felpur's again, and with a twisting move he wrenched the cat's blade right out of his hand. His sword tip danced lightly at the felpur's throat.

"Stop, Bill!" Zorth's voice.

Bill snapped, "I thought rudeness didn't go unpunished hereabouts." Eyes on the now cringing felpur, he added, "Or does that only apply to your kind?" He suddenly lowered his weapon and turned to the five felpurs he'd saved just yesterday. "I see I'm an embarrassment to you here," he said bitterly and turned for the tavern door.

His only thought was to lose himself in the reveling crowd. He heard Zorth shouting his name, but he didn't turn. He resented that the felpurs he'd helped yesterday hadn't lifted a hand to defend him today. He'd been stunned—and yes, frightened—when the felpur whipped out his blade with such practiced speed.

The hilt of his sword in his hand still pulsed. What kind of weapon was it? He'd been as surprised as anyone when he'd disarmed the cat so effortlessly. Had it been his old skills or this strange sword? He recalled that moment when the tip of the blade paused menacingly at the felpur's throat. Just a tiny lunge on Bill's part, and the cat would be dead.

The fight crowd poured into the cavernous doors of an establishment called the Twisted Tail, a building that dwarfed the Prancing Robe. It occupied more than a New York City block. Preoccupied, Bill followed the others inside.

He discovered a dimly lit amphitheater with seating for thousands, all facing a central arena. A painting of Cobran the lizardman hung beside booths where bookies were taking bets at fifty–to–one odds.

Bill by now understood that free–roaming humans were unwelcome in Trillius. Accordingly, he found a table in a darkened corner. A Gnome waiter brought him a tankard of ale. He tossed a few copper, silver, and gold coins onto the table. The Gnome scooped up a copper and left. Bill grinned as he lifted his drink. Evidently, they hadn't heard about inflation here.

He brooded. Did the confrontation at the Prancing Robe mean the loss of his only friends in this place? He regretted his high–and–mighty refusal to respond to Zorth outside the tavern. Blowing the frothy head of his ale aside, he took a deep swallow. He couldn't afford to be proud. So what if the felpurs hadn't leapt to his defense? He was lost in a land peopled by walking, talking dragons, lizards, cats, and dogs, a land where gnomes, hobbits, dwarfs, and elves were unremarkable–but an unchained human brought stares–he couldn't be too choosy about the few friends he had.

Sitting alone in the semi–dark, he admitted that his deep–down fear, as much as the felpur's insults, had goaded him to the brink of killing again. Discovering that his sword would do just about anything he wanted hadn't helped, either. He'd only been in this world about twenty–four hours, and already he was a stranger to himself.

He felt tired. His mind strained and strained to make sense of his predicament. Part of him still insisted this was all just a dream, an illusion. He'd wake any time now...and what? Find himself strapped in a strait jacket, lying in a padded cell?

That was what one part of his mind both hoped for and feared. The other part feared something much worse: that he'd never waken and would come to realize he was really here to stay.

He ought to go find Zorth and apologize. He ought to be

looking for a way to get home. He ought to be doing many things besides sitting here, drinking alone in a strange place among decidedly strange creatures. Instead of rising, he motioned to the Gnome to refill his tankard.

For the moment, he could think no more. He couldn't even make himself move. He just wanted to sit in this dark corner and drink himself silly.

Chapter Two

Out on the street, Zorth fluently cursed Bill. "Temperamental, furless, bone-headed human! Where could he have gone?"

"It's a big town," Quatar replied.

"He questioned my honor! My manners! It wasn't my fault Hovra behaved like a boorish fool." A powerful emotion, one he didn't care to examine too closely, filled Zorth. "Temperamental, furless, bone-headed human! Where could he have gone?"

"Bill is a stranger to our ways," Quatar said, unperturbed by her brother's anger. "He just may have assumed, since he helped save our lives at great risk to his own, that we would do more than just stand by while he was subjected to insults and threats. But as you said, he's a barbarian." She shrugged, adding sarcastically, "He should have known better."

"Are you trying to make me feel worse?"

"We must remember that he's not from our land. Did you see the way he looked around as we passed through the city? I bet he's never visited any place this large or grand. From whatever village he hails, they must never see any outsiders—no elves, or dracons, or even a mook. He can't know how he's expected to react when someone like Hovra challenges him. He's probably just not used to his friends letting their friends draw steel on him."

Zorth sighed at his sister's admonitions. "I should have stopped Hovra."

"Yes—for Hovra's sake. Did you notice how Bill's sword seemed a part of him? Hovra's fortunate to be alive." She smiled. "He was trembling by the time Bill finished with him. I've watched Hovra fight before. He's quick and as deadly as he is ill-tempered, but Bill easily disarmed him."

"I suppose I'll have to apologize," Zorth said. "To a human. Me, a member of the Seven Families, a Priest of Yalor, humbling himself before a hairless monkey whose clothes smell like..."

"Like the abomination leading that pack of orcs who would have killed us if not for Bill. He may be a barbarian, but we are not. We're supposed to behave better." Looking into Zorth's eyes, she asked, "If you had been alone in the woods, lost, and saw a raiding party of orcs about to jump a group of humans, would you have warned them?"

Zorth's eyes shifted away from his sister's steady gaze.

"Until a few days ago, either of us would have gone our merry way. We would have seen little difference between an orc and an human. We might even have found it amusing to watch them kill each other. Certainly, we would never have risked our own lives to save Bill, had the tables been turned. You know it, and so do I."

She put a hand on Zorth's shoulder. "I'm just as guilty as you are. I've never liked humans. We've been taught not to believe those who claim they're lower forms of life —and intellectually, I accept that. But in my liver? No. When I first saw Bill in the meadow, I came close to dropping him with an arrow. I thought he was trying to trick us. When the orcs attacked, I figured he was with them, part of their trap. If I hadn't been jumped by an orc, my next arrow would have pierced Bill Evans' heart."

Zorth put his hand over hers, smoothing her fur. "Your wisdom, like your arrows, is unerringly on target," Zorth said.

"I'm just saying that he may be human, but he's a re-markable human, and we've treated him horribly. We never even thanked him properly, because we let our prejudice get in our way. I feel guilty, and I don't like it, so I'm taking it out on you."

"You're doing a fine job, too. So, where do we find this remarkable human?"

"We'll have to check the taverns."

"Do you have any idea how many taverns there are in Trillius?

"I think we're about to find out. While we're searching for Bill, we can also ask about our litter brother."

"That's true." Zorth grinned. "We'll probably find Portnal sitting in some tavern soaked in beer. He's probably explored every house of pleasure in the city."

"I wish I could really believe that."

Zorth's grin failed. "I do, too. But I can't shake this feeling that he's here, somewhere, and that he needs us."

"I just hope he's alive," Quatar said. "The elders were not too clear about the dangers we'd find in Trillius."

"They probably didn't know. We just have to be very care-ful. Something evil lurks in this city."

"You're certain we can't just convince Cobran to throw the fight?"

Bill couldn't remember how many tankards he'd drank. He didn't know how long he'd been asleep, either. He'd rested his head on his arm and slipped off. Waking now, he over-heard two strangers in a nearby booth, talking in low voices. He didn't bother to lift his head from his arm. He was too comfortable. Besides, the conversation interested him.

"Someone once suggested that he throw a fight," one speaker said. "The crazy reptile killed him." He snapped his fingers. "Just like that! Broke his neck."

"Doesn't he understand the crowds don't come to watch him anymore? The gate receipts are way down. The bookies tell me no one will bet against him. If he'd throw this fight, we'd be richer than the Regent. A few well-placed bets. Won't he listen to reason?"

"Listen to yourself, Klorgo. He's a lizardman. Killing is all he understands. His pitiful excuse for a brain makes it impossible for us to reason with him. He doesn't care how many people show up. He's not interested in the money. He likes being the champion, likes the way the crowd shouts his name, likes the way they part when he walks into a room. The only way he'll give that up is if he's killed in the ring himself."

"That could be arranged."

"What are you talking about?"

"It's simple," the one called Klorgo said. "We bet every-thing we have against him. Everything. Then we poison him. He dies, and we're rich."

"You're crazy. They'd know."

"Not if we use a poison that doesn't kill him right off." Klorgo added, "I know of something that would just disori-ent and slowly drain him."

"What if he beats the challenger before it takes effect? It's too risky. With our luck, he'd die after he won the match."

"There's a way to fix that problem," Klorgo insisted. "We doctor his weapons to make sure they break. Then, he can't kill the challenger. It would explain why he lost, too. A freak accident. Meanwhile, we're rich, and no one's the wiser."

Bill, his head still on his arm, could almost hear Klorgo's skeptical friend thinking.

At last, Klorgo's cohort responded, "It could work." He laughed cautiously. "It could make us very wealthy."

Bill recalled the exhibition match in which he'd watched Cobran behead his opponent. Though he had no desire to spend time with the likes of this lizardman, Bill felt touchy right now on the subjects of justice and fairness, right versus wrong. Yes, he'd had quite a bit to drink, but this Cobran didn't deserve to be poisoned. He deserved better than to have a fight rigged against him.

Bill opened his eyes enough to see the speakers, two dracons, leave their booth. They noticed Bill, and Klorgo seemed startled. He glared at Bill with the look a dog gives just before it bites. Bill tensed.

"Just a drunk," the other said. "He didn't hear us."

"Maybe we should kill him to be sure?" Klorgo was already reaching for his dagger.

His companion grabbed his arm as the waiter returned. "Don't be a fool," he hissed. "We don't need to draw any attention to ourselves today. He's just a human. He wouldn't understand what we were talking about even if he was awake and sober. Who would listen to him, anyway?"

As they walked away, Bill whispered to himself, "I think we'll be seeing each other again." He stood, a bit unsteadily. "That's powerful ale," he muttered.

He waited to make sure he didn't run into the dracons

again as he left the inn. Standing in the street, he looked up and down its length. "So where to?" He didn't know where he was, didn't know how to get home. He didn't even know where "home" was anymore. The only friends he had were cats with bad manners.

He shook his head. Upset as he was with the felpurs, they were his only friends now. He was walking along a narrow way amid unknown dangers and had to use whatever stepping stones he could find. He headed toward the Prancing Robe.

Zorth and Quatar sat alone at a table. They rose when Bill entered. "Thank the Gods," Zorth said, pulling out a seat.

"We thought you'd never return," Quatar said.

"We wouldn't blame you." Zorth, still standing, looked both relieved and uncomfortable to see Bill. "I must apologize, Bill, for acting so badly. I forgot the debt we owe you—as well as my manners."

"Let's forget it," Bill said.

Quatar leaned forward across the table. "You saved our lives, and we repaid you by standing idle while Hovra insulted you."

"We've never known a human before, and, well, we were ashamed to admit in front of our friends that we knew you. We have dishonored ourselves, our litter, and our clan by our actions."

Bill hadn't expected anything like this. Obviously, Zorth wasn't the type to apologize easily. "Look, you're the only friends I have in this world. Where I come from, we have a custom of drinking together to show there are no hard feelings. Sit down, and we'll have a toast."

Zorth sat stiffly, motioning a waiter to bring a tankard for Bill. "I'm again in your debt. If someone acted toward me the way I have toward you, I would have challenged him to a duel."

"You forget," Bill said, "I'm only a human, a barbarian with no sense of manners." He laughed. "I don't like to fight with my friends. I don't like this talk about how you owe me, either. It makes me think you would have nothing to do with me otherwise. In my culture, you do what you can to help your friends, simply because they're friends."

Quatar rose and lifted her tankard. "Here's to our friendship!"

"To friendship." Zorth joined her.

The three drank deeply.

Seated again, Zorth wiped his mouth and smiled self-consciously. "Your customs seem strange but pleasing."

Bill grinned. "Now, let's forget what happened earlier. I want to talk about this championship fight tomorrow. The one with Cobran."

"What possible interest could you have in that?" Quatar asked.

"From what I know, it's simply lizardmen tearing one another apart," Zorth said. "Such amusements divert the people here. They like blood and gore."

Bill told them about the conversation he'd overheard.

"What does that have to do with us?" Zorth asked. "So someone is rigging a fight? These things no doubt happen wherever large sums of money can be made by the lazy and the wicked."

"I don't think it's right," Bill said, surprised by his heat.

"I'm tired of standing by and letting others get hurt. How do I contact the authorities about this?"

"If you're asking who is in charge of the fight, I suspect it's the very people you overheard," Quatar said.

"Well, then, who is in charge of the city?"

The two felpurs looked blankly at him.

"This place must have a city hall, a government, someone who enforces the law."

"Laws do exist," Quatar said slowly, "but..."

"Who is the leader?"

"Of the kingdom?"

"The kingdom? Then, there's a king?"

The two felpurs' ears flattened against their skulls. "Have you lost your mind?" Zorth hissed, while Quatar's eyes darted around the room to see who might be listening.

Relaxing, she said, "You must not speak of Him, must not ask about Him. No one does."

"I can't believe you would be such a fool," Zorth muttered.

"Easy, Zorth. Remember, this world is new to him. He doesn't know the danger in what he said. It's all right. No one heard."

Zorth let out a sigh, visibly relaxing. "I apologize again, Bill, for speaking too quickly."

Bill said, "You act as if I'd asked about the devil himself."

Again Zorth looked around the room. "Keep your voice down. You're speaking of things you know nothing about. A living devil, one that walks among us and feeds upon us."

"Shhh," Quatar placed her hand on her brother's wrist. "If someone hears you..."

"I don't understand," Bill said. He was surprised at their

obvious fear, which was even greater than when they were attacked by the orcs.

Zorth looked him steadily in the eye. "My friend, we are ruled by the Unnamed One, a demon-spawn possessing powers beyond our ken. To even speak of Him can draw His attention, some say. As a Priest of Yalor, I know that's not true. I studied enough of the mysteries to know the Unnamed One cannot actually hear us, but I know enough of the world to realize His spies skulk everywhere. They might hear, or someone in this tavern might tell His minions, just for the gold that crosses the palm of those who would turn us in."

"You're a priest?" Bill asked.

"I have studied the healing spells of Yalor as closely as the mace and the flail. I have much more to learn, but I've gained the wisdom to know that powers exist that even Yalor would be hard-pressed to stand before."

"This Unnamed One is that powerful?"

"You have no grasp," Quatar said. "Though He pays little attention to these lands. He rules from the Forbidden City to the north. We pay our tribute to His minions. Most of the time He ignores us. He appointed an Arch Regent to live in the castle at the heart of Trillius. She looks after the city for Him. She's as black-hearted and nearly as powerful as He.

"But as you've seen, the lands surrounding the city grow wilder. His orcs and other creatures walk freely, attacking unwary travelers. They come here to spend their booty. It's said the dead walk the darker streets at night. As a Monk, I've traveled far, studying the mysteries of Thea, unlocking the secrets of the mind; but the minds of those who do His bidding are beyond my ken."

"If He pays so little attention," asked Bill, "what stops people from eradicating these orc things? Challenge His rule, get a new monarch—if He's as evil as you say."

Zorth glanced around nervously. "Keep your voice down. If someone hears you, we'll be on the gallows—or worse—by dawn."

"If you knew more, you wouldn't ask such questions," Quatar hissed. "He pays less attention, because He's already crushed those who once stood against Him. He constantly extends His rule."

"Say no more," Zorth said abruptly, eyeing a gnome in a corner, staring back with rapt attention. "I don't think he heard us, but better to discuss such matters when fewer ears are nearby."

"Okay," Bill said, "but to whom do I turn to put a stop to this fight. There must be someone I can warn about what they plan to do to Cobran."

Quatar said, "The Guildlords run Trillius' civic affairs: the Gambling Hall Guildlords, the Tavern Guildlords, the Joy Guildlords—they run the houses of pleasure and so forth. If a problem arises, they resolve it in the Guild Council. When they need to quietly deal with a source of irritation, they turn to the Assassins' Guild. They all pay their tithes to the Arch Regent, who manages the royal affairs. If She shares in the profits of this scheme you've described, She'll be content."

"So there's no Office of Consumer Affairs, no bunco squad?" Bill's question drew only puzzled looks from his companions. "Who maintains order in the streets?"

"Each guild employs guards from the Warriors' Guild.

The Arch Regent has her Royal Guard—who are as likely to arrest you as to look at you."

"I'm on my own then."

Quatar said, "It's none of your concern and none of ours. Trillius can be an enjoyable place." Her shiver contradicted her words. "It offers delights for every sense. Stay out of its affairs, though, or you'll find it dangerous beyond comprehension. Do not intrude in the business of the Guildlords. They are ruthless."

Bill said nothing.

"You're not listening, are you?" Zorth said. "You hear our words, but they have no meaning.

"If the Guildlords even suspect you of interfering with them, they won't send their warriors after you. They'll send a Ninja trained to kill with a single blow. The assassins dress in black. They are masters of stealth and cunning. From childhood, they are taught only one thing: to kill, quickly and without detection. They never give up, once they accept a contract. If one fails, another takes up the challenge. No one has ever escaped them, at least no one brave enough to stay around and boast of it."

Chapter Three

The three friends took rooms for the night. Zorth and Quatar's felpur escorts had already left to return to their village. Bill offered to help search for the felpurs' brother, but the two needed to visit places frequented by their own kind. Bill napped while Zorth and Quatar resumed their search for Portnal. They agreed to meet for a late dinner.

Refreshed after sleeping off the effects of the ale he'd drunk, Bill decided to explore Trillius on his own. A few blocks down a side street, he came upon a disturbing sight: a caged human. He remembered the felpurs saying they hadn't seen many humans roaming free. Also, they had said they didn't share the views of those who believed all humans should be caged. At the time, the comments slid by him, as did Hovra's slurring demand to know where Bill's chain and master were. Now, everything became clear, including why Zorth and Quatar had been reluctant to admit their connection with Bill to their city friends.

The caged beings now before him explained it all, and the bland expressions of the bystanders indicated this was not an unusual sight.

A dozen chained and desolate-looking humans sat inside one cage, several men and one woman. Another man stood on an auction block, head bowed, shoulders slumped. Yet another crouched in a set of medieval-looking stocks, while a dracon enthusiastically whipped him. A crowd counted the strokes aloud in unison, apparently delighted by the man's cries of agony. Children, mainly little dracons and lizardmen, along with a few felpurs and dwarfs, taunted the caged human with sticks.

The adults eyed the man on the block with practiced expressions. One dracon stepped up to open the man's mouth to examine his teeth, then felt his biceps and thighs.

"He'd make a good worker in the mines," the auctioneer shouted. "Let's get the bidding going. Who'll start at a silver piece? These gentle creatures—they're not all like that one in the stocks —have been well broken. They're used to hard work. They were born for it. They just need a firm hand and proper direction."

A red-cloaked dracon leaving the auction muttered, "Who would want one? Disgusting, vile, sweaty creatures. They should all be exterminated." Bumping into Bill, the horned, scaly beast looked startled. "What in the name of the Gods is this?" he howled, stepping back and brushing himself off furiously, as if he'd touched something unclean. "How dare you touch me, you foul, pest-ridden piece of offal? Where's your master? How dare he let you walk around this way? What's that?" he shrieked, growing more hysterical as he pointed to the sword Bill fingered. "Who has allowed a human to be armed as if he was a citizen?"

"I don't want any trouble," Bill said. "Why don't you just go about your business?" The sight of his own kind being subjected to such humiliation and pain affected him deeply. He was already edgy and didn't know what he might do if this dracon didn't lay off him.

The dracon, however, had no intention of withdrawing. "Insolent orc-spawn! You maul me, then you insult me..."

At a loss for words repellent enough to express his disgust, the dracon resorted to a shove. "I'll have you whipped. I'll have your master whipped for releasing you from your cage. Imagine a creature such as yourself, prowling the streets, attacking decent citizens like a skulking jackal."

Bill recovered from the shove but a dark, unreasoning rage filled him. His hand clenched the hilt of his sword. He felt the weapon pulse to life. "I've heard enough nonsense," he growled in a low voice.

"How dare you speak to me that way." The dracon threw back his red cloak to draw a gleaming scimitar from his belt. "Prostrate yourself before me, or I'll cut out your entrails and strangle you with them!"

Bill drew his own sword. He smiled at the dracon as he felt the now familiar pulse electrify his hand and arm. "You talk too much, you scaly maggot. If you say one more word, I'll split those horns and use them to pluck your eyes out of your snout."

In the back of his mind, he wondered what he was doing, where all this anger came from. He couldn't pause to analyze his behavior now, though, not when the crowd's attention had shifted from the auction block to the confrontation in their midst. He heard gasps of surprise as the onlookers realized that at least one human hadn't been properly "broken" yet.

Even the humans stared in amazement. The one in the stocks craned his head, his bloody welts momentarily forgotten. The dracon with the whip stopped, too. The children pulled their sticks out of the cages to gape at Bill with wary shock.

Bill gave the dracon before him a look of contempt. The

creature stepped back, surprised that the sight of his scimitar alone hadn't cowed the "piece of offal" into submission. He drew courage from the expectant eyes of the crowd, however, and quickly regained his belligerence.

The thoughts seeping in the back of Bill's mind pushed forward: *I don't really want to fight anybody; I'm not the kind of person who wages battle with others.* But looking at the slaves around him, he knew he could never face himself again if he didn't wipe the smirks off the mouths of these onlookers. He'd start with this swaggering cock-of-the-walk in front of him.

"I'll give you one last chance," the dracon said, raising his voice for the benefit of his audience. "I don't want to kill anyone's property. Prostrate yourself, and I'll be satisfied with a simple whipping."

Bill sneered, "Is that blade merely for show?"

The dracon swung his sword in a fluid movement that would have severed Bill's head if his own blade hadn't caught it in mid-arc. He grunted as the collision of steel rang. The beast was strong, but Bill's hand and arm pulsed as his blade came alive. He again flicked the scimitar aside, and deftly snicked off the dracon's left horn. The creature squealed as blood spurted, pouring down into one eye. Bill felt squeamish at the sight. Had he done that? Really?

Seeing the deadly scimitar again coming toward him, he quickly recovered. He doubted that the dracon would feel any misgivings about letting his blood.

"I'll pluck your eyes out with that horn," he said, dodging a blow and responding with a slash to the dracon's knee. The creature's leg buckled. "Prostrate yourself before *me*, and I'll settle for a good whipping!"

The dracon shrieked in anger and tried to drive toward him with a stabbing motion. Bill stepped aside and watched his sword dip as if with a will of its own, lopping off the creature's head with a single stroke.

He feared he might throw up as he saw the dracon's head fall and roll in the dirt. At the same instant, a whip cracked across his back. As he arched in pain, he heard a voice shout, "Kneel or die, you insolent scum!"

Staggered by the unexpected blow, he heard a second crack of the whip. This was no time for second thoughts about defending himself. As he turned to face his new attacker, his blade shot out faster than his own eye or mind could follow, or that his past training could account for. The next thing he saw, the whip's leather tail lay on the ground. The dracon holding its handle stared in wonder. Bill's sword, on its own volition–he could honestly say he did not initiate the action–again leapt forward and stabbed the dracon in the chest.

Four others pulled their swords and came at him from different directions. He stepped toward the one to his right, spun, and with his sword, neatly spitted the dracon behind him. He pulled his blade free just in time to parry a thrust. Everything happened so fast, so intuitively, that he lost track. His blade moved everywhere at once, dancing with a life of its own, thrusting, parrying, slicing through the air, carving through leathery skin. He poked one beast in the eye, penetrating its brain. He lopped off an arm that got too close, cracked open a skull, slashed a throat.

Stepping back from the slaughter, he became frightened by what the sword in his hand had achieved. He felt the pulsing of the sword, as if it had a heart that beat, lungs that breathed. He turned, expecting a new assailant, but noticed that the crowd had drawn far back. Wary and frightened eyes studied him.

The changed expressions on the faces of the onlookers gave him a renewed sense of confidence strengthened by the reassurance the sword gave him. Bill walked straight into the crowd, which parted to make way for him as he advanced to the auction block.

"I bid one copper," he announced. "Who dares to bid against me?" He held his gory blade aloft for emphasis. "Come, come my good auctioneer. I bid one copper."

"For that man on the auction block?" the startled dracon asked.

"For the entire lot."

"This is entirely irregular," the auctioneer said. "I don't sell humans to humans."

"You don't?" Bill asked in what he hoped was his most menacing voice. "Then, maybe it's time you start. My money is just as good as anyone's." He looked at the crowd. "Does anyone care to question that?" he asked. "Does anyone question my right to bid?"

Though most of them would have liked to challenge his right, their eyes couldn't help but drift to the six dead dracons only a few yards from them.

"I can't sell this entire lot for one copper. Don't be ridiculous," the auctioneer said.

"You can't?" Bill asked. "You think you can get more from someone else? Do you really think that anyone else wants to buy these humans after my demonstrating how easy it is for us lowly humans to kill dracons? Do you really think any of them will ever again prostrate themselves at your feet? If they do, you'd better watch your feet, or you'll lose them.

Whoever told you that you can break humans forgot to mention how easy it is to un-break them. Just look at them if you don't believe me."

The sharp collective intake of breath suggested that his words were not lost on the audience. Anyone could see the change the humans had undergone. They were obviously awakened. They stood straight, unbowed.

Bill suspected the humans had listened just as closely and had taken their cue from his speech and actions. Although they didn't exactly look ferocious to him, they did seem less compliant and broken. A few shouted curses at the crowd. "Unchain me," the man in the stocks shouted. "I'll rip your throat out."

Bill smiled. "I'm doing you a favor," he said to the auctioneer, trying to sound reasonable. "I'll take them off your hands. You know you can never use these humans as slaves again, that you cannot allow them to mix with your other slaves. Word will spread, how easy it is to kill a master. The price for your slaves will drop.

"I'll give you two silvers for the lot." He eyed his sword, still dripping with blood. "You don't want to insult me, do you?" he asked, looking more intensely at the auctioneer.

"Take them and go far away," the auctioneer said. "I don't want them around here. I don't want you around here."

Bill removed two silvers from his purse and tossed them at the auctioneer. "I like doing business with a reasonable man. Perhaps I'll attend your next auction."

The auctioneer clearly wanted to say something in response. He almost choked on the words he held back. Instead, he unlocked the cage and set free the man in the stocks.

Bill motioned to the bodies on the ground. "Strip them,"

he said to the humans as they came out of the cage. "Bring me any money you find, collect the weapons, and see if any of their clothing is still of any use."

A few in the crowd leaned forward and murmured as if to protest, but remained still—their eyes riveted to his sword.

"Hurry up," Bill cried. "Pick a weapon, if you can find one. Put on those clothes. We don't want to stay here any longer than necessary."

He knew these folks were none too happy with the idea of armed humans. The freed humans had to act quickly before the crowd decided to squelch the arm-toting humans before it became a trend.

The humans seemed to understand the need for urgency. Within minutes, Bill held several bags of coins in his hands, and fourteen humans stood in the ill-fitting dracon clothes. "Let's get moving," he ordered.

As they left the stunned crowd of slave owners, the human who had been on the auction block ran up alongside Bill. "Master, forgive me, but I must speak to you," he said as Bill broke into a jog.

"Don't call me master," Bill snapped, his head craning behind him for any signs of pursuit.

In barely the time it took to look back, the slave had fallen prostrate before him, lying on the ground, his face in the dirt. "Forgive me, I do not know how you wish to be addressed."

"Get up! We don't have time for this foolishness. My name is Bill, just Bill. Now, let's go."

"Just Bill," the man said. "Your parents named you well. Bill the Just One. I am Pasham."

Bill shook his head in frustration. "Don't ever get on the

ground in front of me again. You're a man. Where I come from a man would die before he'd crawl before someone else. Unless you people want to be slaves for the rest of your lives, you'd better show some pride. If you act like slaves, you'll be treated like slaves forever."

"Forgive me, but I humbly suggest we get off this main street and head toward a part of the city where humans won't stir as much notice," Pasham said. "The Slave Guild will send the Warriors Guild after us as soon as they finish beating the auctioneer."

Bill hesitated, recalling the warning his felpur friends had given him about interfering with the Guildlords. He suspected that killing customers and freeing slaves might be considered an intrusion. "Lead the way, Pasham."

As good as his word, the ex-slave led them into a side alley. Even here, the large group of humans drew attention. But as they passed deeper into a seedier section of the city, fewer took notice of them.

Squat, ugly tenements loomed up several blocks into the city, but Pasham led them deeper. Bill's concern that they would be pursued began to diminish. No one could stand the sickening, overpowering smells.

The narrow, cluttered streets wound deeper into the city, like a dank maze. Sunlight seldom fell into what passed for thoroughfares. The buildings appeared pregnant. Additions jutted overhead, seemingly added on by builders who cared less about aesthetics than the need to jam as much into as little space as possible.

"Where are we?" Bill asked.

"It's known as Darktown," Pasham said. "Most of Trillius ignores this place, but it houses delights that are unavailable elsewhere."

"It doesn't seem delightful," Bill muttered.

"Appearances can be deceiving in Darktown. If one knows where to go, one can find certain pleasures found nowhere else. And the key that unlocks these treasures is gold.

"Behind these doors reside people who can provide you with substances that can transport you to places in your mind you've never before explored. Oh, in Uptown you may find houses of pleasure where women of any race do your bidding. But here in Darktown, the houses cater to even more exotic tastes. Magicians can sell you magical items to enchant the woman of your dreams or to punish your enemies. Alchemists can provide you with poisons. Witches can offer you talismans that bring you luck or destruction upon your enemies. In Darktown, you are limited by the size of your purse and the boundaries of your own imagination."

In this section of the city, few citizens looked directly at Bill and his companions. The unofficial motto seemed to be Mind Your Own Business. Free-roaming humans appeared everywhere here—poorly dressed, some obviously underfed, but nonetheless, human.

Bill's hand went to his sword. "Orcs," he said, involuntarily tensing as he noticed a group swagger by.

Pasham placed a nervous hand on Bill's. "Many of them frequent Darktown," Pasham whispered. "They won't bother us if we don't bother them. Let them be, lest we draw the attention of their masters."

A battered sign marked a tavern called the Royal Falcon. Pasham led them inside its dimly lit, smoky interior.

The Falcon apparently had seen better days, and today was not one of them. The place was empty, and Bill would have thought it closed had he not noticed a fire in the hearth and the ever present pot bubbling above it. The group took a large table that, apparently, had barely survived innumerable bar fights. It tipped unsteadily when he leaned against it, the surface scarred and battered by more than tankards of ale.

A portly man greeted them at their table. "I don't want you here if you don't have any money," he announced. "Either drink or get out. I'm not operating a social club for misfits."

Bill was surprised and pleased to see a human working at the tavern, but the man's rude greeting grated on him. "Give us a round of drinks and watch your mouth," he said evenly.

The tavernkeeper seemed ready with a retort until he noticed Bill's hand straying to his sword. He brought them ale.

Bill poured out the contents of the purses taken from the dracons and divided it into fourteen equal piles, one for each freed slave. It came to three gold pieces, two silvers, and three coppers for each. "It's not much, but it should help."

"You joke, master," Pasham said. "This is more money than I've ever held in my hand in my life. You rescued us, fought for us, and now you shower us with riches. Surely you must have a great task for us."

"No," Bill said, "unless you can shed some light on a few things for me, like why humans are slaves around here."

The group exchanged surprised glances, caught off guard by the question. "Surely, you know," said the man who had been imprisoned in the stocks. "He has ordained it."

"Whom?" Bill asked.

"He whom we must not name. I am Yorth, Just Bill. Since my father's day, He has ordained that humans be set apart as slaves. He says we have no souls, that we are spawned by darkness, that we are unfit to walk in the light."

"It's said that He hunts us for sport," said Pasham. "He mates humans with orcs and even worse things. Most of us not killed outright, end up in the mines or enslaved."

"I don't understand," Bill said. "I saw humans on the street here. A man runs this place. Why does He leave them alone?"

"The people of Trillius don't want to live here in Darktown. It's too close to the castle," Yorth said. "The castle is inhabited by creatures that make them uneasy."

"They blame humans for the evil that has befallen this land," said Pasham. "When they punish and mistreat us, they feel it atones for the Collapse. They blame us for the Unnamed One defeating the forces of the Realm and conquering this land."

"That doesn't make any sense," Bill said. "Why blame humans for the ills of this land? Everything I've heard seems to suggest that the real problem is this King."

"Quiet, blasphemer!" shouted the innkeeper, who had returned to fill their tankards. "I won't have that kind of talk in my establishment and find myself hung or sent to the mines. I won't have it. You have gold, I see that, but gold won't buy my life if His agents come for me. I spoke harshly to you when you entered, and for that I apologize. Most humans who come here have nothing to pay for what they order. But drink in peace and leave me in peace. Cease this talk that will cause only misfortune."

Yorth brandished his sword before Bill could react. "Have a care, innkeeper. An hour ago I was a prisoner in the slave market." He pulled down his shirt for emphasis. "See the welts left by the dracons? They are still fresh with blood. My blood! They tortured me to teach me manners, because I did not lower my eyes fast enough to suit the auctioneer. For that offense, I was put in the stocks and whipped to remind me of my place in this world.

"This stranger," Yorth pointed to Bill, "freed me from the stocks and killed the dracon who whipped me. He liberated all you see here, and brought us to safety—even shared his gold with us. Bill the Just can say what he chooses, when he chooses, and where he chooses. I don't know how long the slavers will let this insult remain unavenged, but I refuse to spend what little time I have left cowering."

The innkeeper's eyes widened as he listened to Yorth's account. "You killed a slaver and freed these humans from the slave pens?"

"He killed six of them," Pasham said. "Fought four at once and slew them all just as casually as you swat a fly."

The idea seemed too much for the innkeeper. He pulled out a chair, sat down, and poured himself a drink. "I'll buy this round." He passed the pitcher around the table. "Freeing humans from the slave pens? That's never before happened in Trillius. The whole city will be in an uproar. The Guild Council will be called into session. Every slaver in the city will demand your blood. They'll send the Warrior's Guild after you. And here you are in my establishment! They'll talk about this for years to come."

"Do you want us to leave?" Bill asked. "We have no right to place you in danger. If they will send this Warrior Guild after me, I should be on my way."

"I again apologize for my outbursts," the innkeeper said.

"My name is Orwynn. I'm just a frightened, ill-tempered old man. I was once a successful innkeeper. Before the Unnamed One came to our land, good King Liam himself sometimes sneaked out of the castle to enjoy a drink by my fire. Ah, there was no better man than Liam."

"It is death to speak of Liam," whispered Pasham.

The remark brought howls of laughter from the innkeeper. "For everything you've done and said today, the punishment is death," Orwynn said, trying to stifle his laughter. "Only moments ago, I feared that someone might hear your dangerous talk–and now you warn *me*. It's been a long time since I had reason to be proud of my kinsmen. Today, I celebrate a great deed performed by a man. Let us not worry about the spies, the Guilds, or the punishments they dream up for humans, even as we speak. Your actions have reminded me of happier days when a great man, Good King Liam, ruled this land and all creatures respected men."

"The king was a man?" Bill asked.

"That's the true pity of today," the innkeeper said. "It's death to speak of Liam. It's death to speak of the time before the Unnamed One killed him and began to rule our land. It's death to recall that only thirty years ago, men ruled this land, justly and wisely. He doesn't want people to remember those days, so He kills anyone who dares to mention it."

"How can the people go along with this?" Bill asked. "I've seen the way they act and talk. They really believe men are inferior and deserve to be slaves."

"It's a long tale," Orwynn said. "After His forces con-quered the land, they claimed that King Liam had sold them out, that he and the humans had secretly worked to enslave all the other creatures. The Unnamed One claimed He invaded the kingdom to rescue it from the evil conspiracies of humankind. At first, no one believed it, then they began to ask why our forces had fallen before His army so quickly. Though many knew it was because He had corrupted the captains, rumors spread that men had lusted for the properties of the other creatures.

"The Unnamed One announced evidence of new conspiracies to enslave the creatures of the kingdom. As He gave the estates owned by humans to the other races, He decreed it only right to then enslave them, to ensure they never again threatened the peace of the kingdom.

"Every time He issued an unpopular edict, He blamed humans for it. His secret police, He claimed, was established to protect the other races from the humans. He corrupted the people by giving them the belongings of the humans and setting up a scapegoat to blame for all their troubles. The enslaved humans give the people something to mistreat when they're really angry with Him."

"You say the people accept this? They believe this nonsense?" Bill asked. "I find it hard to believe that everyone has been fooled."

"No one wants to admit they have no rights to the humans' property, so they convince themselves that humans are inferior. The failure of King Liam to protect them conveniently proves that he and other humans are guilty of all the crimes for which they are blamed."

Bill said, "Surely there must be those who dispute all this absurdity."

"Yes, there have been those who felt it was wrong and tried to enlighten others. They were branded as traitors and ruthlessly killed. Their lands and titles were confiscated and distributed to those who parroted the lies of the new rulers."

Orwynn paused to drink from his tankard before continuing. "When the Arch Regent was installed in Trillius, she turned it into a pleasure city to divert the populace. She encouraged the formation of the Guilds, giving power to the landless and the corrupt, and winning allies to Her cause by offering an easy path to riches. The honest merchants who opposed her lost their businesses to those who were willing to cater to the lusts and cravings of the people."

"Yet, you still have your inn," Bill said.

"I could see which way the winds were blowing," the innkeeper said. "I gave it to a trusted gnome who had worked for me. He has never believed the lies spread by those who have gotten rich from the new regime. As far as the authorities are concerned, I'm a slave operating this inn for my master."

"Aren't you in danger by having me here?" Bill asked.

Orwynn seemed unconcerned. "When the Warrior Guild comes into this section of the city, I know long before they arrive. The Guilds leave us who live in Darktown alone for the most part," the innkeeper said. "They seldom venture into this part of the city, coming in force when they come at all. Orcs and other creatures from the castle walk in our midst. Some of us have banded together to protect our lives and our properties. I will be told if they come here."

"By whom?"

"Bill, I admire what you've done today. I can choose to put my own neck at risk by speaking of things that are considered treason, but until I know you and your companions better, I cannot speak too much of others."

Chapter Four

The door to the inn burst open. "Orwynn! The Warriors' Guild has entered Darktown!" a young gnome shouted excitedly. "A hundred of them, dressed in full battle gear. They're looking for a band of renegade humans who went on a murder spree in the slave market and have started a revolt all over the city."

Orwynn looked from the gnome to Bill. "Your fame grows."

Yorth drew his sword to salute Bill. "If I must die today, I'll die as a free man, standing by your side."

The others scrambled to their feet, raising tankards and blades to Bill, repeating Yorth's oath.

Seeing this display, the young gnome's eyes widened. "These are the renegades?"

"Peace, Morko." Orwynn chuckled. "These friends haven't murdered anyone, nor organized a revolt. The Slavers' Guild is just trying to scare Trilliuns into helping them recover some missing property. Now tell me, what are the warriors doing and how long before they arrive here?"

"They haven't come to our street yet, but they're asking everyone about a free band of humans, and someone is bound to tell them you have them here, Orwynn. Make them leave. They have no right to endanger us."

"Hush, lad," Orwynn said. "What would your grandfather say if he heard you? You know better than that. We cannot just abandon them. Now settle down and think as your grandfather would."

Morko didn't seem too pleased, but at the mention of his grandfather he paused for a moment. "We have to split them up. They're looking for a group of fifteen. Anyone who noted them coming into Darktown at all probably didn't look too closely at their faces. And the Warriors wouldn't recognize them, even if they saw them. If we can separate them and hide them in different places around town, after a few days the Warriors will conclude they've fled the city."

"Ah, that's my lad," Orwynn said, clapping his hands. "You make me proud. Now, will you take three of them to your grandfather's home?"

"Me?"

"Of course. You've developed a brilliant plan. Your grandfather will be proud of you for personally rescuing these humans right out from under the nose of the Warriors' Guild."

"Yes, I guess he would be pleased," Morko answered uncertainly.

"You know he and your father want you to carry on their work. Our work." Orwynn turned to the freed slaves. "Three of you shall go now to Morko's father. He'll know what to do. After you've gone, I'll send another three to Morko's house."

Morko said, "I could be killed if they're found there."

Orwynn looked at him, as if surprised at the remark.

Morko looked from the humans back to Orwynn, then to the door, as if listening for the tramp of boots. "I guess I can do no less than my father or grandfather." He sighed. "But what of the rest?"

"I'll find a place to hide them," Orwynn said. "You don't have to worry." He pointed at three of the humans. "Go with Morko, and do what he says."

They looked to Bill, who told them, "Do as Orwynn says."

Reluctantly, they followed Morko out a back door. Orwynn gave directions to a second and third group on how to find Morko's and his father's houses. He wrote a note for them to give to Morko's father. "In a few days, someone will take you to a safer place. They'll say I sent them, so you'll know they can be trusted. Now quickly, go."

Yorth and Pasham remained seated. "We will stay here with Bill," Pasham said, in a tone that brooked no argument.

"Oh, all right," the innkeeper said impatiently. He pointed at the others. "But you—the rest of you must go."

Bill nodded his head toward the remaining group. They departed, leaving only Bill, Yorth, Pasham, and three other slaves. The innkeeper motioned. "Come with me."

"I appreciate all you have done for us," Bill said, "but every one would be safer if I left."

Pasham and Yorth protested. "We go with you, Just Bill," Yorth said. "We can protect you."

"I don't think so," Bill said. "They're looking for a group of humans, not one man. They won't look for me in the center of the city with my friends. Orwynn, I entrust these people to your hands," he said and reached into his tunic for a purse taken from the dracons.

"Don't insult me," the innkeeper said.

"This is to help you with whatever expenses come up. I'll be back in a few days. We can talk more then." Bill rose and walked toward the back door.

"Don't leave that way," Orwynn said. "Come with me. I want to show you something important." He led Bill alone to a back room and down a set of stairs to a wine cellar. When he pressed a hidden button, a passageway opened. "Take this torch." He handed Bill the torch and pulled a map from underneath a wine cask. "This passageway leads to the labyrinths under the city. Dangers lurk down there, so keep your sword ready. I think they'll be watching Darktown tonight, but you can get back into the main part of the city through here without being detected. Now tell me where it is you intend to go and where I can find you if I need to locate you?"

Bill said, "My friends are at the Prancing Robe. I don't know very much about your city, but if you need to find me, I suspect I'll be there or at the Twisted Tale."

"I know both places," Orwynn said. "I like the Robe. I sneeze a lot when I'm there, but they have fine ale. I have nothing against felpurs, but they make me sneeze."

He marked the map. "This path takes you close to the Robe. If possible, return in two days. You can come back the same way."

"These tunnels go under the city?"

"Yes. Few know of them, and they are rarely used, because of the things that prowl the darkness there. It's bad enough here in Darktown. Under the city, things are far worse. Most entrances are blocked, but if you find a crescent moon near a doorway, you can open some of them with this." He handed Bill an object shaped like a crescent with a handle. "Now go—carefully. I must hide your friends before the Guild arrives."

After Orwynn closed the passageway, Bill found himself

in a dark stone-lined tunnel, with only the flickering and sputtering of the torch to guide him. He drew his sword, comforted by its pulsing power. Checking the map, he set out for the Prancing Robe.

The thick cobwebs proved how few people used the underground passageways. The stone walls were slimy. Small creatures scurried away from the light of his torch. "Rats. I can see this isn't a major tourist attraction."

Orwynn closed the door to the secret passage behind Bill, checking that no one saw what lay behind it. He walked back upstairs into the tavern where Pasham and Yorth waited impatiently. The other three slaves seemed nervous.

"The Warriors' Guild will arrive soon. I want you to go with a friend of mine out of the city."

"What about Bill?" Pasham asked. "Will he go, too?"

"I can't answer that."

"Then I will remain in the city until he returns," Yorth said. "I do not leave until he leaves."

"I must stay, too," Pasham said.

"I admire your courage if not your good sense," Orwynn responded amiably. "I'm afraid that you other three must go, though. It's going to be dangerous for humans here." He scrawled a note on one side of a sheet of paper, and hastily drew a map on the other side.

"Take this two blocks down the street," he said, pointing to the map. "When you see Anorexa's House of Joy, stop and ask for the lady of the house. Give her this message, and she'll help you leave the city. And—this is terribly important—tell her to send Zynaryxx to me. I must see him."

"Who is Zynaryxx?" Pasham asked.

"Forget you heard that name," Orwynn said. "If any of you are caught, you must promise me that you will not say that name. Tell them anything else you must, but pledge on your lives and your newfound freedom that you will not reveal that name." Orwynn looked at all of them. "Promise me," he repeated.

They promised.

When the slaves left, Orwynn directed Pasham and Yorth to go upstairs to scrub the floors. "The Warriors' Guild could arrive at any moment. If they discover you, they might believe you're just household slaves."

Yorth and Pasham were diligently scrubbing the floors to the inn's rooms when they heard Orwynn moving about downstairs. "Is it the warriors?" Pasham whispered.

"Shhh," Yorth hissed.

"I wish Bill was here," Pasham said.

"Get hold of yourself," Yorth said, fingering his blade. "And be quiet before you give us away. I want to hear what they're saying down there."

Straining, the two freed slaves could hear the sound of two voices below them.

"Orwynn, I hope you had a good reason for dragging me out of Anorexa's," a strange voice said. "The good woman brought in some new pixies just for me. The frightened sprites were pleased to have me welcome them to the city."

"Still, you rushed over the minute I sent for you."

"I did rush," the voice answered. "Is it my fault that at my age some things take longer than they did in my youth?"

Orwynn chuckled. "Zynaryxx, you're an old goat. We must talk of something more important than pixies. A human came in today who might be of interest to the League. His name is Bill Evans, a stranger to our city and our land."

"The kingdom is filled with strangers these days. What's another more or less?"

"This one is quite different," Orwynn said. "He killed six dracons in the slave market today and freed fourteen slaves."

"Here in Trillius!"

"I thought that might pique your interest. I don't know where he's from, but certainly nowhere near. He knew nothing of the king, the Arch Regent, or the Guilds, and seemed quite disturbed that humans were slaves. The Guild Council claims he's started some kind of revolt. I spoke to the slaves he freed, though, and they'd never seen him before today. It seems that he acted on his own on the spur of the moment. The Warriors' Guild is searching Darktown even now, looking for him."

"You're not thinking he might be the one?"

Orwynn sighed. "I'm an old man. I've waited a long time, Zynaryxx. I've been a member of the League too long to let my hopes cloud my judgment. I don't yet know enough to answer your question, but he bears watching. I also think the League could use someone like him, regardless of whether he truly is the one."

"Why, Orwynn, I haven't seen you this excited about someone in years!"

"We need a man of action. The League has grown too complacent. Our enemies hardly even think of us, much less fear us. The country has begun to think of the League of the Crimson Crescent as some myth, romantic in its own way but lacking in substance. The Arch Regent believes She's secure. Her minions roam the streets of Darktown too freely. I suggest we start a rumor that the League had a hand in freeing the slaves today."

"It would be easy enough," Zynaryxx said. "I have to wonder, though, whether we want to draw so much attention to ourselves and our activities."

"Our activities?" Orwynn spat. "What have we done lately? What cause for hope have we given our friends? What fear have we struck in the hearts of our enemies? This League has become nothing more than a glorified debating society dominated by frightened fools and nervous nabobs."

"Our members have much to lose if we act too rashly," Zynaryxx defended.

"Lose? The only thing we stand to lose is our lives. They've taken everything else. And what of the lives they've left us—nothing but shadows. We fear to walk our streets. We fear to roam the city lest we end in the slave pens. We fear to speak our minds lest His spies hear us. I think we have far too *little* to lose."

"Orwynn, what makes you so excited?"

"I don't know. I had fifteen men in here today, quite unlike the men I see every day. Hope shone on their faces. They spoke freely. They were willing to die for the right to speak their minds. A few hours before, they'd been slaves. They tasted freedom, and it made them hunger for more. They swore they would never again bow before their oppressors. I'd forgotten how that felt. This city is a tinderbox. If we can strike but one spark—"

"We shall burn ourselves," Zynaryxx interrupted.

"Perhaps. Perhaps. I prefer to think we could light a torch

from which men could take hope."

"It's a noble thought, my friend. Keep in mind, however, that most torches only draw moths so mesmerized by the flame, it consumes them," Zynaryxx said.

"If you are too frightened, then I will act without you," Orwynn snapped.

A long pause hung in the air.

Upstairs, Yorth and Pasham strained to hear. The pure, precious freedom Yorth felt sharpened to the point of pain. He would never be a slave again, thanks to Just Bill.

"I do believe you would, old friend," Zynaryxx said, amiably. "I think I must meet this Bill Evans who had such an effect on you."

"I'm sorry I accused you of being frightened," Orwynn said. "I know better than that. But it's time to act."

Zynaryxx said. "I agree that the League has been too quiet for too long. We've allowed caution to become a habit. It's all this soft living and visits to houses of joy, I suspect. But you've piqued my interest. Bring this Bill Evans out."

"He's not here," Orwynn said. "He had to rejoin his friends at the Prancing Robe. He said we could find him there or at the Twisted Tale."

"Ah, the Robe," Zynaryxx said. "He has a fine taste in ale, I see. I like him already. If the Warriors' Guild is searching for him as intently as you suggest, though, didn't he take quite a chance in walking there?"

"I gave him a map and a key to the caverns," Orwynn said. "I asked him to return here in two days."

"You gave him a map to the caverns? You gave him a Crescent key? Did you give him a roster to the League's membership while you were at it? I really must meet this man who inspires such trust so quickly."

"I'm sorry if you don't approve," Orwynn said stiffly. "As you said yourself, it seemed too great a risk to send him through the streets."

Zynaryxx laughed. "You must stop taking me so seriously. I'm just not used to seeing you so decisive. You're beginning to make me feel like I'm one of those nervous nabobs you spoke of. But how much did you tell him about the League?"

"Nothing," Orwynn said. "He just considers me a kindly tavernmaster. I wanted to talk to you before I confided in him. That's why I'd like to have you check him out yourself before we bring him into the League."

"Very well," Zynaryxx said. "But for now, I must be on my way. The streets are deserted enough that our friends from the castle should soon take their leave. A cool ale at the Robe would do wonders for me."

Pasham and Yorth hurried into the tavern's main room just as Orwynn closed the door. "What is it, my friends?" he asked, jovially. "Have you cleaned the rooms upstairs so quickly?"

"Who was that?" Yorth demanded. "What are you getting Just Bill into?"

Orwynn's jovial expression faded, as if the sun were shut off by a cloud. He met the freed slaves' accusing stares with a level gaze, ignoring the way Yorth's fingers strayed to his sword handle. "Your loyalty speaks well for you, my friends. I've wondered if slaves could shake loose from the mental bonds ensnaring them after their physical restraints were gone. I won't reproach you for listening in on what I thought was my private conversation. If I were in your shoes, I'm sure I'd do the same."

"You haven't answered our question," Yorth said.

"No, I haven't," Orwynn said. "Nor will I. Suffice to know that my friend will see to it that Bill is safe. Believe me, he is far more capable than either you or I to ensure Bill's safety."

"What is this League you talked about?" Pasham asked. "It sounds dangerous."

"Dangerous?" Orwynn asked more to himself than to the two men before him. "Yes, it's dangerous, though life would be far more dangerous for Bill without the League's assistance. For now, though, I suggest that the two of you forget what you've heard tonight. Put aside your suspicions. The sun has set in Darktown. The streets pose enough dangers to keep us busy. Meanwhile, we can expect a visit soon enough from the Warriors' Guild. They will have heard that a group of humans came in here this afternoon. There are too many eyes and too many open palms to let that slip by unmentioned."

Chapter Five

Bill made his way cautiously through the labyrinth. Using his torch, he examined the map and finally found the doorway closest to the Prancing Robe. "Let's hope this gadget works," he muttered as he wedged the crescent key into a quarter moon–shaped indentation he found in what he hoped was a door. Tugging with all his strength, he felt it give. With a final pull, it opened, and a blast of fresh air rewarded his effort.

He stepped out into a darkened alley. He hid in the shadows as he listened to a column of marching feet nearby. "Have you seen any humans?" a gruff voice demanded. "A group of them staged a revolt in the slave market today. They're armed and dangerous. Murdered everyone they found, hacked up babies and children, sparing no one."

"Human?" a voice familiar to Bill answered. "What do you take me for? I don't allow the nasty creatures near me."

"Well, keep your eyes open. One's been seen in the neighborhood. We think it's the same one that has been staying in a room at the Prancing Robe. It was gone by the time we got there, and if it returns, we'll know soon enough. The Council is rounding up any we find loose. Too many free–running ones have started to give the slaves ideas. A taste of the lash is what they need, if you ask me. Let's go, boys."

After the soldiers stomped off, Bill poked out his head. "Quatar," he whispered, "is that you?"

"Bill! We've been looking for you for hours. Stay right where you are until I find Zorth. It's not safe for anyone to see you. Stay put until we figure out what to do."

She dashed back toward the inn, returning minutes later with a bundle and Zorth beside her. "Put this on," she said, tossing Bill a hooded cloak.

"If no one looks too closely, we can get you into my room," Zorth said. "The Warriors questioned me about you. I told them we met you on the road and that you'd taken a room with us, but otherwise I didn't know much about you. I told them you had left us today to wander the city. They're watching the Inn in case you return. The whole city is looking for humans. If someone sees you, they might think you're the renegade that started all this commotion."

"I'm afraid I am." Bill threw the cloak around him.

"What?" Zorth demanded. "How could you lead a slave rebellion?"

"It wasn't a rebellion. I went for a walk and found myself in this slave market. I bumped into a dracon who thought he could run me through for sport. When I defended myself, I found another five of them trying to skewer me. I figured that since I was already in trouble, freeing those poor caged people couldn't make matters worse."

"Of course not," said Zorth heavily. "How could it?"

Quatar shook her head. "The whole city is searching for him, armed troops on the alert, and I'm standing in an alley helping to disguise him, nodding my head as if it's all so reasonable. I, too, must be going mad."

"You don't have to put yourselves in danger," Bill said. "I appreciate the loan of this cloak, but I don't think it's safe for you to take me back to the inn."

"Nonsense," Zorth said. "We haven't searched for you for hours to allow you to go off and get captured. You're returning with us to the inn and you're going to eat a hot meal. I shudder to think what mischief you'll get into if we leave you on your own again."

"What if someone recognizes me? The inn is being watched. You don't need any more trouble."

"We'll decide how much trouble we need," Zorth snapped. "You just do what you're told for once. We can take care of ourselves—and you. Our three litter brothers have left. We'll take their rooms."

"I'll come," Bill said, "but keep your swords handy."

Inside the inn, the trio stayed close together as they moved through the crowded dining room. Evening traffic at the Robe had drawn more than just felpurs. Creatures held forth in animated conversations, the chief topic being the slave revolt, of course.

"I tell you, the humans have been planning this for months," a fat elf told a dracon. "The massacre in the slave market is but the first step. One of these nights, our house servants will slit our throats. Mark me. There's rebellion in the air."

"I hear it's the work of the League," said a gnome. "The League of the Crimson Crescent is behind all of this. They say that the League's membership has grown."

"The League is just a bedtime story," the chubby elf retorted. "I can't believe any organized resistance to the crown even exists. It's just the humans spinning tales to frighten us."

"I say we exterminate them all," the dracon retorted. "I've never trusted them. I've seen the way they whisper to one another when they think no one's listening. It was a mistake to ever let them into homes. I hear the council's going to ban them from the city."

"You're all being ridiculous," a tiny creature sitting on the tavern's bar scoffed.

Bill couldn't take his eyes off the tiny, well-dressed figure. A cloak thrown over its shoulders, the creature leaned over a small mug, dipping a ladle into the ale. Although his features were delicate, he didn't sip delicately. He guzzled with gusto.

"If you ask me, some folks are deliberately blowing this all out of proportion," the creature said, directing his comments to the dracon. "They're trying to frighten everyone so they'll have an excuse to crack down on us even more. We'll have the Warriors' Guild searching our homes, all in the name of snuffing out this so-called rebellion. Citizens who never even speak to humans, but who have made the wrong people angry, will end up in the castle dungeon on some trumped up charge or another. The numbers of people dragged off to the dungeons continues to increase, and this kind of hysteria makes it all the easier for them to haul away yet more citizens."

"No one asked you." The dracon spun on its heel to face the little man. Stooping, the dracon grabbed him by his tiny collar, hoisting him in the air. "I've never liked faeries much, either. You give me the creeps the way you sneak around. You're too much like humans, always poking your noses in others' affairs."

Without first stopping to think, Bill stepped forward. "Put him down before I peel your scales," he said in a low voice to the dracon.

The dracon dropped the faerie, startled by the interruption, but found itself unable to turn to face Bill as Zorth and Quatar pressed in from either side.

"Felpurs!" the dracon snarled. "I'll teach you to butt in."

"We haven't time to teach you anything," Zorth said. "I would advise you, however, to sharpen your sword before you say anything more."

Zorth and Quatar's grim expressions gave the dracon pause. "I was just trying to enjoy an ale when everybody started bothering me," he said defensively.

Nearby, the fat elf said nervously, "Well, it's time I hauled my belly upstairs to bed. Uh, good night, all." He slipped away softly.

Zorth, still staring down the dracon, stepped back. "Very well, then. As long as you keep your hands to yourself." Without another word, he and Quatar turned their backs and hustled out of the dining area toward their lodgings.

"Why didn't you pull off your cloak while you were at it?" Zorth whispered through clenched teeth. "Why not announce that you started the slave rebellion?"

"I couldn't let that oversized iguana grab that little guy," Bill answered. "I guess it wasn't too smart. I appreciate the two of you helping me out."

Inside their room, he asked the felpurs about faeries.

"I mentioned them when we came to town," Zorth said. He was visibly trying to put the confrontation downstairs behind him, but his smile was the kind put on bravely despite dire pain.

Quatar chuckled more naturally. "And he gave you the same blank look he wears now."

"What are they?"

"They're an ancient race," Zorth said. "Some call them sprites. Some call them pixies. They can be quite elusive when they want to be. They usually keep to themselves. Most don't have much contact with the other races, especially in cities. Only a few rub shoulders with the rest of us."

"I'm surprised the dracon managed to grab that one," Quatar said. "They're usually too fast and agile for that. The old-timer must have been quite drunk. That dracon is lucky we stepped in when we did. Most faeries spend most of their lives studying magic. Some of them are quite adept at the mysteries."

"What do you mean, magic? Would the faerie have turned him into a toad or something?"

Zorth looked perplexed. "Faeries have a long-standing, intimate relationship with nature that gives them a deep understanding of fire, water, air, and earth. Many of them devote their entire lives to the study of thaumaturgy."

"Thaumaturgy?"

"The study of harnessing the elements," Zorth said. "I've studied some of the art but not in the same field."

"I don't follow you," Bill said. "Does it really work?"

"Sometime, you must tell me where you come from," Zorth said. "Of course, magic works! Your sword works, doesn't it? A skilled mage with the proper training and experience can harness powers you can't imagine."

"Okay, I'll accept that for now," Bill said. "What did you think of the faerie's assessment of what's occurring in the city?"

"Of course, he's right," Zorth said. "The Arch Regent will love this slave revolt. They'll round up all of their enemies under the pretext that they were involved in some fabricated conspiracy."

"Your friend the faerie will probably be at the top of the list," Quatar said. "If the Regent's spies hear him, it won't be long before he'll be hauled away. With our luck, we'll be in danger, too, for defending him."

"We can worry about that tomorrow," Zorth said. "For now, I'm going to get us something to eat, then I want to hear how you got into this mess."

Over hot bowls of stew, Bill recounted freeing the slaves, hiding in Darktown, and meeting Orwynn.

"So, you've been to Darktown," Zorth said. "That's good. I'm going there in the next few days. I haven't found anyone who knows much about my litter brother, though someone recalled that he was with some people from Darktown. I'm going to talk to someone who may know their names. Perhaps this Orwynn can help me."

"I'm sure Orwynn will," Bill said. After a moment, he added, "Something puzzles me. In the tavern, I heard someone speak of the League of the Crimson Crescent. What is it?"

"Don't put much stock in tavern talk," Quatar said. "People always conjure up conspiracies."

"They said it was some kind of resistance movement to the crown," Bill said.

"That's what they claim," Zorth said. "Apparently, when the Arch Regent took over Trillius, a group proclaiming to be a fellowship of all the creatures formed a league of some sort. They oppose slavery and advocate the rule of law that existed under the old monarchy. Supposedly, they have sworn to overthrow the Regent. Tales describe some very daring exploits by these rascals who supposedly can magically appear anywhere in the city. If you believe what you hear, they pop right out of the ground. Most people don't put much stock in it. They've been quiet for years. Whatever members they may have had must now be rotting in the dungeons."

"They appear anywhere in the city, as if by magic?"

"Yes," Quatar said. "No one ever knows where they come from or how they make their escapes."

Bill showed them the crescent key he had tucked in his vest. He unfolded the map of the underground network beneath the city.

"Where did you get these?" Zorth whispered.

Briefly, Bill recounted his journey underground and how the key opened an entrance way to the alley off the Prancing Robe.

"By the Gods." Quatar examined the map wide-eyed. "Look at this network of tunnels! No wonder they say the League's members appear as if by magic. Do you have any idea what the Regent would do to you if you were caught with these?"

"Probably the same thing She'd do if She knew I caused the slave revolt. If I've become Public Enemy Number One, I don't suppose it can hurt to be friends with all the other Public Enemies."

"That map could be useful," Zorth said. "Guard it closely."

"If Orwynn is a member of this League, I wonder why he took the risk of giving me these? He didn't seem like a member of a clandestine resistance organization."

"Do you imagine they all walk around in long dark cloaks, furtively dashing from shadow to shadow?" Zorth asked. "They need people with wide-ranging sources of information. Who better than a tavernkeeper? Members could drop in for an ale without arousing any interest. Taverns are excellent listening posts for learning someone's political leanings. After a few ales, a person speaks freely about anything."

"He never said a word about the League to me. He just told me to come back to see him day after tomorrow."

"The League couldn't have survived this many years if they told everyone they met that they were sworn to overthrow the crown," Zorth said. "I suspect they are checking you out through their own means. When you go back, they'll probably offer you membership."

"What if I refuse?" Bill asked.

"Then they'll have to decide whether they want someone who is aware of their secrets walking loose," Quatar said.

"That's a cheery thought," Bill said. "Let's not worry about the League, though. Tell me what you've discovered about your missing brother."

"There isn't much to tell," Zorth said. "He arrived in the city, and for some reason, he met with some people from Darktown. Tomorrow we'll see if we can find out more. You must promise to stay here until we return. The streets are too dangerous for you. I know you don't like being kept inside, but keep in mind that if you're arrested, they'll link us to you. Then they'll want us, too."

"That isn't fair," Bill said. But the next morning, when the felpurs left in search of news of their missing brother, he remained behind. He spent the day resting and studying the map Orwynn had given him. It showed a twisting, turning underground labyrinth that could pose serious difficulties for the uninformed. Even with the map, Bill suspected he might get lost if he strayed from the outlined paths.

The sound of footsteps outside his room interrupted his

solitude. "He's in there," a voice muttered. "Zorth and Quatar are keeping him inside their room."

"Is this wise, Hovra?" a second voice asked.

"It's our duty, Petra. The filthy creature attacked me. For no reason at all, it pulled a sword on me and nearly killed me. Luckily, the creature was so frightened when I called its bluff that it ran away."

"That's not the way I recall it," Petra said.

"Are you questioning me?"

"I'm just wondering if it's wise for us to break into Zorth's room."

"I'm telling you we have to do it for Zorth's own sake. You saw the way Quatar and Zorth behaved after I chased it out of the tavern yesterday, as if I'd done something wrong! They're obviously under the filthy creature's control in some strange fashion. It's dangerous. I think it may even have had something to do with that slave revolt. If it can enchant Zorth, then it's capable of anything."

"Shouldn't we notify the Warriors' Guild?" Petra whispered. "They're looking for these humans. We ought to let them handle it."

"I did," Hovra snapped. "They're waiting for my signal."

"Why don't we let them take him?"

"You sound frightened," Hovra said, pulling a key from his belt as he began fiddling with the door's lock. Bill watched the door's handle turn. Without hesitating, he pulled open a window and jumped outside, rolling as he hit the ground.

"It's getting away," Hovra shouted behind him.

Pulling the hood close around his face, Bill ran into the street, ducking into the crowd as a troop of warriors charged out, responding to Hovra's shouts of alarm. Bill dodged among the street revelers, trying to put distance between himself and the Warrior troop. As he ran, he heard shouts of fear and confusion. A horn sounded. All around him, people began to run.

The shouts turned to screams. An arrow skittered alongside him. A dracon fell before him, another arrow pierced its side. A rawulf, not far ahead, stumbled as a feathered shaft penetrated the back of its head.

"The Warriors are firing into the crowd," a hobbit cried as it stumbled, a missile puncturing its throat.

Bill saw a line of riders armed with lances charging around a corner into the running crowd.

"They're going to kill everyone on this street just to get me," he said aloud, as he drew his sword. Next to him, an arrow punctured a gnome's skull.

In front of him, the crowd turned before the onslaught of riders. Confusion reigned as people attempted to flee. The riders systematically impaled runners with their lances or simply rode them down, crushing them under their horses' hooves. Others slashed them with swords or bashed them with heavy war axes.

As a rider bore down on Bill, he held his ground. His sword swung up, fending off the rider's weapon, blocking the swing. He thrust up into the rider's stomach, spitting him neatly.

Bill grasped the saddle and jumped onto the horse's back. He pushed the dying rider off, and with a yank on the reins, turned the horse and rode away from the slaughter, through the line of startled riders.

As he turned a corner into an alley, he heard a shout and the sound of pounding hooves. He'd been spotted.

Where the alley emerged into a side street, he leaped off the horse, turning it loose. He ran into another alley as the sound of riders approached. He sprinted the alley's length, hoping the riders would search the street for him.

Meanwhile, he traced his movements in his mind and decided he was only a few blocks from the Twisted Tail. He sheathed his sword and pulled the hood closer around his face. If he could put a few blocks between himself and the riders, he might elude them before they blocked off the street and mounted a house-to-house search.

Briefly, he considered searching for an entrance to the labyrinth. It might be safer in the caverns beneath the city, but he was too curious to see how the city could justify the unprovoked slaughter of its citizens.

A short time later, the Twisted Tail's shadowy interior suited his need to maintain his anonymity. At a small table in a darkened corner, he ordered a pitcher of ale, keeping his face averted from the hobbit that waited on him.

Nearby, news of the massacre had already become the hot topic of conversation. A rawulf told a group sitting at a table, "I was standing at the door when a Warrior told old Ironsides that the humans had staged an uprising on the street. They started killing anyone they saw. It was a bloodbath—just terrible—women, children. Those escaped slaves from the slave market did it. They murdered the Warriors sent after them yesterday, stealing their clothes and armor, then launched their attack in broad daylight just a few blocks from here. Some people mistook them for Warriors, if you can imagine. They just began killing everyone in the street. Luckily, a mounted column was nearby and managed to get most of them."

An elf said, "I saw it, and I saw Warriors on horseback. I was walking down the street when a crowd came running this way. Warriors were chasing the people...and they were not humans or escaped slaves. The troops shot arrows into the crowd, and those on horseback lined up and charged at full gallop with their lances down. They slaughtered everyone, without any warning. I hightailed it here as quick as I could, to get off the street. It didn't seem too healthy to stand around. I doubt they want witnesses."

"That's ridiculous," interrupted a dwarf. "The Guild Council may be high-handed, but they'd never sanction that. There's no profit in it. They need tourists. You can't let armed troops run amok, slaughtering your customers in broad daylight. It's bad for business."

"Those weren't Guild troops," the elf retorted. "They wore the Arch Regent's colors. I doubt whether She cares what the Council thinks."

"You're saying She ordered it?" the rawulf asked.

"Who else would dare? The city's been in an uproar since that killing in the slave market. Everyone is searching for this League of the Crimson Crescent. I suspect what happened had to do with that."

"If it was the Regent, it may not be wise to question the official version," the rawulf said. "You never know who might be listening. She has ears everywhere."

"I don't care," the elf said stubbornly. "I'm tired of wondering every time I open my mouth whether I'm going to feel a tap on my shoulder. It's getting ridiculous."

"You can say what you want," the rawulf said, rising

from the table, "but I'd prefer you didn't say it around me. I've never seen the castle dungeons, and I have no desire to do so."

"It's people like you that make it possible for this to happen," the elf said hotly. "You're so afraid that someone might realize you have a thought that you just close your eyes to everything. You parrot the official line. And if any-one opens your eyes to the truth, even for just a moment, you run away from it."

"Say what you like," the rawulf answered. "I have a wife and children to think about."

"What kind of life is in store for them?" the elf demanded. "What will they think when they grow up and realize that their father was too afraid to do what was right?"

"What's *right*? All you're doing is shooting your fool mouth off, coming very close to treason. I came here to watch Cobran kill this challenger tonight. I don't want to talk about politics. We don't know what happened today. I don't care what you think you saw. I say, let the Guild Council handle it."

When the elf started to respond, the dwarf shoved him off the bench. "No more nonsense. I want something to eat, then I want a good seat for the fight. I have money riding on Cobran."

The elf picked himself off the floor and stalked away in silence.

"Stupid fool. He's got more mouth than sense."

"What if he's right, though?" a hobbit who had remained quiet at the table asked. "What if the Arch Regent did order troops to slaughter people in the streets?"

"What if She did? Will it make you feel any better know-ing that as you rot inside Her dungeon? It makes no sense to meddle in these affairs. Worse things have happened and will happen again. The only thing you can do is make sure they don't happen to you. That's what that elf needs to realize. You can't make a difference. No one can. That's why I'm not going to worry about it. I'm going to enjoy the fight tonight."

Bill considered the dwarf's words as he sat nursing his ale. Could one person make a difference? He'd freed fourteen slaves yesterday. He'd made a difference in their lives—and indirectly, he'd cost lives today. He'd set off a massive massacre, causing anguish and agony for untold numbers of people. He suspected that even more would die as the Empire relentlessly searched for him.

Did everyone who had ever defied a totalitarian regime suffer these same misgivings? Did he have the right to jeopardize others? Those who suffered probably didn't think so. Those who had been murdered wouldn't think so. The great majority probably preferred being left alone to enjoy Trillius' illicit delights.

Yet today's outrages had upset the pleasant facade that made it so easy to ignore the more brutal aspects of this society. Despite whether he had the right to upset that false tranquillity, Bill knew he had no choice. He had no way to change what had happened. They would continue searching for him, and they'd kill him if they caught him.

The conversations he'd overheard here and at the Prancing Robe showed that many citizens knew they were lulling themselves with a false sense of safety. If the powers that controlled the city were willing to massacre their own citizens in broad daylight just to get one man, was anyone in Trillius really safe?

Chapter Six

Bill decided the apathetic citizens of Trillius needed another shock. When the waiter came back, he ordered a large dinner and a candle. Keeping his face to the dark corner, he studied the tunnel map as he ate. *This just might work*, he thought to himself.

Rising from the table, he pulled his cloak and hood tight around him. There was no reason to let anyone know that Public Enemy Number One was on the prowl. As he left the inn, his eyes darted along the street. No one paid any attention to him. Checking his map, he confirmed the nearest entrance to the caverns.

He walked to a nearby alley. *This should be the place.* Despite a meticulous search, however, he found nothing that looked right, no outline of a door, no crack in the wall. He touched the bricks, examining them one by one.

As he was about to give up, his fingers slipped into a groove in the brick. He looked it over carefully, but saw only parallel lines. His fingers, however, felt something different than his eyes saw. They traced the familiar quarter moon shape. *It must be disguised with some sort of optical illusion*, he reasoned.

He glanced up and down the alley, double-checking to ensure he was still alone. Reassured, he inserted the crescent key and pulled, but the ancient lock resisted. He tugged harder as he jimmied the key, until, slowly it gave way, and a door opened before him.

Drawing his sword, he slipped into the cool darkness, pulling the door closed behind him. With no torch, he had to trust the drawing he'd memorized during his dinner. He stepped carefully, feeling for any loose stones or holes in the floor. He felt along the wall for the next crescent indentation. "It's got to be here," he muttered.

"What does?" a voice in the darkness asked.

"Who's that?"

"A friend," the voice answered. "You did me a service, and I've been watching you. You nearly lost me when you got on that horse. However, I'd heard that you frequent the Twisted Tail, and sure enough, you went there after losing those Warriors."

"You've been following me?"

"Don't make it sound so sinister," the voice responded. "I was impressed that you discovered how the key works. Most people depend too heavily on their sight. They are unwilling to trust their other senses."

"Who are you?" Bill demanded.

"In good time, my good man. I only now chose to announce myself when it became clear that, at the rate you're going, you'd never find the key hole you seek. You miscounted your steps."

"How do you know what I'm looking for?"

"How else could I have followed you in here?" replied the voice from the shadows. "Take ten steps to your left."

"Why should I trust you?"

"Why should you not? If I were your enemy, I could have turned you in any time today. If I wanted to harm you, what better opportunity would I have than a few moments ago when you were completely unaware of my presence."

Bill considered this, then began edging to the left, counting ten steps, using his sword for a staff to test the floor for hazards.

"Why don't you just tell me who you are?" he said.

"In good time," the voice said. "For now, content yourself to know someone is looking out for you. Move your right hand slightly to the left."

Bill's fingers felt the familiar crescent indentation.

"When you need me most, I'll be there," the voice said.

Bill fumbled with the key and jerked open the entrance. As torchlight entered the passageway, he sensed that he was again alone.

As he stepped through the doorway into a darkened room, he heard the clink of ale glasses overhead and smiled. He was in the basement of the Twisted Tail.

After closing the passage door, he felt for the crescent indentation and marked the spot in his mind. He might be in a hurry when he returned.

As he walked through the darkened hallway, he could see the ring where the evening's fight would take place. His steps quickened as he approached the arena. Only a few people had taken seats in the front row. An empty seat awaited him next to a pillar.

All around, the crowd's excitement mounted. A steady stream of people took their seats. "I've bet a lot on Cobran tonight," said a dracon next to Bill. "I'm counting on him to finish off Yobo in the first round."

By the time a stout dwarf sauntered into the ring, the amphitheater's seats were filled.

"I hope old Ironsides doesn't waste time talking tonight,"

the dracon muttered. "The slug always takes his time up there, hoping that if he talks long enough, everybody will get thirsty and hungry and buy more of his slop."

The evening began with what Ironsides called "the preliminaries."

A young dracon battled a scarred rawulf who had seen better days. The dracon made short work of him, drawing hisses from the disappointed crowd.

"They always do this," the dracon announced at Bill's elbow. "They give these young bucks easy marks to build up their records. The bettors just look at their win–loss records. They don't bother to check out what kind of hacks they butchered. Then, they're surprised when their challenger with the so–called thirty–to–one record gets cut down the minute he steps into a ring with a real fighter."

The second bout of the evening featured a young lizardman against a faerie.

"I like these novelty fights," the dracon said, prodding the silent Bill. "You'd think a lizardman could crush one of those little winged buggers. But you can't crush what you can't grab, and those little faeries are fast."

The lizardman carried a sword. He paced the ring, padding back and forth, trying to back the faerie into a corner. The faerie was armed with a wand.

"Those wands don't look like much, but they can whack you quick and hard," the dracon observed.

The lizardman dashed in for a quick thrust, hoping to end the fight quickly. Like lightning, the faerie dodged the blow, parried, and slashed across the lizardman's eyes. Temporarily blinded, the lizardman backtracked hurriedly, ripping the air with his sword to keep the faerie at a distance.

The tiny sprite pursued, diving low to deliver a nasty crack on the lizardman's knee. The injured lizardman hobbled, balancing on one leg, as he futilely ripped the air with his blade.

The crowd applauded, hooting with enjoyment as the faerie darted in close to slash his face, once, twice, three times.

The dracon beside Bill let loose a huge barnyard laugh. "Faeries don't hit all that hard, but those wands deliver their own smack. People think faeries are soft and cuddly, but they can be cruel when they've got you down."

As if for emphasis, the faerie cracked the lizardman on his remaining good knee. He collapsed but rolled to his feet again in a fluid movement, catching the faerie off guard. When the lizard suddenly came in for a killing stroke, the sprite found it had stepped too close. The lizardman managed to smack it with the side of his sword, sending it sailing across the ring.

"That could be all she wrote," the dracon said.

The creature's wings slumped, their edges crumpled. It rose to its feet with difficulty. The lizardman limped toward it, favoring one leg. When within a few feet, he again swatted the faerie with the side of his sword, knocking it end–over–end across the mat.

The faerie slid into a corner, still desperately hanging onto its wand.

Applause exploded from the crowd, which approved of the victor's decision to play with his opponent now that the end had come. As he stooped to pick it up, however, the faerie jabbed its wand into its attacker's eye, then bashed the lizardman's skull several times for emphasis. The lizardman shrieked in pain, stumbling backward, senseless from the blows. The faerie followed, relentlessly cracking the lizardman's bad leg as he tried to back away.

"It can't fly," the dracon said. "It figures it'll bring the big guy down to his level so he can finish him off."

The crowd, on its feet, applauded wildly, caught up in the bloodlust as the lizardman delivered a punishing kick to the faerie, sending it sailing across the mat. With a blood-thirsty roar of anger, he took two steps and dove after the faerie, landing squarely on it.

Rolling off, he chopped twice with his sword, severing its crushed wings. The faerie screamed a sharp keening cry. The lizardman pounded its head with his clenched fist, silencing it. Without hesitation, the lizardman chopped again with his sword.

In expectant silence, the crowd watched as he slashed again and again, cutting the once delicate creature to pieces. A few members of the crowd began clapping in unison with the swings of the lizardman's blade, and soon the entire crowd clapped along with the rhythmic thrusts.

The lizardman grabbed the faerie by its torso, lifted it to its mouth, and bit off its head. The crowd cheered. Bill felt nauseous.

"That young fellow has a future," the dracon said. "He knows how to entertain a crowd. They'll be talking about this one all week. I bet everybody here was rooting for the little guy, but the lizardman really charmed them.

"Most of these youngsters just hack and slash," the dracon went on. "They don't take any chances. They protect them-selves, waiting for the other guy to make a mistake. They don't show any spirit. This fellow gets mad, he gets even. He'll be a big draw if he's half as good with someone his own size.

"You sure are quiet." The dracon nudged Bill. "I hope I'm not bothering you." He nudged again. "Well, am I bothering you? I just thought I'd advise you on the finer points."

Bill was saved from responding by Ironsides' reappearance on stage. "I know what you've been waiting to see tonight," the dwarf shouted. "Are you ready?"

"Bring on Cobran," an elf shouted.

"Who?" Ironsides teased.

"Cobran!" several people yelled.

"Are you talking about the Empire's Champion?"

"Cobran!"

"You mean the undefeated winner of 257 matches?"

"Cobran! Cobran!" the crowd shrieked.

"Do you mean the most dangerous and powerful creature alive today?"

"Cobran! Cobran! Cobran!" the crowd chanted in a frenzy.

"Bring him up here," Ironsides said.

The crowd went wild, shouting Cobran's name in unison as the powerfully built lizardman Bill had seen before climbed onto the stage. Cobran deliberately ignored the crowd, though the amphitheater rang with his name. As the chant grew in intensity, his arms—along with his scimitar—rose to acknowledge the homage. He repeatedly thrust the blade into the air, delighting the audience as he parried and feinted with an imaginary foe, dodging faster and faster to the rhythm of the crowd's chant.

Stopping abruptly, the lizardman raised his blade over his head with both hands as the crowd's shouting reached a crescendo.

Now, Yobo entered the ring. His snakelike mouth opened, and his tongue darted out as if to taste Cobran's presence.

In the back of the arena, a few voices shouted his name. Cobran glared in their direction, tensing, as if he might spring into the audience to silence them.

"He's a mean customer," the dracon whispered to Bill. "I once saw him go into the crowd after someone who ticked him off. Made short work of him, too."

With a bellow from both corners, the two reptiles squared off. Yobo moved quickly, swinging a sword in one hand and an ax in the other. Cobran's two–handed blade crashed down on him. Yobo parried with the ax and tried to jab with his free blade. Cobran anticipated the maneuver. Swinging his sword free from the ax, he blocked the thrust. Yobo swung his ax, but Cobran blocked it with his sword.

As the two weapons crashed in mid–air, Cobran's blade cracked and fell from his sword's handle. The champion stared in surprise. Yobo bellowed in triumph, shaking his two weapons. He moved in quickly, swinging his ax and jabbing with his sword, throwing the champion on the defensive.

Cobran backpedaled, trying to keep his distance from the sword Yobo used to herd him into the corner. The challenger's plan was obvious. He'd use the greater reach afforded by his blade to keep his competitor off–balance. When he found an opening, he'd use his ax to fell Cobran like a log.

The two circled the ring, looking for an opening until Yobo grew tired of the cat–and–mouse game. Flourishing his sword above his head, he swung down on Cobran. The champion stepped into the swing, using his sword handle to block the blow. His other muscled arm darted out, grabbing Yobo's ax arm.

The two wrestled until Cobran faltered. Yobo kneed him

in the stomach, sending him staggering back. Following quickly, Yobo swung his ax. Still stunned from the last blow, Cobran stepped under the swing. Nonetheless, Yobo managed to rap his skull with the hilt of his weapon. Cobran staggered, shook his head, lurched unsteadily.

Yobo thrust his sword. Cobran intercepted with his sword handle. But Yobo struck a glancing blow to his opponent's forehead, sending the champion tottering backwards.

Cobran hesitated in the corner, his head swaying as Yobo played to the crowd while he readied himself to advance for the kill.

"It's show time," Bill said to the dracon as he jumped to his feet. He vaulted into the ring. Yobo spotted him as he leaped the ropes. The crowd did, too. Bill heard startled gasps as he faced the surprised challenger.

With a cry of rage, Yobo bore down on him. Bill drew his own sword. "Don't fail me now." Meanwhile, his heartbeat took off.

His blade met Yobo's with a clang. He stepped aside as Yobo swung his ax at him. He neatly dodged the weapon, positioning himself between the reeling Cobran and the enraged Yobo.

"Cobran!" he shouted to the confused creature against the ring's railings. "Try not to move too much! They've poisoned you."

Bewildered, Cobran tried to focus his eyes on his rescuer. "Who poison Cobran?"

Yobo's blade darted dangerously close to Bill's midsection, interrupting the conversation as Bill deflected it with his sword. He spun, flicking his weapon near the lizardman's eyes to keep him at a distance.

Cobran seemed on the verge of collapse. Bill knew that if he didn't act quickly his efforts would be in vain.

Bill lunged at Yobo, who circled to the side in order to get closer to Cobran. "Cobran's mine," he hissed, his tongue darting out. "I taste a human. After I chop you down like a weed, I'll cut out your heart. I'll peel your skin and make a cap with it."

Bill dodged a swipe from Yobo's ax and advanced toward his opponent, stabbing at his throat. Yobo brought his ax down in a jarring blow, but Bill parried it. The force of the swipe partially numbed his arm, however. He jabbed his sword into the lizardman's forearm, cutting a deep gash in the leathery skin.

Yobo screamed as his ax fell from his hand. Recovering with a shriek of rage, he swung his sword in a wide arc that Bill neatly blocked. Bill darted forward, using the opening Yobo had left. He thrust, surprising Yobo as his blade slipped past the lizardman's defense and pierced his armor, impaling his midsection.

Stepping back from his shocked antagonist, Bill plunged his blade a second time into the lizardman's chest.

Yobo stood motionless, gasping both with pain and surprise. Tottering toward Bill, he stepped too close and quickly found Bill's blade slashing across his throat.

The crowd continually jeered Bill—until he chopped Yobo's arm. They were surprised and chagrined that an unknown could even draw blood against a fighter of Yobo's prowess. When Bill actually stabbed the challenger, some cheered. As they watched Yobo stagger back, blood pouring from Bill's final thrust, they began applauding wildly.

Bill seized the moment to pull his hood back and reveal

his face.

"He's a human! A human is the new champion!"

Yobo collapsed, blood gurgling from his mouth. Without waiting for the crowd's next reaction, Bill ran to Cobran. He grabbed the confused champion by the arm. "If you want to live, come with me."

"You champion?"

"We've got to get out of here," Bill said. He yanked the champion's arm, but found it was like yanking a wall. He yanked again. Dazed, Cobran came with him, stumbling to the ropes lining the ring. "We've got to jump it," Bill shouted.

Bill vaulted the ropes, with Cobran closely following him into the dimly lit hallway.

Behind them, the crowd rose to its feet, some cheering him. Others simply stared, their mouths agape in bewilderment. Some, enraged, shouted that the match had been rigged.

Bill grinned. "I wonder how the gamblers will pay off after a match like this one?" he muttered. Cobran seemed too bewildered to understand.

The grin quickly left Bill's face at the sight of several dozen heavily armed warriors, weapons drawn, advancing toward them. They were close enough to cut him off before he could reach the passageway.

"I don't think they're coming to crown me," he said.

A blinding light exploded in the faces of the warriors, dazzling them and leaving them sightless. Bill blinked, and his own vision returned instantly, though the soldiers and the crowd seemed to remain dazed.

"Maybe we can make it." He pulled Cobran along with him.

"Why you save Cobran?" the lizardman asked.

"We don't have time to talk right now." Bill urged him down the corridor.

"Where do you think you're going?" a vaguely familiar voice shouted. Bill spun and recognized one of the two dracons who had plotted to poison Cobran.

"You've ruined me," the dracon snarled. "I've lost everything." He seemed to recognize Bill. "You were in here yesterday. You weren't passed out, you were listening to us. I should have killed you when I had the chance. I'll correct that mistake now." He unsheathed his sword.

"Cobran, this is the guy who poisoned you and rigged your sword so it would fall apart," Bill said.

"Me kill." With a spurt of energy, Cobran darted from Bill's grasp. Lurching toward the dracon, he grabbed the surprised creature's throat. Bill heard the dracon's neck snap.

Bill fitted the crescent key into the indentation and yanked, opening the door. "Let's go, Cobran," he said as he stepped into the secret passage.

"Cobran got him." He staggered after Bill into the hole in the wall. As the sound of running feet neared them, Bill found the keyhole and disappeared into the labyrinth.

Chapter Seven

"They'll have fun figuring out how we escaped," Bill said. "Come on, we've got to find you some help, Cobran."

"Cobran feel funny." The lizardman lurched down the dark passage. His arms flailed as he lost his balance.

Bill paused to steady him. "Lean on me."

"Why we run away?" Cobran halted suddenly. "Cobran never runs. Cobran's enemies run, not Cobran."

"I'm sure that's usually true," Bill said, "but you're not feeling well right now."

"Yes," he agreed, putting more of his weight on Bill for emphasis. "No understand. No like."

"It's the poison. That's why you couldn't fight Yobo. They rigged your sword to snap and slipped you a poison so you couldn't defend yourself. If we don't find some kind of antidote, it'll kill you."

"Cowards kill with poison. Cobran find them, smash them, pound them, tear arms off!"

"I believe you will," Bill said, helping the husky lizardman down the passage. The lizardman grew heavier with each step.

Bill concentrated, trying to recall the map. His plan had worked perfectly. He'd given the people a shock from which they would not soon recover. They'd have a tough time reconciling their attitude toward humans with what they'd seen tonight. Every time they looked at one of their human slaves cowering before their whips, they'd think about what they'd seen tonight and wonder. He smiled. Only one question remained: What was he supposed to do now? It was clear Cobran had taken a lethal dose of something.

Bill considered his options. The Prancing Robe was out. Zorth could help, but the inn would be under surveillance. Orwynn seemed his only hope—if Cobran could walk that far.

"Why you help Cobran? No one help Cobran. You kill Yobo, but you can't be champion if you not kill Cobran."

"I don't want to be champion. At the Twisted Tail yesterday, I heard a plot to kill you. They wanted you to throw the fight, but you wouldn't, so they rigged your sword and poisoned you. I decided to try to help. Simple as that."

"No one ever help Cobran before." The lizardman clumsily patted Bill on the arm. Then his foot slipped, and he fell, taking Bill with him.

Bill tried to help him up, but Cobran couldn't rise. "Cobran tired."

"He'll die if he goes to sleep," a familiar voice spoke in the darkness. "That would be a pity. You took such a chance getting into that ring. Cobran himself would have killed you if he could have."

"You again!" Bill shouted. It was the voice of whoever had helped him find the Twisted Tail.

"Did you notice that little burst of light that halted those warriors? I gave you one of the great exits of all time. They'll be talking about it for years. I told you I'd be there when you needed me. They're still searching that corridor, talking about how a human vanished into thin air. They think you're some kind of magician who walks through walls."

"If I was a magician," Bill said, "I'd know how to cure Cobran. He's dying."

"I can cure him," the voice said. "Pour this down his throat."

Something hit Bill in the chest and fell clanging to the floor. Bill fumbled for it.

"Perhaps a little light might help," the voice said.

A soft glow appeared a few feet from Bill. It emanated from a thin wand held by a tiny bearded man, wearing a cape.

"You're the faerie from the Prancing Robe. The one the dracon grabbed."

"And you and your friends helped me out. I was testing you. He couldn't have grabbed me if I hadn't allowed it. It's a good thing you and your felpur friends convinced him to let me go. I was tempted to incinerate the imbecile, though I've found that advertising my abilities can be extremely unhealthy. Now hurry and pour that vial down Cobran's throat."

The tiny cylinder was easy to find in the wand's glow. Bill uncorked it and poured it between Cobran's lips, even though the white color around the lizardman's mouth, like the underbelly of a fish, repulsed him.

"Who are you?" Bill asked the stranger.

"They call me Zynaryxx," the faerie said. "Orwynn sent me to look after you. He's quite taken with you. He told me to size you up for myself. I must say, he's right. I've never seen anyone upset this town so terribly and in only a few days. Quite remarkable."

"If Orwynn sent you, you must be part of this League of the Crimson Crescent."

"Bright too! Orwynn assured me he said nothing about

the League to you, but he underestimated you. Yes, I must agree with him, the League needs you."

"I'm not sure whether I'm interested in joining," Bill said.

"We don't force anyone to join us. I assume that you'll keep our little secret."

"I will," Bill said. "But I'm surprised you're so willing to trust me. You don't even know me."

"I know enough," the faerie said. "I've watched you closely. Besides, I think you'll join the League. After all, you agree with our aims. And whether you like it or not, everyone in Trillius already believes you're part of it. With the whole city searching for you, the League is the only organization that can help you. And you'll need us to rescue your felpur friends."

"What's happened to them?"

Zynaryxx shook his head. "You were in their room when the warriors were sent in after you. When they didn't catch you, they kept the room under tight watch, hoping you'd return. You didn't come back, but your friends did. I suspect they're being questioned about you right now."

"Why didn't you tell me sooner?" Bill demanded, jumping to his feet.

"It happened shortly before Cobran's fight. I had someone watching the inn with instructions to intercept Zorth and Quatar. Unfortunately, he missed them. By the time he got to the Twisted Tail to tell me, they'd been taken in, and you were in the ring. I caught up with you as soon as the passage was unoccupied for a moment."

Cobran stirred. He seemed to be regaining his color.

"Our lizard friend is coming around," the faerie said. "He'll need this potion to help him recover his strength. And I suspect we'll need his help to free your friends. It's a restorative.

He suffered quite a bit of damage from that poison."

"Are you some kind of magician?"

"You mean these healing potions? I just buy them from priests I know. Usually, I don't go in much for healing. My studies took me in an entirely different direction. I guess you could call me a magician, although we prefer the term mage. I've spent most of my life studying the intricacies of thaumaturgy. It occasionally comes in handy in the pursuit of my other studies."

"Which are?"

"I've been studying the Empire. That's one of the reasons I'm interested in you. I suspect that the Empire is growing quite curious about you."

"Me?"

"Don't play dumb with me. You've set off a slave revolt, escaped the Warriors' Guild on three separate occasions, been proclaimed the greatest warrior in the Kingdom, and reinvigorated the only existing conspiracy against the Empire. That's not bad for a few days in town. But the Arch Regent becomes quite concerned when Her control is threatened. So we must move quickly."

Bill said, "Granted, I've experienced an interesting few days here, but I can't imagine how anyone could consider me a threat to this Empire. I've seen the kind of control they exercise. I don't care about politics; I don't really care about Trillius. I've just seen people in trouble and did what I could to help them." He realized that he felt a bit ashamed saying this, for there had been a time when he ignored people in trouble.

"That's the point," the faerie said. "The Empire's entire strategy for maintaining control has been based on convincing its citizens not to get involved. They keep their noses out of what you call politics. Avert their eyes, glad it's not them being hauled away. Trillius is a city of a thousand entertainments, designed specifically to keep the populace diverted from what's occurring right under their noses.

"But you've rubbed it in their faces," Zynaryxx went on. "To make matters worse, the authorities can't catch you. You have no idea how much that must grate on the Arch Regent. She's unaccustomed to not getting Her way. The people of this city believe that anyone who challenges Her gets crushed immediately, without pity. When they see you undermining Her authority—a human, supposedly the lowest of the low—they wonder if they might reach out and help someone they care about.

"Believe me, She's thinking quite a bit about you. She can't afford to have you helping people. It could start a trend.

"Meanwhile, your friends are being held by the Warriors' Guild. Once She learns they're connected to you, She'll order the council to turn them over to Her. That's why we have to move," the faerie said, leading the way down the corridor.

Bill roused Cobran and helped him to his feet. "This isn't the way to Darktown," he said to the mage.

"We've got to get to your friends."

"What are we going to do? Walk in and say, 'Release my friends?'"

"This, the man who leaps into the ring of a championship fight to save someone he's never even met, someone as likely to kill him as to look at him, criticizing my plan before he even hears it."

"What's your plan?"

"All in good time, my friend."

Cobran had recovered his strength. He seemed groggy, but his step was sure as they made their way through the labyrinth. The faerie led them on a twisting path, up and down passageways, through doors Bill didn't realize were doors until Zynaryxx opened them.

"Are you sure you know where you're going? I've got my map if you want to check."

The faerie paused briefly. "Who do you think drew that map?"

Bill considered the time it must have taken to gain such knowledge of Trillius' underground. "You said I'd need to join your League if I wanted its help to free my friends," he said.

"We don't have time to bring in more of the League right now. Too many of the members would waste the entire night debating the issue. By the time they had decided, your friends would be in the hands of the Arch Regent. Then, we'd have a debate about whether to risk Her anger."

"Why are *you* helping me? It can't be healthy for you to challenge this Council."

"But it'll be fun," Zynaryxx said. "Orwynn got me to thinking that the League really has grown too cautious. We sit back talking, talking, endlessly debating about the right time to act, while conditions worsen, our enemies grow more powerful, and the people become more listless. Organizations rot when they only talk about their noble principles. The League needs to act if it's to give Trillius any real hope. If we show you can strike with impunity, the citizens will rally. We'll gain recruits and strike fear in the hearts of the Arch Regent's minions. The real power of any despot is the power to convince the people that they have no hope."

"But why help my friends and me?" Bill persisted.

"It's precisely your friends we must help," Zynaryxx said. "For years now, the people have heard that humans are the lowest of all creatures, little better than orcs, betrayers of the people, the foulest scum ever created, deserving of enslavement. Imagine the stir when the whole city talks about how a human saved a lizardman and won the championship. Think what they'll say when they hear that this same human, along with a lizardman and a faerie, risked their lives to rescue two felpurs. The very idea! I couldn't dream up a better piece of propaganda to demonstrate the fellowship of all creatures."

Bill looked at Cobran, who hadn't spoken for some time. "Cobran, we will soon face some difficult fighting. Do you want to be involved? We could take you up to the street."

"Cobran great fighter." His eyes sparkled at the idea. "Cobran go with Bill."

"If you do, you'll be in trouble. They'll hunt you. You won't be able to go back in the ring again. The city will be angry that you helped me. They won't let you be champion again."

The lizardman impatiently shook his head. "Cobran champion. Always champion. No one tell Cobran what to do.

"Hunt Cobran!" he snorted. "Cobran hunt hunters. Cobran kill hunters."

"I don't think you understand," Bill said. "The whole city is after me. If you stay with us, they'll be after you, too. Everywhere you go, they'll be after you."

Cobran looked at Bill impassively, his reptilian eyes unblinking. "Cobran was dying. Cobran have no friends. People hurt Cobran. Try to kill Cobran. Bill help Cobran. Save Cobran. Cobran help friend Bill. People try to hurt Bill must kill Cobran first. Cobran not easy to kill."

As if tired from such a long speech, the lizardman became silent, satisfied that he'd settled the issue.

"Remarkable," the faerie said. "Quite remarkable indeed."

A half hour later, he halted, motioning for silence. "Through here," he said in a low whisper. "The anteroom off the Council's private dungeon. The guards hang out here while the inquisitors perform their work."

"The inquisitors?"

"At times, the Council demands answers, and people decline to cooperate. The inquisitors have ways that help loosen tongues, although they tend to loosen other joints and major organs, as well. When we go through, we'll need to move quickly. The element of surprise will be our major weapon. Don't hesitate. Just go directly into the passageway."

Zynaryxx pulled out his own crescent device and inserted it into a featureless wall. He tugged twice, but nothing happened. Bill grabbed it and tugged, but found no response despite his own exertions.

"Cobran help." Grasping the device, the lizardman pulled, straining motionless against the rock. With a snap, a doorway opened into darkness.

The trio stepped quietly into the corridor as Zynaryxx extinguished his wand. "I don't want to let them know we're coming," he whispered.

They followed the dark passageway, the stillness interrupted only by their breathing and padded footsteps. After several steps, Bill felt the faerie pause in front of him. "Get ready," Zynaryxx said. "Keep your eyes closed when we first enter. When I say *go*, count to three before you open your eyes."

"Let's go," he whispered.

Even with his eyes tightly closed, Bill felt the brightness exploding in the chamber they entered. He drew his sword as he opened his eyes. The room was better suited to banquets than to a lounge for heavily armed men. Tattered tapestries hung on the ancient granite. Sputtering torches stood in holders attached to the walls, though the warriors didn't need the torches. They had obviously been blinded by the faerie mage's fireworks.

Bill dashed through the chamber, ignoring the stunned warriors groping blindly for their weapons, shouting for assistance. Cobran paused, hauled one guard from his seat with one muscled arm, while yanking the guard's sword from his sheath. The lizardman smiled as he examined the blade he had taken, dropping the guard back into his seat before casually backhanding him with the sword. The guard slumped from the blow, his head lolled back in an unnatural way.

At the end of the chamber, a closed door barred the way. Bill pushed and pulled at its handle, until Cobran shoved him aside.

Putting his shoulder to it, the lizardman thrust himself against it, ramming it the way a linebacker crashes into a tackling dummy. Hinges snapped as it collapsed into the inner room.

The warriors' cries had evidently alerted those inside. As Bill followed Cobran, he could see Zorth and Quatar strapped to tables with wheels that were apparently used to stretch apart the tables. Five black-masked inquisitors pulled wicked–looking sabers out as Bill and Cobran stormed into the room.

Cobran smiled, his tongue snaking out as if to taste their presence. "Cobran tastes fear," he said, eyeing them.

Pointing his sword at his adversaries, the lizardman advanced on them, studying them warily as he positioned himself in front of the captives.

Bill ran to Quatar, slashing the leather thongs binding her wrists to the rack.

"You tamper with prisoners of the Crown," an inquisitor said. "We have received orders that they are to be transferred to the Arch Regent. You interrupt us at your peril."

"Fool," snapped another inquisitor. "This is the human we're looking for!"

The inquisitor stepped toward Cobran. "You have no reason to consort with a human," he said. "Put your weapon down as we subdue him, and we will remember your loyalty."

Snorting derisively, Cobran darted forward, plunging his sword into the inquisitor's chest. "Good blade. Cobran like," the lizardman said as he pulled the bloody weapon from the masked man's chest.

With a startled yelp, the remaining four inquisitors attacked Cobran, wildly swinging their sabers. While Bill slashed the thongs tying Quatar's legs, Cobran deftly repelled the attackers, slashing, thrusting, parrying with the ease of a gladiator.

The inquisitors, who were used to their adversaries lying helpless while they practiced their evil craft, clumsily swung at Cobran. With snakelike grace, the lizardman strode into their midst. His blade flashed in the torchlight as it pierced the mask of one inquisitor, puncturing his eye.

As the creature screamed in pain, cutting its hands as it clawed at the blade that had pierced its eye, Cobran seemed to smile. The lizardman drove it deeper into the socket as the inquisitor collapsed.

Whipping the blade out of his victim and to the side, Cobran slashed at an advancing inquisitor. "Black masks hurt Bill's friends. Not fight fair. Tie up friends." Cobran shifted as he darted in toward the inquisitor, his sword slashing high, forcing the masked man back against the wall.

Another inquisitor tried to rescue his colleague, leaping at Cobran from behind. The gladiator spun, his sword flashing with deadly accuracy, splitting his assailant's skull, cleaving it to the neck.

Turning back to his prey still frozen against the wall Cobran feinted, advancing with deadly intent. The inquisitor looked like some rodent paralyzed in fright, its eyes fastened on the lizardman's unblinking snakelike eyes. Cobran's tongue slithered out.

As Bill freed Zorth from his bonds, Cobran's sword hacked off the arm of his victim. His sword again shot out, carving off the other arm. The lizardman smiled as he spitted the inquisitor's abdomen and watched it collapse on the floor, writhing in agony.

A fifth and final remaining inquisitor shrieked in sheer terror as Cobran turned to face it. He shouted. "She will find you. She will punish you. You will experience agonies beyond your imagination when She is done with you."

Cobran's sword danced out, knocking the inquisitor's blade from its hand.

"You will pay dearly," it shouted.

Cobran dropped his sword. The inquisitor paused,

stunned. The gladiator stepped closer to the masked man, his muscled arm reaching out to yank his adversary off his feet. Effortlessly, he picked him up with both hands raised him over his head, knelt with fluid grace, and dropped the inquisitor. Bill could hear the inquisitor's back snap as it smashed against the lizardman's knee.

"How did you find us?" Zorth asked, attempting to rise from the table, his fearful eyes fixed on Cobran. Tenderly rubbing their wrists and ankles, the two felpurs stood up from the torture devices.

"Again, we owe you our lives," Quatar said. Her nostrils quivered and her jaws bunched, as if she were trying not to wretch.

"We don't have time to talk right now," Bill said. "Can you walk?"

The two felpurs nodded, gingerly taking a few steps before collapsing on the floor.

"Great," Bill said.

"Cobran help Bill's friends." The lizardman scooped one up in each arm and flung them roughly over his broad shoulders. "We go now. Find little man."

Neither Zorth nor Quatar looked very comfortable hanging like feed bags over Cobran's shoulders, but Bill knew they didn't have time to worry about it.

They ran out of the torture chamber back into the guardroom only to see Zynaryxx throw a fireball into the midst of the warriors, some of whom had recovered from their temporary blindness. The faerie created a wall of fire between the guards and their escape route.

"Hurry," he shouted, heaving another fireball into the guards' midst.

Frightened by the flames, some warriors ran away, shouting. Others, who had not yet recovered their sight, shrieked in terror. Several went up in flames, their shrill screams of agony adding to the confusion of the growing inferno. A guard armed with a bow fired an arrow at Cobran. The arrow pierced his side, and Cobran staggered but kept his arms around the felpurs.

The mage threw a third fireball at the bowman, who exploded into a ball of flames. Landing amid the confused guards, the fireball ignited the tapestries, rapidly spreading around the room. The mage collapsed, exhausted.

Bill grabbed him, picked him up, and ran into the corridor they had used to enter the room. Cobran limped behind him. Bill hurried through the dark corridor with the mage in his arms.

The faerie opened its eyes. "Close the door. I didn't want to create a fire storm, but I couldn't take a chance. There were too many for you. By tomorrow She'll know I was there."

"How will She know?" Bill groped for the door to the passageway.

"We go back a long way, She and I. She thought I was dead. By tomorrow, however, She'll have no doubt that the League of the Crimson Crescent has returned. She'll even know we used the labyrinth. Then, it will become very dangerous down here."

Handing his wand to Bill, he whispered, "Use this to guide us back to Orwynn's tavern. It will fade whenever you take a wrong turn. It'll brighten every time you take the correct path." Zynaryxx' eyes closed with exhaustion.

Chapter Eight

"Can you make it, Cobran?" Bill asked.

"Cobran go with Bill."

The wand guided them through the passageways. The lizardman staggered behind Bill and Zynaryxx, his jaw clenched, his breathing labored.

"Bill, we really need to stop," Zorth said. "I'm not certain which torture is worse, the rack or being lugged around by your friend. I can help, if we stop for a moment."

"I don't like the idea of resting here," Zynaryxx sighed. "Creatures we don't want to meet may be already stirring in these passageways."

"Please," Quatar said.

"Very well, if Zorth thinks he can help, we'll give it a try."

"Put them down, Cobran." Bill ordered, taking a seat on the passage's floor next to Zynaryxx. He hadn't realized how tired he was until he let himself rest.

Zorth and Quatar leaned against the stone walls, looking uncertainly from Bill, to the drowsing faerie, to the lizardman. "This is Cobran, the fighter?" Zorth asked.

Bill said, "I told you he was in trouble. I couldn't leave him to the mercies of those gamblers. It's a good thing I didn't, too. You saw the way he handled those inquisitors. We'd still be in there if he hadn't been there to carry you out."

Quatar moved unsteadily to bow to the lizardman. "We

are in your debt. Our litter stands ready if you ever need our assistance."

Zorth attempted to do the same, but failed. "I must beg your forgiveness, Cobran," he said weakly. "When Bill told us he planned to help you, I tried to convince him to not attempt it. Once again, I have been proven too hasty in my judgments. I can only hope that you will accept our friendship and excuse our error."

Cobran gazed steadily at the two felpurs. "No one ask Cobran to forgive before. Cobran like new friends. Furry. Cobran glad could save furry friends from bad masks. Not have friends before met Bill."

"I think we can help you, Cobran," Zorth said. "But first, we'll have to pull that arrow out of your side."

"Cobran pull arrow out."

Grasping the wooden shaft in one hand, he yanked it out of his side, gasping as the barbed point pulled loose.

Zorth raised his hands, murmuring words Bill didn't understand. They sounded soothing. Cobran's gaping wound closed, and the bleeding stopped.

"What did you do?" Bill asked.

"It's a healing spell," Zorth said. "One of the simpler spells of the priests of Yalor, although it takes quite a bit from me."

Zorth again muttered an incantation, over himself, Quatar, and Zynaryxx. The faerie stirred and opened his eyes.

Both felpurs seemed more relaxed, though Zorth seemed wearied from his effort. "Since we must be on our way, I can give Cobran, Quatar, and myself the additional stamina we need to complete the journey, although I warn you the effort will later drain me."

"None of this would have been necessary if it hadn't been for me," Bill said. "They wanted me. Hovra told them I was in the Prancing Robe."

"Hovra!" Zorth said. "I knew I should have killed him. He will pay for that. I can assure you that his own clan will turn him over to me when they learn of his treachery."

"I barely managed to escape," Bill continued. "They waited outside the Tavern. They sent Hovra in after me, but I escaped through a window and slipped past them. They butchered everyone on the street in an effort to get me."

"We heard about it," Zorth said. "Only we heard a slightly different version. In that story, the humans attempted to revolt and slaughtered everyone on the street until the Warriors arrived. The humans supposedly were dressed like Warriors in the Arch Regents colors, part of some elaborate ruse to make the people of Trillius think that the Crown could not be trusted."

"Many people on that street saw for themselves that there were no humans dressed up as warriors," Bill said. "They know the truth. I can't believe no one challenges the official line. Can an entire city be so frightened that they lie to themselves while their own government slaughters its citizens?"

"Don't be so quick to judge them," Zorth said. "You have no idea of the horrors they have seen. You are an outsider. While my clan lives far from Trillius, we have experienced the fear that the Unnamed One visits on our kingdom's people. Even questioning the Crown can cost one his life or even worse.

"If you had a wife, children, loved ones whose lives would be forfeited, you'd think twice before challenging the authorities," Zorth said. "You're only risking yourself."

"I see your point," Bill said. "You wouldn't have been taken prisoner if not for me."

"We accepted that risk," Zorth said. "We knew the possible consequences when we brought you into the Robe. But you shouldn't blame yourself for our capture. Hovra will pay dearly for it. When he betrayed you, he knew that we'd be taken in as well."

"Exactly what happened to you?" Bill asked.

"We spent the day searching for our litter brother," Quatar said. "We knew he'd been seen in Darktown. We traced him to The Mercenaries Martyr, a tavern close to the castle where hired thugs congregate. Some of them work for the Warriors' Guild, some for the Arch Regents forces, some as private troops for the various Guildlords. Still others hire out as freebooters. They're a rough crowd. We don't know what our brother may have been doing there, but Aleka will know."

"Who is Aleka?"

"We don't know that yet," Quatar said. "We were hoping that your friends in Darktown might be able to help."

"I've heard the name before," the faerie said. "I'm certain Orwynn will know more if we can just get to his tavern before the Arch Regent's troops start to search the labyrinth for us. If you feel well enough, I think we should move on."

"Why are you so convinced She'll know you were involved?" Bill asked. "You act as if you're old friends."

The faerie paused, giving Bill a somewhat bemused look. "We are," the faerie said. "Not in the usual way, but a long, long time ago, I knew her very well. But no longer. Today, if She could find me, She would kill me. However, I shall say no more while we're in this dark place. The shadows are Her friends now. I will tell the tale some time when we are in the light."

Turning to Zorth, the faerie bowed. "I salute you priest of Yalor," Zynaryxx said. "You have studied the healing mysteries well. I feel quite refreshed, thanks to your work."

Zorth's head bobbed. "Thank you, but after watching you bring a fire storm on our enemies I can only say that my sister and I still owe you a great debt," the felpur responded. "I have met few mages as adept at harnessing the forces as yourself. I suspect that when we first met at the Prancing Robe, you were only toying with that brutish dracon."

"That may be, but you had no way of knowing that when you offered to draw steel in my defense."

"I see that my friend Bill has once again chosen wisely in his friends," Zorth laughed. "Who would have imagined that I would owe my life to a man, a lizardman warrior, and a faerie mage in so short a time? A few days ago, I was a Noble of the Seven Tribes. Today, I'm hunted by the Crown and allied with the League of the Crimson Crescent."

"It may be time for the hunted to hunt those who sought to prey upon them," Zynaryxx said.

"Cobran like to hunt," the lizardman interrupted, evidently bored by the conversation.

Smiling, Zynaryxx led the group on its journey through the underground.

When they arrived at Orwynn's establishment, the faerie went in first, to make certain they'd be safe. He discovered the worried innkeeper anxiously awaiting them.

"It's about time you got here," the innkeeper said as Zynaryxx entered alone. "By the Gods, the city is in an uproar! The Warriors came this morning demanding to know about the humans who had been seen here yesterday. I told them they paid for their drinks, then I made them leave, because humans are bad for business.

"The tavern was full tonight. First, everyone talked about how the escaped slaves launched an attack in the middle of the city. Then, a dracon claimed he saw a rogue human break into the middle of the championship fight and spirit off Cobran himself. Later, we heard a rumor that the League had broken into the Guild Council's chambers, set them on fire, and escaped with some especially prized captives involved in this conspiracy against the Crown. Then, the Warriors came again and closed us down. They've imposed martial law, declared a curfew, and I'm told the Arch Regent has warned the Council that if they don't bring those responsible for this chaos to Her, she'll take control of the city herself."

The faerie grinned at the news. "She must be in a rare mood indeed," he said. "I don't think I could have planned this better myself."

"But don't you understand?" Orwynn said excitedly. "It's happening. The city's rising up. We're not alone. Others have begun to fight the Crown. I can feel rebellion in the air."

"I wouldn't get too excited too quickly," the faerie cautioned as he walked back to the passage and signaled to the others to come in. "I don't think it's fair to say the whole city is in rebellion."

"But don't you see it's not only us any longer?" Orwynn said. "Humans battling troops in the streets, an attack on the Council's very chambers to free captives! The rebellion has begun. The people of the city are rising to our side."

"That's quite true," Zynaryxx conceded. "But before you say anything else, you'd better meet the rebellion."

Orwynn seemed near tears when the faerie explained that the battle in the streets had just been Bill trying to escape from the Warrior troops. He seemed impressed to meet Cobran in person but was dumbstruck to discover that the attack on the Council chambers had been no more than the faerie, Bill, and Cobran.

"You mean to tell me that the five of you caused all this?" he demanded. "I thought we had discovered others who shared our common fight."

"Orwynn," the faerie said. "You're missing the point. If five of us have caused this much turmoil by accident, just think of what we can do on purpose. As I recall, just a day ago you told me that the League had degenerated into a debating society."

Orwynn remained crestfallen. "I guess I got carried away with my hopes," the tavernkeeper said.

"Orwynn, don't carry on so," Zynaryxx said. "A week ago, you were a tired, angry, cynical retired revolutionary frightened of his own shadow. Yesterday, you were a firebrand, plotting to bring the Crown down in flames, even if you had to do it yourself. Today, now that the first steps actually have been taken and the city is in an uproar, you're depressed, because the revolution may take longer than a day. Come now, pour us some ale. New friends have joined us. We must make plans."

Orwynn grinned at Zynaryxx's good-natured jibes. "It's true what you say," he said. "Just yesterday I was trying to shame you into action."

"And I acted," the faerie said. "And we have new recruits

to show for it."

Bill hadn't noticed the chill of the stone tunnels until he entered the basement of the tavern. The heat enveloped him like one of his grandmother's thick down quilts.

"The mightiest fighter in the kingdom," Orwynn said, looking at Cobran.

Cobran took his cue. "Cobran like ale," he said.

Orwynn laughed. "And ale you shall have." He strode to a keg to fill a pitcher.

After a drinking fest that lasted into the evening, the tavern keeper showed them to upstairs rooms. "We don't get too many overnight guests here, anymore," he said. "But I think you'll find the beds satisfactory. Here in Darktown, we keep the lanterns lit at night, even in our rooms, as a precaution. The night brings too many unwanted visitors to this part of the city. Darkness serves only as an invitation to them. Tomorrow is soon enough to make plans."

As he showed Zorth into his room, the felpur turned to the innkeeper. "My sister and I would ask a favor if we may. We're seeking our litter brother who has been missing for some time. We heard that a person known as Aleka might know his whereabouts and that we might find her here in Darktown, at the Mercenaries Martyr."

"You'll find her there, all right," Orwynn said. "She owns it. But be careful. The Martyr is a dangerous place frequented by rogues and cutthroats—and Aleka is just as dangerous as any of her customers."

"We have no choice," Zorth said. "Our clan has sent us to find him. Wherever the trail leads, we must go."

"I'm not sure you understand how dangerous it is," Orwynn said. "It's only a block from the castle. The castle's staff gathers there to amuse themselves, and what they consider amusing isn't something you want to be mixed up in."

"I am a priest of Yalor, chosen by the Seven Tribes to bring back my brother," Zorth said stiffly. "I am not concerned with risks. My brother would do no less for me. Tomorrow, if you can provide me with the directions to this place, I will see this Aleka."

"I didn't mean to suggest that you might be frightened off. I'm simply urging you to exercise caution. In the morning, I'll give you whatever assistance I can."

Bidding him a good rest, Orwynn went downstairs and barred the front door with an oaken beam. He locked the windows with double guards that even Cobran would have difficulty unlatching. He didn't turn out the lights, though. In Darktown, no one invited darkness into their quarters after midnight.

Bill woke up abruptly at the touch of a hand slipping across his face. With a start, he tried to jump up, only to find himself slammed back into the bed.

"Quiet," a voice commanded in the darkness.

Bill had left on the light as Orwynn had insisted when he went to bed. But the intruder had apparently put it out. He squinted in the darkness, trying to size up his attacker. With no lamps or moonlight from a window to silhouette his adversary, Bill found himself unable to discern what (if any) dangers stood before him.

He was sure the Inquisition had somehow found him. He shoved, trying to push himself up, only to find himself forced back on the bed.

"I said, be quiet!" the voice ordered again, the hand across his face stifling. "We need to talk."

Bill drove a fist into the intruder's face, loosening the grip long enough to roll out of bed. He jumped to his feet, just in time to be knocked across the floor as his attacker slammed into him. Bill butted his forehead into his opponent's head, breaking himself free from his grip.

"What's happening?" Bill heard Cobran shout as the lizardman stormed into the room.

Though Cobran's speech, lacking as it was in grace and style, implied the lizardman was intellectually slow, the gladiator took no time to size up the situation unfolding in the room. With a roar that startled Bill, Cobran launched himself at Bill's opponent, knocking him off Bill and across the room.

From the light of the hallway, Bill could see that his adversary was dressed completely in black from head to toe. A tight-fitting black mask covered his face, except for his eyes. Bill recognized the outfit. A ninja had slipped into his room.

Cobran lunged toward his foe only to find the ninja had dodged out of reach. The lizardman spun, his foot snapping out at his enemy's side. The ninja took the kick and managed to grab it in midair, twisting Cobran's leg enough to topple the champion to the floor.

As Cobran attempted to rise, the ninja's leg flashed out, knocking him back to the floor.

Bill lunged at the ninja, hoping to distract him long enough to give Cobran time to get back on his feet. But he found himself diving past where the ninja had been.

With no sign of exertion, the ninja's foot stabbed out at Cobran again as the lizardman attempted to stand, again knocking him to the floor.

Zorth and Quatar burst into the room. "What's going...?" Before Zorth could finish, the ninja launched himself at the two felpurs, slamming them against the wall.

Bill and Cobran dove at the ninja from behind. Spinning on his toes in a pirouette, the ninja thrust both hands out, jabbing both Bill and Cobran in the stomach. His hands flew up, striking both under their chins.

Bill reeled from the blows, crashing onto the floor. Cobran grunted but stood his ground, his own powerful fist chopping out into the ninja's face. Their antagonist back–flipped across the room, putting distance between himself and Bill's companions.

He saw, out the corner of his eye, that Zynaryxx had entered the room. The faerie muttered an unintelligible chant, his hands passing in the direction of the ninja.

The ninja collapsed in a heap on the floor.

"What did you do to him?" Bill asked as Cobran helped him to his feet.

"I put him to sleep," the mage said. "When I saw how successfully the four of you were handling him, I thought I'd better act quickly before he killed you all."

Cobran approached the still figure and drew his sword.

"What are you doing?" the faerie asked.

"Cobran kill ninja," the lizardman said matter–of–factly. "Cobran kill now, before ninja wakes and attacks Bill again."

Kneeling down next to the black figure, Cobran pulled its hood off, revealing long blonde tresses. The lizardman seemed puzzled. With a yank, he pulled the mask off to reveal an elfin woman's face.

"Pretty elf," Cobran said, prepared to slit her throat.

"Don't be ridiculous," the mage snapped. "Put that sword down before I put you to sleep, too."

"I don't think that's wise," Zorth said. "I, too, see no honor in slitting the throat of a downed and defenseless enemy, friend Zynaryxx, but we have little other choice. She knows where we are. We can hardly let her go and expect her to keep our secret. If we allow her to escape, she'll only come back with more of her friends. The Arch Regent would pay dearly for the information she carries. As much as the idea of killing a sleeping enemy, much less a beautiful woman, turns my stomach, I suggest we let Cobran go ahead with his work."

"My friends, I must say that all of you disappoint me. The faerie gave them the sort of solemn look you give someone in an hour of bereavement. "I really expected more of you. Slitting the throat of a sleeping enemy–I've done it myself on more occasions than I care to count. But I really must insist that you leave the ninja alone."

"I take it you want to first question the ninja," Quatar said. "Makes sense to me. For all we know, she may have friends awaiting her return."

"Quatar, I surely expected more from you. A fine group of revolutionaries we have here," the faerie said, sadly snaking his head. "First, you need to learn what really happened here before anyone begins to talk about slitting someone's throat.

The faerie asked Bill, "What exactly happened?"

Bill told how he had been awakened and had immediately assumed that the Inquisition had found him. Then, he had struck the ninja, causing the commotion that brought Cobran to the room to investigate the noise.

"Did she say anything to you?" the faerie asked.

"She said we had to talk," Bill said. "She told me to be quiet. But I must say, she can disguise her voice. She sounded like a man."

"Doesn't it strike you as peculiar that she only wanted to talk to Bill?" Zynaryxx looked at the companions.

"I just assumed that she wanted to question me," Bill said. "I'd seen the Inquisition's methods of questioning earlier tonight. Zorth and Quatar still ache from their little question–and–answer session."

The faerie shook his head. "Look at her," he demanded. "She's a ninja. She's not an Inquisitor. She's a member of the Assassins' Guild. Doesn't that tell any of you anything?"

"Forgive me, my good mage, but I'm afraid it tells me that we ought to heed Cobran's suggestion," Zorth said. "From everything I've heard, the members of the Assassins' Guild are the most cold–hearted killers in Trillius. They strike without warning, dispatching their victims with a knife, poison, ax, sword, or their bare hands. If even half the stories are true, they are the most feared killers in the kingdom. They spirit away, slipping into the shadows before their deeds are even suspected. I've heard they can kill with a single blow of their bare hands."

"It's quite true," the faerie said, approvingly. "Now what does that suggest?"

"Cobran kill!"

"No!" the faerie said, stepping between the lizardman and the ninja. "My friends, you aren't paying attention. You aren't even listening to yourselves. The Assassins' Guild has not built up its well–earned and much–feared reputation by having its members waken their victims for little chats before assassinating them. They kill quickly, silently, then slip back into the night. If this ninja had wanted to kill Bill, he'd be long dead. If her aim was to kill, some of you would be dead right now.

"This particular ninja showed remarkable restraint. Outnumbered by foes that would have killed her without a second thought, fighting one of the greatest gladiators the kingdom has ever produced, she still fought only to protect herself."

"If she was only trying to protect herself, I'd hate to see her try to kill someone!" Zorth said.

"Put her on the bed," the faerie directed.

"Don't bother," the ninja interrupted. "I'm quite comfortable here on the floor."

"You're awake?" Zorth said.

"You'd be surprised at how quickly talk of slitting your throat rouses you from even the deepest slumber," the ninja said, still motionless on the floor. "I was contemplating how many of you I could take with me if you didn't listen to the faerie."

"I must apologize for them," Zynaryxx said, turning to face the black figure. "We're a bit jumpy today. Everywhere we've gone for the past few days, strangers have tried to kill my friends, especially Bill. Powerful people would give quite a bit to know he'd met with an unfortunate accident. As his friends, we are a bit hesitant to welcome intruders who break into our rooms in the middle of the night for little chats."

"I see now that I should have tried a different approach," the ninja said. "I apologize. I had hoped to explain my intentions to Bill before I met all of you. You see, I'd like to offer my services to you."

"Do you have a name?" Zynaryxx asked.

"My mother named me Nagano," she said.

Zorth snorted. "You have a strange way of offering your services, my black–suited friend. Why are we supposed to believe you?"

"If I had wanted to kill Bill he'd be dead by now and I'd be long gone," the ninja said. "He's alive. And if I'd truly meant any harm to the rest of you, some of you would be lying beside me right now. You're not. I think that alone says more than any words I can say."

"Then tell us, assassin, why do you wish to join us?" Zorth asked. "You don't appear stupid. You must know that the Arch Regent's forces search for us even as we speak. Why would someone want to join a group all the kingdom's swords have been drawn against?"

"True, the odds are not favorable," the ninja said. "But I have no other choice. This afternoon, the Arch Regent killed my mother. Still, the Regent and those who serve Her believe that I am searching for you. She expects me to perform my usual service. I probably would had the Regent's forces not killed my mother. For that, the Regent Herself must pay. To kill Her, I'll need help—your help."

Quatar sighed in exasperation. "That's why you're here? You want us to help you kill the Arch Regent? Maybe you want us to storm the castle itself?"

"I don't think a frontal assault would be advisable," the ninja said.

"Not advisable! A madwoman! She sits there as if she hasn't a care in the world, suggesting we plot to kill the Arch Regent."

"And just what position do you think you're already in?"

the ninja snapped. "They freed you, Her prisoners, right from under Her nose. You free a group of slaves and challenge the royal edict that enslaves humans. Do you people not consider that a plot against the Arch Regent? You think this League of the Crimson Crescent aims any lower than to kill the Regent? Just how do you intend to free this city? By asking Her nicely, please?"

The ninja glared at the five companions.

Zynaryxx seemed unperturbed by the outburst. "She's really quite right. We can play revolutionaries all we want, but only for so long. Sooner or later, all of you will realize that killing the Arch Regent has to be our major goal."

Zorth's laugh broke the tension gripping the room. "You can't honestly be serious," he said. "Our only real option is to get out of this city as soon as I've located my litter brother. If most of you were wise, you'd leave even sooner. I can't believe any of you would pay attention to such nonsense."

"I understand your fear," the ninja said, ignoring the flash of rage that crossed Zorth's eyes at the accusation. "Earlier today, I, too, would have considered it madness. My Guild sent me to the Prancing Robe when we learned Bill was hiding there. Unfortunately or fortunately, depending on how you look at it, the Warriors' Guild arrived ahead of me. I watched from the shadows when Bill made his escape.

"I was close to earning my fee when the Warriors' Guild began their massacre. My mother was on that street. I saw her struck down by an arrow, her body trampled by the Regent's troops. For that, the Regent will pay in blood.

"I trailed Bill all day, but I lost him when he went into that tunnel beneath the city. When I heard they'd captured his friends, I waited at the Guild Hall, because I knew he'd return for them. I needed someone willing to take that kind of risk. I nearly lost you again when you went in the tunnel, but I managed to pick that rather clever lock, and I followed you here."

"So just like that, you decided to join us?" Zorth said. "You betray your Guild. You forsake your oaths. You decide to become a revolutionary. It all sounds quite simple."

The ninja effortlessly bounded to her feet. "There is nothing simple about it," she snapped. "Her thugs killed my mother. I care nothing for you or your revolution. But killing is something I know a great deal about, as you may find out if you continue with your snide insults."

Bill stepped in between Zorth and the ninja, his hand on his sword. "I apologize for the rudeness of my friends," he said. "But the strain we've been under makes us forget our manners. I am sorry for your loss."

"I didn't come here for your sympathy," the ninja said, defiantly. "I came here, because I believe that my talents might be of service to you. And I believe that your skills might help me achieve my own goals. I'm not here to ask for your friendship. I don't need it. I only need your talents and your courage."

"Of course she needs us," Zorth spat. "She probably wants us to serve as a diversion while she gets herself killed. We have nothing more than her claim that they killed her mother. But even if it's true, so what? Going into the castle would be madness. It's the worst kind of folly."

"I can't argue with you," Zynaryxx said. "I didn't say I considered it risk free. I only say it's necessary."

"I'll have no part of it," the felpur said. "We need to leave this city as soon as possible. We need to do the sensible thing for a change."

"The sensible thing," the ninja said, her voice dripping with disdain. "Be glad your friends didn't consider the sensible thing when the two of you were being questioned by the Inquisitors. When they broke in the chamber and fought to save your lives, were the two of you shouting, "Do the sensible thing?""

Zorth ignored the insult, although it was evident that the effort dearly cost him. Turning to Bill, the felpur's voice sounded almost pleading.

"It's not your fight, Bill. It's not our fight. We can't free the entire kingdom. Tomorrow, my sister and I hope to find our litter brother. After that, I hope you'll leave with us."

"I can't, Zorth." Bill shook his head. "I understand your feelings, and I appreciate all you've done for me, but I have to see this through. If I leave with you, what have I gained? Wherever I go in this kingdom, I'll be a marked man. If they can't find me in the city, they'll remember I was last seen with you, and they'll come looking. I can't put your family and your clan in that kind of danger. And I don't know how to get back to my own home, so my only chance to ensure my own safety is to follow Zynaryxx's advice. I have to make this city safe for humans."

"You can't be serious!" Zorth exploded. "You don't owe these people anything. This so-called League is powerless to help. They have great dreams, certainly. But for thirty years they've remained impotent against the dark forces. My clan can protect you."

"Will they?" Bill asked, his eyes level with Zorth's. "You and Quatar would stand beside me against them. But you know your people better than I do. How many Hovras would risk their children and families for a human?"

"You question my word? My honor?" Zorth's eyes flashed.

"No. You know I don't," Bill answered. "I have no doubt that the two of you would argue my case in the councils of your people. But think back to the way the two of you thought a week ago before you met me. You yourself told me that you were ashamed to admit to the felpurs at the Robe that you knew me. Can you really imagine that your friends would stand against the Arch Regent's troops to shield me?"

Zorth's gaze wavered.

"The felpur have been told for thirty years that humans are the lowest creatures alive. They may not feel that all humans should be caged. But, I doubt that they'd consider me worth their own families' lives."

Zorth and Quatar looked each of their companions in the eye, then, without a word, they turned and left.

Chapter Nine

The ninja started to say something, but a look from Zynaryxx silenced her. "I suggest we, too, get some rest. We'll be busy tomorrow." He directed the ninja to a room where she could spend the night. "I suggest you refrain from any late–night chats. My friends still feel a tad nervous about you."

She nodded in agreement.

Zynaryxx returned to Bill. "I'm glad you decided that our fight is your fight. I wouldn't blame you if you thought it too dangerous."

"I really have little choice."

"We always have choices. They are seldom the choices we want, but they exist."

"Where could I go?" Bill said. "Nowhere in the kingdom is safe for a human. I can't hide anywhere. And I can't go home–I don't know how to get there."

"Since I first heard about you, I have wondered just where it is you come from. I know it's not anywhere near here, but how is it you don't know your way back to your own home?"

The mage listened intently as Bill told his story, questioning him in detail about his life before he'd slept in the cave.

"I've spent my life traveling and studying the greater mysteries," the mage said. "But I confess, I've never heard of a place such as you describe, much less within three or four days of travel."

Seeing the look of disappointment on the man's face, the faerie's voice softened. "Don't despair. From all indications, your journey has been for a reason. I believe you've been called here. You apparently entered a cave that serves as a portal, a kind of gate into this world. I know something of astral gates. Demons use them to cross the temporal planes from the darker regions into this world of substance. I have, on a few occasions, created gates to send them back, although I've failed more times than I've succeeded."

"Could you create a gate and send me back?"

The mage shook his head. "It's not the same kind of gate," he said. "The astral gates I've dealt with don't send creatures to a place anything like what you described. They lead to the fiery pits of the dead and the damned. You don't ever want to go there. But I do know such gates exist. You and I will just have to find someone with more knowledge on the subject."

Bill perked up at the thought. "I was starting to think I was doomed to remain here forever," he said.

"I can't promise you results. All I can promise is that when we've finished our mission, I'll devote my time to helping you."

"What do you mean when you say I was called here?"

"We think you are the One," Zynaryxx said. "Some know the legend in this land of the Unnamed One, though it is death to repeat it. However, one more crime can't worsen matters for me. So, I will tell you.

"It is said that a strange man shall come out of the mountains with a sword of ice and fire. This man will befriend the races of the kingdom. He'll unite them against the Evil One, and the cleansing fire of his blade will send Him to the pit to join the forces with which he has aligned himself."

"You've got to be kidding."

"Do I look like I'm joking?" the mage asked. "You said you came here from the mountains. You are a stranger. Your companions are a faerie, a lizardman, two felpurs, and now an elf. You are a man."

"What about that sword of fire?"

"Tell me about your sword," the mage said.

"Well..." Bill drew the sword from its sheath. "Strange lettering has been etched upon it," Bill said, telling him of how he found it in the cave. "When I draw it, I feel it pulsing with a strength that I know I alone do not possess. It practically fights my battles for me. Sometimes, it glows with a kind of blue fire."

"Fire and ice," the mage said. He took the sword, intently examining the lettering. His hand passed over it a few times, his eyes glazed over as he stared at the weapon and mumbled strange words.

The blade began to glow, the lettering brightened. The mage continued to speak in a strange tongue. Then, he looked up. "We've waited many years for your coming. It's the Demon's Bane," Zynaryxx said. "The final proof. You are the One foretold by legend."

"That's ridiculous," Bill said. "I'm not a legend. I'm just a guy who got lost."

"You don't understand. Have you not wondered why the King hates humans? Haven't you asked yourself why He's gone to so much trouble to raise every creature's hand against them, to enslave them? Men frighten Him. He knows the legend I've told you about. He knows that a man will come some day to destroy Him. That's why He took the humans' property from them as soon as He took control of the kingdom. He knows that even He and His agents can't be everywhere at once. So, He keeps them in servitude, and He had devoted Himself to cultivating the hatred against humans that you've experienced. He's waited years for your coming, and He's spent that time preparing."

"I'd say He's done a good job."

"Hardly," Zynaryxx said. "Look at your companions. The legend doesn't say how many of each of the races you'll unite. It doesn't say how many it will take to destroy Him. For thirty years, the league and I have waited for the moment to strike. You may think it's hopeless, but you also know you have few other options. I have no desire to throw my life away. I wouldn't be willing to try this if it was just some fool's errand. When the Regent realizes She is facing the One, She'll be beside Herself with fear."

"How will She know?"

"You don't know Her," Zynaryxx said. "I do. Her agents have already told Her how a man braved the gladiators' ring to rescue a lizardman. By now, they've told Her that same man even dared to break into the Guild Council's Chambers to rescue two felpurs. She's heard that he was accompanied by the lizardman he saved, as well as a faerie. Never underestimate Her intelligence or Her cunning. When She discovers an elf ninja has joined us, She'll see the pattern—as will the people of the city. Combined with the League's efforts to remind everyone of the Legend, this pattern will convince people that the races are uniting against the regime."

"You're forgetting the felpur are leaving us."

"I'm not," the mage said, as he turned and went to bed.

Once again, Bill did not soon fall asleep. The dark behind his eyelids was alive with fear and hope.

The next morning, Zorth and Quatar got directions to the Mercenary from Orwynn. They left without a word to their companions. The street was unnaturally quiet after the previous day's events. The city blazed with sunlight and throbbed with stillness. "I don't feel good about leaving them," Quatar said after they'd left the tavern.

"Then go back to say your good–byes," Zorth snapped.

"I don't mean this morning," Quatar responded. "You know exactly what I'm talking about. I don't like the idea of leaving them to walk into danger."

"And you think I like it?" Zorth asked. "A week ago, I didn't even like humans. Today, I feel the same way about Bill as I do about any of my litter. But the path he's taking is nothing more than idealistic madness. That mage will lead him to disaster. That ninja will cut any of their throats if she thinks it will help get what she wants. And Cobran, for all his courage, hasn't the brains to know when he's facing impossible odds. I don't like leaving Bill with them any more than you do."

"Do you think they can free the kingdom?"

"She'll kill them the moment they set foot in the castle. They have no idea what they face."

"But, for the sake of argument, what if they did kill Her?" Quatar asked.

"It's stupid to even discuss what can't happen," Zorth said. "But say they did. You've spent time in Trillius. You've talked to people. Do they really seem like they want a revolution?

How many have you met who would give their lives...let me rephrase that; how many would even cross the street to help a human?"

Quatar offered no response.

Zorth forged on. "They don't like the Arch Regent, but most of them feel She poses no real threat to them. As long as She leaves them alone, they're content to just sit back and complain."

"But what if they did kill her?" Quatar persisted. "What would happen?"

"Nothing," Zorth said. "That's my whole point. You can't free a kingdom that doesn't want to be freed. If the whole city rose up against Her forces, you might have a chance.

"But the populace is content with its diversions; that's why Trillius exists. It distracts them from their problems, offers them a place where they can run away from whatever bothers them. People busy gambling, sampling houses of pleasure, and enjoying other delights don't care who runs the city. If they're poor, they think that with just one lucky bet, they can make enough to be happy for the rest of their lives. If they're unlucky at love, they see the pleasure houses as a place where they can buy what they can't get otherwise. And if all else fails, they can find happiness in a needle or a pipe.

"Even if Bill and his friends do manage to kill Her, the Arch Regent's forces would still be in control. The King would replace Her. The only difference would be that the Unnamed One would concentrate his attentions on crushing whoever disturbed Trillius."

Quatar shook her head sadly. "I still don't like it," she said, "I feel like we're running away."

"I feel that way, too, but we don't have time to worry about it. We're here." The felpur stood in front of a tavern with two swords crossed over a shield. The Mercenary Martyr was venerable even among the old buildings of Darktown.

Inside, its clientele appeared to have little concern for the time of day. Despite the early hour, the tables were filled with surly looking drinkers. Many of them paused in their conversations to eye the intruders.

"I don't think we're going to win any popularity contests here," Quatar whispered to Zorth.

Pushing his way to the tavern's bar, Zorth signaled for two tankards of ale. "We're looking for Aleka," he said to the creature pouring the drinks.

The creature looked more like an orc than anything else, but it was evident that it also had dracon in its bloodline. Its lips curled as it looked over the two felpurs. "What makes ya' think Aleka would conduct business with the likes of you?" it asked in a voice that went straight through Zorth's bones.

"What makes you think that she wants you standing between her and a chance to make money?" Quatar asked mildly. "I don't think she'd appreciate it very much if she found out your ill manners had cost her a chance for gold."

"Gold?" The word seemed to brighten its spirits.

"What's in it for me?" it asked. As Zorth reached for his purse, Quatar caught her brother's arm.

"After you take us to Aleka," Quatar said.

The creature snarled but jerked its head to a door in the corner of the tavern. "Come on with me. But you'd better be telling the truth about the gold, or I'll slit your throats."

When they got to the door, the creature motioned them

to go first. Zorth stepped through, only to find himself in a shadowy dead—end alley. Quatar staggered behind him, propelled by the creature's hard shove.

The tavernkeeper joined them in the alley, followed by three other orcs who blocked the door and the way to the open street several hundred yards away. Zorth didn't even have time to yearn for the clear sunny morning, the bright edged openness that lay beyond his reach.

"They've got gold and smart mouths," the tavernkeeper growled to his cronies. "They say they want Aleka, but she don't have no business with them."

The orcs drew their weapons and began advancing on the felpurs. "Give us the gold, kitties," one smirked. "Give us the gold, and maybe we won't skin you and use your hides for my new coat."

Zorth and Quatar drew their own swords, warily watching the orcs. "Your mistress will not be happy when she discovers you tried to cheat her," Zorth said. "She's not going to like this at all."

"I'll take care of Aleka," the leader flashed an evil grin, flecks of drool dripping from his yellowed fangs. "She don't like being disturbed this early in the day. She don't like sunshine. And she don't like dandies."

"Does she like you?" Quatar asked, reaching out as her blade traced figure—eights in front of the advancing orcs.

With a snarl, one of the orcs pulled a nasty looking ax from beneath its cloak. The curved blade told the felpurs that this ax had not been forged to fell trees. Shrieking, the creature swung it at Zorth, who barely managed to block it with his sword. Zorth's feet slipped from beneath him, but kicking the orc in the chest, he regained his balance in time to ward off a blow from another club–wielding orc.

The tavernkeeper swung a heavy steel mace that clanged as it fell upon Quatar's blade. The smaller felpur found herself stepping back as the orc rained blows down on him. The fourth orc was notching an arrow in its bow when the door smashed open and two figures crashed out.

Zorth looked at the doorway, hoping for rescue, but the steel–eyed dwarf woman clad in armor and the ebony clad rawulf warrior hadn't come to help the two felpurs.

Nonetheless, the four attackers froze uncertainly at their entrance.

"What's this all about?" the woman said.

"They wanted us to wake you," the tavernkeeper said. "We brought them out here to beat some manners into them."

"They wanted to steal your gold," Zorth said, interrupting the orc, trying to catch his breath. "We told them we had business with you, but when we told them we had gold with which to pay you, they tricked us into coming out here so they could steal your gold."

"He lies," the tavernkeeper snapped. "I'll cut out his lying tongue. These filthy cats will say anything. You can never believe a thing they say."

The dwarf woman gazed into the orc's eyes until he looked away. "We were standing at the door," she said. "I heard everything. You told them you'd take care of me. What did you mean by that?"

The tavernkeeper's eyes wavered. "I meant that I'd make sure you got your share," he stammered.

"My share?" she said. "Your saying *my share* suggests that you and your little friends also deserve *a share* of my gold.

What makes you think I intend to share with you? You and these thugs were going to keep some of my gold for yourselves, is that what you're saying?"

"Aleka, we was just having fun with these dandies. It don't seem right that you should get worked up over them. We didn't mean nothing by it."

"Since when did I give you permission to use my name?" she asked softly. "First, you decide that you and your boys are going to steal my gold. Then, you become impertinent."

The tavernkeeper's eyes narrowed. "Don't be taking on so. I'm just as important as anyone else. Me and the boys don't appreciate the way you carry on sometimes. We don't like the way you've been taking on airs, making us feel like we're not good enough," he said.

"So, I'm carrying on, taking on airs, and you disapprove." Her eyes flashed. "I suppose you'd like me to apologize to you. Perhaps I should get on my knees and beg your forgiveness."

"You don't have to beg. Me and the boys are just glad you're coming to your senses."

"That's quite good of you," she said. "I've never liked getting on my knees. But I rather enjoy seeing others prostrating themselves in front of me. Perhaps you'd care to humor me."

The orc appeared puzzled. "I'm not quite sure I follow you," he said.

"I'm not asking you to follow me," she snapped. "The thought of you behind me sends shudders of disgust through me. I'm suggesting that you might want to kneel down before me and beg my forgiveness for your offensive behavior, your unjustifiable rudeness, your attempt to steal my gold, and your disgusting and unforgivable ignorance about your station in life."

"Aleka, there's no call for that kind of talk. I've put up with a lot from you. Probably more than I should have. I can see that it's given you a lot of fool ideas, but you're getting a tad too high and mighty."

"I told you to kneel," she said quietly.

"And I told you there's no need for you carry on like this," the orc said. "You act like some kind of royalty. You run a tavern in the worst part of town for the worst kind of people. You're not no fancy lady, and all your fancy talk won't make it so."

"I believe you and the boys need someone to remind you how to behave."

The ebony–clad warrior stepped forward, drawing his sword. "May I have the honor, my lady," he said, advancing on the tavernkeeper.

The orc raised his mace, backing away from the advancing knight. "This ain't none of your business, Blackie. You stay out of it."

Without a word, the knight swung his sword in a tight arc, crashing against the mace. The tavernkeeper's steel weapon cracked and shattered under the impact. The orc's skull did the same.

"Do any others need lessons in manners, my lady?"

"I'm not sure, my lord," she said, eyeing the three orcs, who had dropped to one knee. "I believe they may have seen the error of their ways."

"Bow your heads," she said to them.

They complied. She nodded to the knight.

Without hesitation, his sword swept in a wide arc, lopping off all three orcs' heads.

Zorth felt the release from danger as abruptly as the relaxing of a fist.

"I believe they've learned a lesson they'll have trouble forgetting." The knight looked at the felpur. "Always remove your hat in the presence of a lady."

Zorth pulled off his hat, and Quatar followed suit. "Our apologies, my lady," he said, bowing deeply. "My sister and I have traveled in barbarous company of late. We beg your forgiveness. It's seldom we find gentlefolk in our travels."

"I accept your apology. It's rare that we have the pleasure of meeting someone not raised in a barnyard. But, we haven't been introduced."

"My lady," Quatar curtsied. "I am Quatar, a humble monk. My companion is my litter brother, Zorth, a priest of Yalor who has been sent by the Seven Families and our clan lords in search of our missing litter brother."

"You spoke of gold, as I recall," Aleka said.

"We hoped that you might assist us in our search," Zorth said. "We've been told that our litter brother came to your establishment at one time. We thought that you might be able to help us find out where he might be. We are, of course, quite prepared to pay you for your trouble."

"A felpur," she said, turning to the knight. "I don't recall him. My lord, do you remember a felpur?"

"I do, my lady," the rawulf said. "I never miss them. They're ugly little creatures, no offense to the present company, you understand. I know they can't help the way they look."

"Of course," Zorth said, tightly clenching his teeth. "We felpurs and rawulfs have always felt that way about each other.

It's nothing personal. I certainly understand."

"That's good," the rawulf said, fingering his blade. "I knew you'd understand just how offensive I find your kind. I believe it's the smell. As soon as you walk into the room, the odor fairly chokes me. I've always wondered how a felpur can stand being so close to himself."

Quatar must have sensed the effort Zorth expended to control himself. She asked, "Since you obviously remember him so well, perhaps you can tell us where our litter brother might be, my lord?"

"I didn't speak to him," the knight said. "I wouldn't speak to you if my lady hadn't asked me. I only smelled him when he came in. The stench nearly overpowered me."

Quatar said quickly, "But perhaps you recall those to whom he did speak, who might know his whereabouts."

"The tavernkeeper spoke to him, but I doubt he'll be telling you much," the knight said, motioning toward the fallen orc.

"Is there someone else?" Quatar asked.

"Old Olaf," the knight said. "He talks to the most disgusting creatures: anyone who'll buy him a brew. All that beer's probably killed his sense of smell."

"Is this old Olaf around now?" Quatar asked.

"It's too early for him," the knight said. "He'll be along later, mooching for beer."

"How will we recognize him?" Quatar asked.

"He's a mook. A psionic by trade, actually; quite bright. However, he tends to take up with characters that, if it were up to me, I wouldn't even allow in here."

"My lady," Zorth said. "We are grateful for the help of you and your friend. If we may, we will enjoy the hospitality of your establishment until this Olaf arrives. We will, of course, compensate you for your assistance before we are on our way."

"Of course," Aleka said.

Chapter Ten

As Zorth and Quatar walked back into the tavern, the dwarf woman saw the frown creasing the rawulf's face.

"You don't seem to approve, my lord?"

"I don't understand why we have to wait until they've talked to Olaf to get the gold. You should let me kill them now."

"Your impatience ill suits you, my lord," Aleka said. "I was afraid your insults would anger them into doing something rash."

"They're too cowardly," the rawulf spat. "If anyone spoke to me the way I did to them, his blood would cover this alley. But you saw them. They just stood there asking about their brother, overlooking every insult I hurled at them." His eyes narrowed as he looked at the dwarf woman. "Why won't you let me kill them?"

"Don't you recall those warriors who stopped by last night on their way to the castle?"

"The troops looking for the rogue human?"

She nodded. "They said the human, a faerie, and a lizardman broke into the Guildlords' hall to rescue two felpurs. I want you to go to the castle and speak to the Regent's people. Find out what they know about the felpurs that escaped. The Arch Regent is furious. She's threatening to take control of the city if the prisoners aren't returned to Her. I'm curious to see whether there's a connection with our two friends here."

"They'll track down every felpur in the city," the rawulf said. "That's what we did when I worked for them. Round them all up first and sort them out later."

"Precisely," she said. "That's why I want to offer my assistance. With the city in such an uproar, I want the Regent's people to remember that my presence here at the Martyr is in their best interests. Even if those two are not the ones they seek, the Regent will remember that I have remained vigilant for anyone who may possibly be one of their enemies. If they choose to fulfill Her threat and take control of the city, I want those people at the castle to know whose side I'm on."

"How could they doubt you, my lady? Half their troops spend most of their free time here," the knight said.

"I want it to remain that way," she said. "They know you. They respect you. They'll listen to you."

"I'll go to the guard post," the rawulf said. "I prefer to stay outside the castle. The place gives me the creeps."

"Are you frightened, my lord?"

The rawulf's nostrils flared as he fingered his sword. "Show consideration, my lady. I didn't serve in the Regent's forces for ten years to have anyone question my courage. I've simply developed a healthy desire to avoid the more recent inhabitants of that castle. I don't share the Regent's taste in friends."

"That's why it's important that you go. The Regent's troops know you, they'll talk to you. If my suspicions are correct, we'll get the felpurs' gold and some of the Regent's, too. She will be grateful if we can help Her."

Inside the tavern, Quatar firmly held Zorth's wrist. "You can't go back out there," she whispered. "We have to wait for this Olaf."

"You heard what that mongrel said to us," Zorth hissed. "He dared us to draw steel on him, the insolent fool, swaggering and fingering his blade. I won't return home until I've personally strangled him with his entrails. I'll cut out his heart and feed him slices of it! By Yalor's sacred flame, I'll avenge my clan's honor on that black cur. Talk about stench, will he?"

"Get a grip on yourself, Zorth," Quatar snapped. "We have a more important task than teaching manners to an animal. We can deal with him after we've found our litter brother. Keep your wits about you. I don't trust these people, and I don't like them."

"I agree with you there," Zorth said. "She had that black scoundrel lop off the heads of those ruffians as casually as you would kill an insect. And she stood there while he insulted us. She was amused by it."

"She's helping us," Quatar said. "We're missing some piece in this puzzle. She saw nothing wrong with the idea of robbing us of all our gold. What she objected to was the idea that she might have to share it."

"After we find this Olaf, I'll feel no remorse in leaving this city..." Zorth said. "After I've split that creature's skull."

The door to the alley opened, revealing Aleka and her rawulf knight. He stared at the two felpurs in obvious disgust, his nostrils twitching.

"See his nose wiggling?" Zorth whispered. "I'll have his head if he makes another insulting remark."

"You'll do nothing of the kind," Quatar said. "You'll nod

pleasantly and wish him well until we've finished what we've sworn to do." Quatar smiled at the two as they entered the tavern.

The rawulf snorted in disgust as he hurried out the front door.

"It's well for him that he left," Zorth whispered. "I couldn't control myself much longer."

"Watch your tongue. Aleka's coming our way."

Both Zorth and Quatar rose when the dwarf woman arrived at their table. "My lady," Quatar said. "Will you join us for a moment. We will buy you a drink."

"You are far too kind," she said, taking a seat with them. "I came over to personally apologize to you for the rudeness of my servant. I'm sure you understand how embarrassed I am at his behavior before guests."

"My lady, there is no need for you to even think about such unpleasantness," Quatar said.

"What must you think of me?" she asked. "I should have silenced the fool. His insolence so surprised me that words simply failed me. That two gentlefolk should be treated so under my roof is intolerable."

"Let's not concern ourselves with the bad manners of someone whose lack of breeding is far too self evident," Zorth said. "You are quite blameless in the matter. We won't have you bothering yourself over the likes of him."

Quatar said, "We're in your debt for making him answer our questions. Without your intercession, he would never have told us what we need to know."

"It's just that we so seldom see anyone with any upbringing here," she said. "Mostly it's soldiers for hire, brigands and thugs, even highwaymen, all looking for jobs at the castle.

They don't even know enough to stand when a lady approaches. That's why I find I'm forced to employ that sort. As you can imagine, at times I need ruffians to handle the ruffians who come here."

"It must be difficult for someone of your background to consort with them," Quatar said. "What a terrible strain!"

"My lady, it is a testament to your indomitable character that you manage to carve out an oasis of civility in this rough-hewn environment," Zorth said.

"You flatter me," Aleka said.

Zorth raised his glass. "As you flatter us by your company and the hospitality of your establishment. I drink to you and your continued success."

After the proprietor took her leave, Quatar eyed her brother. "An oasis of civility? Indomitable character?"

"She loved it," Zorth said. "The old battle ax was eating out of our hands. I dare say she would still cut our hearts out without a second thought, but she does like pretty words. Let's hope we can continue to amuse her long enough to find out what we need to know."

"When do you think this mook will get here?" Quatar asked. "It's not often you see one, much less a psionic."

"From the way our black friend talked, it sounded as if this Olaf is a regular here. Apparently, he enjoys a drink."

"He must enjoy them quite a lot to frequent a place like this," Quatar said. "It's hard to believe someone with the training it takes to become a psionic could lower himself to patronize such a place. They train their minds so intensely that one mental blast can drive a person, sometimes an entire group, insane. Victims have even been known to turn on their own companions. Psionics can read minds; they even have healing abilities."

"Quite useful in a place like this," Zorth observed. "One needs some ability to keep from being preyed upon by the cutthroats."

The Mercenary Martyr was little more than just a tavern. Unlike the Prancing Robe, its hearth boasted no bubbling stew and inviting odors, instead, greeting visitors with the smell of stale beer. The stairs at the back obviously led to rooms for rent upstairs, but Quatar doubted they were the sort weary travelers daydreamed about. The patrons evidently used them for quick liaisons with the female patrons of the pub. She suspected that even the Martyr's customers would require many brews before they could find the prospect very enticing.

Aleka surveyed her realm from a raised platform in the rear that afforded her a view of the entire tavern. Zorth suspected that such a strategic vantage point was necessary to keep order. Four dracons served the proprietess. A tavern that catered to warriors and roustabouts would require a sizable force. The cost of maintaining her personal warriors probably didn't strain her financially, since most of them would spend their wages here, drinking, eating, and whoring. With so many out—of—work ruffians frequenting the establishment, she wouldn't have much trouble recruiting staff to rough up the other customers. It explained why she could afford to so casually execute any who displeased her.

A hooded figure stumbled in the door. "It's a mook," Quatar said. "Let's hope it's this Olaf we've been waiting to speak with."

Zorth approached the creature at the bar, where it stood looking around uncertainly.

"You'd better have gold, Olaf," the new tavernmaster snarled. "Your credit's run out. We can't have you bothering the paying customers. Either show me the color of your coin to pay what you owe or head for the door, if you can still remember where it is."

Zorth eyed the old one–eyed dwarf who had replaced the orc. "My friend will have whatever he desires."

"You're in luck, Olaf," the dwarf said. "You've found a live one."

The mook stood unsteadily, his hand resting on the bar to brace himself as he stared intently at the felpur as the bartender poured a pitcher of ale. "Have we met, sir?"

"No," Zorth said. "I've been told, however, that you met my litter brother, who was here last month. His name was Portnal. Do you recall him?"

"Ahh, yes, the felpur," Olaf said, grinning. "I enjoyed Portnal's company. He was quite generous. He and I whiled away many hours over many pitchers."

"My brother and I have been searching the entire city for him," Zorth said. "If you would join us at our table, we would like to speak with you."

Picking up the pitcher and a tankard, Zorth headed to the table. Olaf followed close behind. At the table, Olaf began drinking as if he'd recently returned from a long desert march. "Your brother was a refreshing change from the usual customers I meet in this den of iniquity," the mook said between gulps. "He's a true gentleman, not like the Martyr's regular scum. How is he?"

"We were hoping that you might answer that question for us," Quatar said. "We have been sent by our clan to find him. Aleka's rawulf friend said that you'd talked to him."

"Are you a friend of the lady's?" Olaf asked, peering over his tankard at the two felpurs.

"We told her we'd give her gold if she'd help us," Quatar said.

The mook seemed to relax at the news. "She'd sell a man back his own blood after she'd drained him of it if she could find a way," Olaf said. "Her black friend isn't any better."

"Isn't it dangerous telling virtual strangers something like that outright?" Quatar said. "What if she heard you?'

"What if she did?" the mook said, refilling his tankard. "I may be an old drunk, and they may make fun of me to my face in here, but they seldom raise a hand to me. Even when my head is at its fuzziest, Thea never fails me. Enough of them have found that out the hard way, so they just content themselves with insulting me."

Quatar bowed her head when she heard Thea's name.

"You revere Thea?" the mook asked.

"I am but a simple monk who is not blessed with your talents," Quatar said, "Though I've been privileged to learn some of Thea's teachings in my travels."

"You honor me," the mook said, draining his tankard. "I seldom meet students of the Art in Darktown. In fact, I seldom meet anyone worth knowing. Your brother was different. He showed me respect and many kindness'. I fear that I may have repaid him poorly by providing him with the assistance he sought."

Zorth's ears pricked in anticipation.

"He was quite impetuous. Stubborn. The sort who never lets reality stand between him and whatever he wants to do," the mook said.

"I'm not understanding you, Olaf. What was Portnal setting out to do? How did you help him?" Zorth asked.

"I advised him against it," the mook said, refilling his tankard. "We argued quite a bit."

"What did you argue about?"

"I told him it was crazy. I made it clear to him that I wouldn't be responsible for what might happen to him if he went through with it." The mook drained his tankard again.

As he reached for the pitcher, Zorth grabbed his wrist. "What are you talking about? Where did my brother go?"

Olaf wouldn't meet the felpur's eyes. "To the castle," the mook said. "I helped him go inside."

"The Regent's castle!" Zorth exploded. "You sent my brother in there!"

"I didn't send him," the mook said defensively. "I tried to argue him out of the idea. He demanded that I help him. He was bound to go, said that if I wouldn't help him he'd knock out the guards and go through the gate. That would be suicide. I couldn't sit back and let him do that. When I saw that he was seriously considering going ahead with his plan, I realized I didn't have any choice."

Quatar said, "We appreciate that you were just trying to help. Portnal is stubborn. If you hadn't helped him, he would have stormed the gate alone."

Olaf poured himself another drink.

"Why did he go there? Portnal was always proud and willful, but never stupid. He must have told you why he felt he had to go in there."

"He said something terribly wrong was going on in the city. He felt that in the castle, he could find out whether his suspicions were correct," Olaf said. "I told him that a city as evil as this one was not worth his life. I urged him to return to his own home and people, but he wouldn't listen. He said that if someone didn't stop the spread of evil in the castle, his own clans would soon face the same peril. But when it grew powerful enough to threaten them, it would be too late."

"What was this evil?" Zorth asked. "He must have said."

"That he wouldn't tell," the mook said. "He said that I talk too much when I've had too much to drink. I was quite offended at that baseless insult. I told him that I had learned how to drink long before he began lapping milk from his mother's breast. I couldn't persuade him to confide in me. He kept saying it would put me in too much danger if I let anything slip. If I hadn't liked him so much, I would have taught him a few lessons."

"Why didn't you just read his mind?" Quatar asked. "You're a psionic."

"I never thought of it," Olaf said. "There are times when I can't remember everything I've said the night before, and if I did know what he was up to and let it slip, I might put him in even more danger."

"So how did you help him enter the castle?" Quatar asked. "We're going to have to go in after him."

Olaf's face shut, like a door slamming. "You're as crazy as he is. I can't take responsibility for sending two more to their deaths. I should never have helped your brother, let alone help you share whatever fate befell him."

"Don't be ridiculous," Quatar said. "We're not going to spend any more time inside the castle than it takes to find Portnal, free him, and get out. Besides, I think we know where we can get help."

Zorth looked up sharply at his sister. There was a new

fire shimmering in her eyes.

"We don't really have much choice," she said. "It'll mean going back to them and asking for their help. You know they'll go with us."

"You can't be serious," Zorth said. "Go back and ask them to go inside a castle we swore not to enter? It's really too much to ask me to do. That ninja will laugh at us. I can see her sneering. She'll have a field day. I can already hear her. She'll tell them that when they needed our help, we turned our backs on them. Now that we need their help, we're willing to go. I'd rather go in by ourselves than face that."

"Don't be ridiculous," Quatar said. "Together we have a much better chance of freeing our brother. If we go by ourselves, we'll probably end up trapped with him. Together we have a chance of getting him out."

"But that ninja! She'll say—"

"I'm not interested in what anyone says! I'm interested in getting Portnal out of there. That's the only thing that matters. Not your pride. Not her sneers. Besides, you're forgetting something important."

"What's that?"

"When we go back, we'll know a way to enter the castle," Quatar said, "Because Olaf is going to tell us." She turned to the mook as he reached for the nearly empty ale pitcher.

His hand paused. "You are quite, quite lost to sanity. I can't imagine who would be willing to go into that castle, but I won't be part of it. If the Regent's forces capture you inside, they'll know that someone is telling their secrets. I've been lucky they haven't gotten it out of your brother. It would be stupid to take an even greater chance."

"I thought he was your friend," Quatar said. "You're saying you're content to leave him as their prisoner with no hope of rescue. Thea would be quite proud of her servant."

The mook sputtered. "That's not fair. I didn't ask him to go there. Thea embodies wisdom; I just want to have a few ales. It's wisest to steer clear of the Regent's castle and anyone who wants to challenge her domain."

"I think you mistake wisdom for cowardice," Quatar said evenly. "Anyone willing to turn his back on his friends shames Thea."

"You should talk," the mook said. "It sounds as if the two of you have little to speak of when it comes to abandoning friends in danger."

Not in the least quelled, Quatar gave him a stern glare. "At least we don't make a habit of it."

The mook eyed the two felpurs, torn by indecision.

Chapter Eleven

Just as Olaf was about to speak, the front door swung open, revealing Aleka's ebony clad rawulf knight. "I'm so glad you two waited for me," he sneered at Zorth and Quatar as he entered. "I was worried I might miss the chance to introduce you to some of my friends."

Eight warriors wearing the Regent's colors trooped in behind him. Their leader, a swarthy elf, swaggered to the felpur's table. "They might be the ones the Regent is searching for, all right. If so, She'll reward you well, Blackie."

The rawulf said, "Before you go with these gentlemen, you'll give me that gold you promised." Laughing, he put his hand out.

"Cur," Zorth snarled. "I'll pay you, but not in any coin you can spend. By Yalor's flame, you'll take it with you to the nether regions!"

At a nod from the elf, the warriors surrounded the table, pinning the felpur's arms to their sides and disarming them. Zorth and Quatar struggled, but they were held fast as the rawulf relieved them of their purses.

"Take the mook, too," the elf said, gesturing to Olaf. "We'll find out from him what they're doing here."

The mook's eyes darted wildly. "I've done nothing. I was simply enjoying an ale with these two travelers. I know nothing that would be of interest to the Regent."

The elf said, "I'll leave that to the Regent's Inquisitors to decide. You may not even know whether what you know is important. Sometimes, even a chance remark can unravel quite a bit.

"Take him," the elf said, turning his back.

Roughly, the warriors hauled Olaf and the felpurs out the door.

The bright morning had become an ashen afternoon. The rawulf, accompanying the troops into the street, said, "When you're done with them, let me know. I've always fancied having a felpur coat." He gave Quatar a look. "Especially one as tan as toffee. I couldn't wear it, of course. The smell would be too much."

"I'll not listen to any more of your insolence!" Zorth exploded. He sprung free of two of the Warriors' grasp, pulling one of their swords from its sheath. With a howl of rage, he swung at the warriors holding Quatar, severing the neck of one of them.

Zorth pulled it free before the warriors could react, advancing on the rawulf, who stood frozen, shocked by the felpur's outburst. Zorth swung the blade at the rawulf's uncovered face. As it bit deep into his gaping mouth, Quatar kicked the knee of the other warrior guarding him. As the warrior crumpled, the felpur grabbed its sword from its sheath.

"Take them!" The elf drew his own blade.

Olaf, his arms pinned by the two warriors on either side of him, stood motionless, his face contorted by his fearsome concentration.

Quatar thought she could almost see the wave of psionic energy that swept across the warriors emanating from the mook. It hit them with an almost physical force, knocking the leader and four others to the ground.

The remaining warriors stood stunned to see their leader and their companions fall. Quatar stabbed one in the stomach. Zorth hacked the other lone warrior still standing.

As suddenly as it started, the battle ended. The mook's shoulders slumped in exhaustion at the mental effort.

Quatar stooped to take back his and Zorth's purses and weapons from the fallen rawulf. Zorth busied himself by relieving the elf leader and the warriors of theirs.

They looked up in surprise as the front door to the tavern burst open. Aleka and her personal guard gaped at the scene that greeted them. "You've killed my lord," she screamed. "You'll die for this!"

The five fallen warriors felled by the mook's mental blast rose unsteadily to their feet. Zorth looked around, counting ten facing them.

"I'm afraid I may have acted a bit hastily," he said to Quatar. "I don't rightly know what came over me, except that I couldn't stand another insult from that mongrel cur."

"Better to die here with steel in our hands than in the embrace of the Inquisitors," Quatar said. Before the two felpurs had a chance to defend themselves, however, the elf warrior and his fighters raised their weapons unsteadily and staggered toward Aleka and her personal guard. Unnatural grins were pasted on the faces of the Regent's troops as they attacked the tavern owner's warriors.

Grabbing the mook by an arm, Quatar pulled him up the street. "Your mind flay spell drove them mad. They're attacking Aleka's troops. This should give us the time we need to get out of here," he said to Olaf as the trio began running. "Let's just hope they don't come to their senses until we've slipped away."

Several blocks away, the trio slowed to a walk inside an alley. "I apologize, Olaf," Quatar said. "If you hadn't acted when you did, we'd be imprisoned by the Regent by now or impaled on the swords of those thugs. I misjudged you. Thea must be proud of the courage and the skill you showed today. I hope you can forgive the disrespect we showed you earlier. We had no right to make you feel responsible for what happened to our brother."

"In all my life, I've never seen the like," Zorth said. "Friend Olaf, I thought that we had breathed our last when Aleka's band came out and those five stood up. I doubted that any power on earth could save us. When things looked their worst, those zombies rescued us."

The mook stood sheepishly, nodding. "I didn't have much choice," Olaf said. "I have no desire to try out the delights reserved for prisoners of the Inquisitors. They wouldn't think too highly of me if they learned I knew a secret way into their castle."

"I'm sorry that we have gotten you into the middle of our troubles," Zorth said. "I'm afraid that you can't return to the Martyr. The Regent's and Aleka's forces will both be scouring the city for us."

"I'm afraid that's quite true," Olaf said. "Maybe those friends you were talking about would be willing to let a broken down old mook join their suicidal quest into the Dark Lady's lair."

"You want to go with us into the castle?" Zorth asked. "Before, you wouldn't even tell us how to get inside. Now you want to go in there yourself?"

"What else can I do?" Olaf said. "I can't hide in this city

forever. I've been hiding in a bottle for years, trying to hide from myself. Today, I thought I was going to die–and I accepted the idea. If I'd let them take me like a coward, I'd be killed for sure. It's better to die in a fight, using skills and talents I've spent a lifetime acquiring, battling the forces I'm sworn to stand against."

"We've already apologized for calling you a coward," Zorth said. "It was a mean–spirited thing to say. We only said it because we were desperate to convince you to help us help our brother."

"It was simply the truth," the mook said. "I am a coward and an oath–breaker. I swore before Thea that I'd use the powers she's given me in her service, ridding this land of oppression. Instead of fulfilling that oath, I fled to the bottle, becoming a drunken fool."

"You're no fool," Zorth said.

"I was," the mook said sadly. "I fear what waits inside that castle. Yet, I've spent years lurking around its entranceway, drinking at the tavern that many of its guardsmen frequent. Do you have any idea why?"

The felpurs stayed silent.

"I doubted that Thea could stand against the powers of darkness inside those walls," the mook said softly. "Now I realize my doubts were misplaced. It's not Thea, but me. I doubted my own abilities, yet placed the blame on Her. I turned to the bottle for solace, hiding inside it from my own responsibilities."

"We are always our own worst accusers," Quatar said, placing a comforting hand on the mook's shoulder. "No one is more quick to hold us accountable for our failings, real and imagined, than ourselves."

"You don't have to go with us," Zorth said.

"I need to," the mook said. "Even if I perish inside its walls, I will at least spend my remaining hours in Thea's service." The trio hurried down the alleyway, dodging the troops that had begun patrolling the street.

Captain Grizzle stood on the street outside the Mercenary Martyr, watching his men tie Aleka's hands behind her back.

His eyes surveyed the fallen bodies of his warriors whose bodies had been hacked apart by the tavern owner's personal guard.

"They're getting away," Aleka snapped. "You fool, I'm not your enemy. I helped your men catch them."

"Of course," the Captain said. "That's why you and your men killed my people."

"I killed them, because a psionic drove them insane and ordered them to attack us. Why would I send Blackie to bring them here if I hadn't been trying to help you catch the felpurs?"

"Because you believed you could get away with this little game you're playing. You knew we'd learn that the felpurs we've been seeking were at your tavern. You killed my spy with three of his friends today, because they discovered you were in league with these rebels," the Captain said. "You needed to find a way to protect yourself while still helping your little friends escape the Regent's net. You lure my men here. You make a display of helping them catch these felpurs in your tavern, then ruthlessly murder them outside. You thought we'd believe your fantastic tale that a drunken mook drove them insane so that he and the felpurs could escape."

"It's true, you fool. Why would I betray the Crown? Why would I have anything to do with killing Blackie?"

"I think he was on to you," the Captain said. "You panicked, and this was the best story you could come up with. I don't know why you would join this rebellion. I don't need to know why, and I really don't care. My orders are to round up those involved and stamp it out. The Inquisitors will help you remember the names and locations of your co-conspirators."

With a wave of dismissal, the Captain turned his back as a platoon of warriors dragged Aleka to the castle. He'd sent patrols through the streets of Darktown searching for the felpurs. If experience was any guide, he doubted his troops would find them after so long a head start. Grizzle cursed himself for failing to send enough soldiers to take the prisoners in the first place. He should have anticipated trouble. He should have led them himself.

The past few years in the city had dulled his edge. Out on the empire's frontiers, he'd learned better. Out in the provinces, he would almost never have made these kinds of mistakes. Commanders who failed to anticipate trouble never lived long. They learned to crush rebellions quickly. Blanket the area with informants. Use gold, land, and privilege to buy a network of spies, then use them to unearth the rebels. Keep the population terrified with enough mass executions to deter the rabble from joining the insurrection, and eventually you reduce their recruits. It had worked for thirty years. But here in the city, the troops were soft, the commanders sloppy. The regime's opponents sensed the weakness and were capitalizing on it.

To make matters worse, the Regent's growing anxiety was

affecting the troops. A cavalry commander had been executed for failing to capture a human yesterday. The massacre of everyone on the street had angered the Guilds.

The Regent laughed at the Guild emissaries who had protested the killings on the street. They'd complained that such slaughter was bad for business, that it would cut into Her own profits if it continued. When She'd suggested that any reduction in earnings would mean a replacement of the Guild members with more loyal employees, the representatives had left, their aplomb shattered.

The Arch Regent hadn't minded the bloodbath, though when none of the dead turned out to be the human responsible for the growing chaos in her city, She'd been enraged. She'd been upset when She first learned that the human had freed a group of slaves, but She'd been confident Her troops would catch him. When She learned he had saved Cobran and escaped from the ring, She lashed out at the commander who had failed to catch him in the street. When She discovered that the human, and a lizardman, and a mage had freed two felpurs from the Guild Hall, yet another commander learned what befell those who failed Her.

Grizzle shook his head. He didn't care about his colleagues, but Her reaction to the news that a faerie mage had roasted the troops guarding the prisoners did disturb him. She'd flown into a rage beyond even Grizzle's expectations. She ranted about the mage, shouting, "I knew he'd come back—but he'll rue the day he challenged Me!" Clearly, She knew much more about this mage than She let on to Her officers. Unfortunately, no one dared to question Her. She demanded that the failed commander tell Her more about him. He couldn't. Grizzle suspected his colleague wished he had seen the mage. In any event, he would have plenty of time to contemplate his failures in the abyss She had conjured up to swallow him.

Grizzle might have been next if he'd told Her ahead of time that he'd sent men to pick up the felpur for questioning. He'd learned in his career never to raise his superiors' hopes too early. Now, although his men had been ambushed, he could report he'd captured a rebel killer. She might be pleased to know that, but Grizzle didn't plan to tell Her until he had time to analyze whatever Aleka told the Inquisitors.

He needed some information about the rebellion. Grizzle didn't like the growing frequency of the resistance's attacks. He could be facing an organized insurrection instead of a few hotheaded malcontents. The rumors that the League of the Crimson Crescent was behind these terrorist actions added to the tension in the castle. For years, his troops had laughed at the idea that such a League really existed.

It was harder to laugh at the reality of ambushes, escapes, and uprisings. The idea that they might be facing an organized adversary hurt morale. Too many armies consisted of thugs used to pushing around cowed and helpless townspeople, not battle-toughened troops. These city soldiers weren't used to hardship. After today's ambush, they'd be even more nervous, especially when word spread about the Arch Regent's anxiety.

But the League's open contempt for the Crown's forces posed a more dangerous threat than its actual activities. The citizens of Trillius were probably beginning to pay attention to the talk of the League. In the taverns, customers were probably laughing at his troops' failure to catch these elusive traitors.

Residents of the city wouldn't fear anyone whose mistakes made them objects of ridicule. The dangers to the regime were growing.

Grizzle knew that the Regent's forces needed to act quickly to contain the contagion before it became a city-wide plague of mutiny. He needed hard information about his opponents' activities, interests, and whereabouts. He knew of only one place where he might unearth some clues.

Spinning on his heel for the castle, he decided he'd personally supervise Aleka's questioning. She would tell him everything she knew.

A few hours after the felpur left Orwynn's establishment, the ninja sought out Bill, finding him in the empty tavern's main room.

"You didn't want them to leave, did you?" she asked. "You're worried about them."

"I guess I am," Bill said

"They're not worth it," she said. "They know you need them, still they abandoned you."

"I don't expect you to understand," Bill said. "They're my friends. They were the first friends I made here. I'm going to miss them."

"That's quaint," she said.

Bill said nothing, taking a seat at an empty table.

"In the Assassins' Guild, friendships are not encouraged," the ninja said. "We work alone. The less anyone knows about your habits, your interests, your pastimes, the longer you're likely to live. You make many enemies in my business. I learned a long time ago, it doesn't pay to grow too attached to anyone. They're never there when you need them."

"That's a nice philosophy," Bill said. "You must find it quite comforting."

The ninja ignored his sarcasm.

"So why join us?" Bill asked. "How do you know we'll be there when you need us?"

"I don't," she said. "I don't expect you'll be there when the crunch comes. I'm planning for that, but if you are, I just hope none of you get in my way. I can handle this quite well on my own."

"I must be missing something," Bill said. "Why go with us at all?"

"I've already told you, I need your help," the ninja said defensively. "I'll need your help to get to Her. But killing Her, that's my specialty."

"I'm glad we have some reason for going with you," Bill said.

The ninja stared at Bill crossly. "I know why I'm going," she said. "I can't quite figure out what's in it for you, though. Those humans that Orwynn has stashed upstairs said you freed them from the auction block. You saved Cobran from that rigged fight. And I saw you risk your necks for those ungrateful felpurs who cut and ran on you. Why?"

"If you don't know, I can't explain it."

"I don't need to understand to get your help," she said. "The Arch Regent's no dummy. She'll be well protected. If you get me close enough to Her, though, I'll handle it from there."

"You have a high opinion of yourself," a voice from the side of the table interrupted. Zynaryxx rose onto the table without effort. "I don't like eavesdropping, but I couldn't help it."

"I knew you were there," the ninja said. "I wouldn't have lived this long if I couldn't hear even tiny feet."

"Of course," the mage said. "I was wondering how you were planning to get inside the castle?"

"Unless some other suggestions come along," the ninja said, "I thought I would scale the wall and drop a line down to help the rest of you up."

"It's an idea," the mage said. "It might be too risky with so many of us, though. If any of us was spotted up on those ramparts, we'd make easy targets. All they'd need is a few archers. My way is probably just as dangerous, but they wouldn't be able to alert the entire watch guard when we're spotted—as we will be. With luck, we'll dispatch anyone who discovers us before they can alert the main guard."

"How do you propose to get inside?" the ninja asked.

"Through the tunnels under the city," the mage said. "Once closer to the castle, we'll run into some of the castle's inhabitants, possibly quite a few, but they won't be expecting anyone so foolish as to fight their way through there. If we can survive what we'll face in there, we'll get close to the Regent before She's aware we're coming."

"It sounds dangerous," Bill said. "I don't want you to think of me as timid, but I don't relish the idea of taking on the Regent's entire forces inside Her fortress."

"They won't all be there," the mage said. "I'm arranging that."

"How?" the ninja asked.

"By now Bill probably thinks of the League of the Crimson Crescent as an old man's debating society. We've often thought of it that way ourselves. But we've prepared for the time when we might actually succeed. Now with the One on our side, it's time to act."

"How?" the ninja insisted.

"You've seen what's been happening in the city for the past few days. That's with just a few of us," the mage said. "I intend to have the League begin striking at the Regent's forces throughout the city. She's not used to resistance. Her troops are already jittery enough. She only knows one tactic—swift and massive retaliation. That's exactly what we'll need to draw Her troops out of the castle. The more times and places we hit them, the more She'll send out death and destruction."

"Judging by what I saw on the street yesterday, a lot of innocent people will get killed," Bill predicted.

"You're quite right," the mage said. "That's what we'll need to succeed. The people fear Her, but they put up with Her, hoping She'll only strike at others, not themselves. They sit back watching others dragged from their beds at night, hoping that if they keep quiet and keep to themselves, they'll be spared. If enough of them see the brutality affecting them and their families, they'll strike back, especially if the League shows it can be done."

"Zynaryxx, I don't understand how you can so easily sentence so many innocent people to death," Bill said.

"I?" the mage chuckled. "You watched hundreds of people massacred on the streets of this city yesterday. Did I give that order? Are you responsible for those deaths? Ask the humans who wear chains and go to early graves for the amusement of their owners whether they deserve what happens to them? The past prisoners who have died in the dungeons of the castle in unspeakable torment, weren't they innocents? Every day in this city, the blood of innocents is spilled to feed the hunger of those in the castle. That hunger is growing. That hunger has been gnawing at this city for years, spreading through the surrounding towns, eating away at provinces and kingdoms.

"Some will die in the next several days. In my own way, I will cry for them. If we succeed, however, we can tear out this cancer infecting our world."

Bill considered the mage's words. He studied the faerie's face. "Will it work?"

"It has to," Zynaryxx said. "If we are to succeed, the people of this city must shake off thirty years of fear and cowardice. You can't really free them simply by slaying a tyrant, for another despot can always take its place. The people have to join us, they have to rise if we're to hold this city after we destroy the Regent."

"What if they don't?" the ninja asked. "I've spent my entire life in this city. I've never noticed many of its citizens willing to risk their lives for anything other than a few gold pieces."

"If they don't, they deserve what happens to them," the mage said. "Our responsibility is to give them a chance to earn their freedom. You can take off someone's chains, but the absence of chains isn't freedom. You don't appreciate what you have till you put it at risk. That's the best any rebellion can do—give people the opportunity to take their freedom back from those who have stolen it. If they choose not to, we'll have done our best."

"I can't say that your words cheer me up a great deal," Bill said. "I always assumed that all you had to do was slay the evil ruler, and everyone would live happily ever after."

"Few things are that simple."

In the following silence, the three companions heard a persistent tapping on the front door. "Orwynn!" Zynaryxx yelled. "The door."

The innkeeper came out of the kitchen looking worried. "I doubt it's an enemy. They don't tap," the mage said.

When the innkeeper opened the door, the young gnome Morko hurried in, casting anxious glances over his shoulder. "They're coming," he said, breathing heavily. "My grandfather sent me. Troops are on the street, conducting door–to–door searches of Darktown. You need to get everybody out of here before they get here."

"That's no trouble," the mage said. "I know where we can go."

"You can't come home with me," Morko said hastily, "Or to my father's or grandfather's. We got those humans out of the city, but I was nearly caught by a patrol."

"Don't worry so," Zynaryxx laughed. "We know the risks you took. Your grandfather is still talking about the bravery of his grandson. I have another place in mind. Besides, I suspect they'll be searching your home, too."

"Where will you go?" the gnome asked.

"The fewer who know, the fewer will be in danger," the faerie said. "That's the first rule of any conspiracy. What I do need to know now is, what has prompted this new search of the city."

"They're looking for two felpurs and a mook," Morko said. "The Regent's troops have apparently taken Aleka prisoner for killing some of their troopers. They claim she helped the felpurs and their friend escape."

"Aleka?" Zynaryxx said.

"Zorth and Quatar went to see her this morning,"

Orwynn said. "They thought they could find out where their brother was by talking to her at the Mercenary Martyr. I can't imagine her helping them escape from the Crown. It's not like her at all."

"She'd be more likely to help the Crown catch them," Zynaryxx said. "She's always been willing to turn people in to the Regent's forces if it would help her curry favor. But kill troopers, risk her own arrest? It doesn't make sense."

"It may not," Morko said, "But it has the Castle's troops in an uproar. It's been a long time since any of them have been killed on the streets of Darktown. I've never seen them so edgy. You don't want to be here when they arrive."

"You're quite right, Morko," Zynaryxx said. "Bill, round up everyone and take them to that place I showed you. Wait for me there. Morko, you and I need to go for a walk."

"Where?" the gnome asked suspiciously.

"Toward the Martyr to find those felpurs. Unless I miss my guess, they're heading here. You don't want them here with Orwynn when the troops arrive."

"You want me to help you find them?" the gnome asked.

"You can't expect Orwynn to go out on the streets today," the mage said. "They're probably rounding up any loose humans they find. We obviously can't take Bill. They're probably looking for Cobran. Who else can I take?"

"Me?" the gnome asked.

"I think I should go," Nagano said. "I don't want to sound rude, but if there's trouble on the streets, I'd be better equipped to handle it."

The mage eyed the ninja closely.

"I didn't think you cared for the felpurs," Bill said.

"I don't, and I don't care whether we find them or not. I

do care what happens to Zynaryxx. I need him. And I'm better able to ensure he returns to us than anyone else."

"Very well," the mage said. "I'll go along with your suggestion. Morko, go to your father and ask him to help hold down the inn with Orwynn. I don't want him here alone when the warriors come."

The young gnome hurriedly left, clearly relieved that he wouldn't have to escort Zynaryxx.

"Is it wise to wear your mask?" the mage asked Nagano.

"How often have you seen anyone, even armed troops, provoke a member of the Assassin's Guild?" she replied.

"I won't argue that one," the mage said. Together, they went out into Darktown.

Chapter Twelve

"I'm glad you offered to come," Zynaryxx said. "I wouldn't want to try to keep that young gnome's courage up. He'd faint at the first sight of soldiers."

"If I were the suspicious sort, I'd say you knew I'd come along in his place," Nagano said.

"Me? You think I could manipulate someone as astute as you?"

The ninja grinned, then sobered again. "Enough of that. Right now, we need to concentrate our attention on finding those felpurs. To trap a quarry, you have to think like it would. Now, if we were trying to evade the troops, we'd get off this street."

From the east, the ramparts of night toppled over the city. Ducking into an alley, the two carefully examined the shadows.

"I don't think they'd go into anyone's house or into any of these buildings," Zynaryxx said. "The residents of Darktown may have no love of the castle or its troops, but they're just as wary of strangers."

"That means the felpur must be hiding in one of these alleys," Nagano said. "If they have any sense, they're waiting for full dark to fall."

The two prowled through the passage between the buildings until a shout froze them in their tracks.

"What have we here?" An orc stepped from the shadows.

He reached into his pocket, then blew a whistle. A dozen troops sealed off each end of the alleyway.

"I hope I'm not disturbing you," the orc said. "The two of you seem so intent. Perhaps my troops and I can help you find who you seek."

"I suspect we're both searching for two traitorous felpurs and a mook," Nagano said. "If you fools could find them, my Guildmaster wouldn't have sent me to do the job."

The orc stepped back at the ninja's tone. "We're instructed to bring them back alive."

"You can take it up with the Arch Regent if you have any intention of interfering with me."

"I have no instructions about the Assassins' Guild," the orc said.

"I didn't know that the Regent checked with your Guild before issuing Her orders to mine. These felpur escaped from members of your warriors once before. Now this makes twice. It's not my job to know Her thoughts, but I wouldn't be surprised if She decided to let professionals handle this."

"Those weren't Castle troops the first time."

"They were over—armored bully boys," Nagano responded. "Take away the steel they hide behind and what do you have?"

The orc's eyes flashed, but he kept his distance from the ninja.

"Wait here until I receive instructions from my captain," the orc said. "He will have my head if they are not brought in alive for questioning."

"I suspect She'll be quite interested to learn who is really in charge of the city," the ninja said.

As the orc turned in anger, he kicked at a tarp rolled up

along the alley. The unmistakable sound of a painful grunt
came from beneath the tarp. Drawing his blade, the orc poked
the large bundle.

"Come out, or I'll run you through!" he said.

From beneath the canvas scrambled the two felpurs, followed by the mook, who held his side tenderly.

"Take them," the orc said to his men.

The ninja leaped at the orc, kicking his blade from his
hand, swinging around in a circle and smashing her fist into
his throat. As the orc fell to his knees, it made a low gurgling
sound, then collapsed.

The warriors drew their swords and charged at the five
from the two ends of the alley. Zynaryxx passed a hand before twelve of them charging toward him, and a ball of fire
fell into their midst. Seven of them burst into fiery blazes.

Nagano ran toward the five remaining troops, throwing a
small pellet in front of them. As it exploded, the soldiers
stepped back, temporarily blinded. The ninja fell in among
their midst. Leaping into the air, she delivered simultaneous
kicks to the groins of two soldiers. When they fell to the
ground, Nagano snapped their necks between her ankles.
Three remaining soldiers blindly waved their swords, trying
to follow the ninja's movements from the noises their companions made. Grabbing a fallen soldier's sword, the elf
slashed the blind men's throats.

Both Zorth and Quatar held their blades ready as they
advanced on the charging soldiers at the other end of the
alley. The mook bowed his head in concentration as a psionic
burst reverberated through the passage. Five soldiers staggered, but none fell.

Quatar kicked one who had escaped Olaf's mental blast.

As the soldier staggered, she stabbed him, pulling the blade free in time to parry a blow from another warrior. Zorth smashed a second with his mace. The soldier raised his shield, warding off Zorth's blow, while he drove his sword at the priest's midsection. Zorth dodged the blade and managed to grab the soldier's wrist. He twisted hard, rapping the soldier's arm with his mace. When he heard a bone snap and the warrior's shriek, he let go. A third soldier took advantage of Zorth's focused attention to bludgeon the felpur across the back of his head with his club. Zorth stumbled and fell to his knees. He ducked a sword thrust from a fourth warrior.

Quatar stepped between him and the soldiers. She moved inside a sword thrust, parried it, and darted her own blade into the chest of an adversary.

The felpurs' luck was running out. Zorth slumped on his knees, dazed from the head blow. Quatar faced four warriors, one edging to the side, waiting for his companions to distract her long enough for him to finish off Zorth. Meanwhile, the five warriors stunned by Olaf regained their footing and advanced toward the mook.

Zynaryxx waved his staff at the four facing Quatar. They staggered backward as if an invisible fist had struck them. Three fell to the ground. The fourth, who had been edging toward Zorth, stood dazed, his sword tip dragging the ground. Quatar impaled him.

Olaf stared at the approaching soldiers, his brow furrowed in concentration. A second psionic wave buffeted them like a gale force wind. They swayed, stumbled, and tripped over their feet, tottering like drunks. Olaf walked into their midst, rapping two on the side of the head as if he were testing their reactions. When they fell at his feet, he nodded and walked back to the felpurs.

"They should have gone down the first time," Olaf said. "I don't understand it at all. More of them should have dropped, and now I have a terrible headache. I keep hearing this ringing in my head."

"I think we need a rest," Quatar said, helping Zorth to his feet. "Let's just be glad that Zynaryxx and Nagano were here to help. Olaf, there were too many of them for just the three of us."

The ninja elf and Zynaryxx joined the two felpurs and the mook. "My good Olaf, I'm sure we can analyze what happened after we've left this alley," the mage said. "If we remain here much longer, you may suffer something far worse than a headache."

"That's fine to say, but where do you propose we go?" the mook said. "If we leave the alley, we have to go back out on the street where soldiers are looking for us."

Pulling out his crescent key, the faerie walked to corner of a building in the alley, fumbling until they heard a click. "I believe we can discuss this at greater length in here," he said.

With the ninja's assistance, Quatar helped her brother into the passageway.

"We can't go far with Zorth suffering a concussion," Quatar said. "We'll have to rest here a while."

"I don't believe we have that luxury," the mage said. "They won't be looking for us in here. But the Regent's creatures roam these passageways. We'll just have to tend to Zorth as best we can until we can get back to the Royal Falcon. I'll feel a lot safer with Bill and Cobran guarding our backs."

Olaf said, "I can help Zorth. I'm not as skilled as he is in these matters, but I can help him enough so that he won't be a burden."

Bowing his head, the mook spoke Thea's name as he pressed his hand to the felpur's head.

Zorth's eyes fluttered before focusing. "I feel like someone tore off the back of my head," the priest said. "What happened?"

"We owe our lives to Zynaryxx, Nagano, and Olaf," Quatar said. "If they had not been there, those warriors would have done far worse than merely tearing off the back of your head."

Rising stiffly, Zorth bowed. "Again, I'm in your debt. I intend to make payment in full. My sister and I wish to accompany you on your journey to face the Arch Regent if you will forgive my hasty remarks of yesterday."

"You know quite well that we need you," Zynaryxx said. "There is no need for you to embarrass yourself. What you said yesterday only showed that you had good sense."

"You're too easy on him," Nagano said. "If I know this priest, there's something in it for him. That's the only reason he'd change his mind."

"Peace," Zynaryxx said. "Our journey is dangerous enough without questioning the motives of a friend. If Zorth and Quatar choose to help us, I need no more."

"It may be enough for you," the ninja snapped. "I see no reason, however, to travel into danger with comrades who have been faithless. I want to know why they've changed their minds."

"I would be angry with Nagano, but some of her words are true," Zorth said. "Our brother is being held in the

Regent's dungeons. Olaf has told us that Portnal broke in on some mysterious errand of his own. We hope to free him, if you will take us with you."

"Then you will desert us again," the ninja said. "Your offer of help was no noble gesture of gratitude. You'll use us until you get what you want, then leave us to face the perils of the castle as best we can."

"What do you know of noble gestures?" Zorth said hotly.

"Nothing," the ninja said. "I don't pretend to. I don't use empty words. I let my actions speak for me, as I did just a few minutes ago when I saved your lives. Your gratitude, as always, overwhelms me."

"I'll forget this conversation for now, assassin, for I owe you my life." Zorth said. "When the debt is paid, however, I may remind you of your harsh words."

"You'll forgive me if I choose not to worry too much," the ninja said. "My hair will have long turned gray before you do any more than flap your tongue with idle threats. From what I've heard, you and your sister have been rescued repeatedly, yet your ingratitude only grows. You call me assassin as if it were an insult, but among my profession, the word of Nagano has served as an inviolate bond. Never have I been known to walk away without fulfilling a contract or paying my debts in full. That is more than you can say."

"Is it now?" Zorth said. "What of your contract to find and kill Bill? Haven't you broken your word? Are you perhaps planning to fulfill it once he has helped you even your blood score with the Regent?"

The ninja angrily started for Zorth. Quatar stepped between them. "We owe you our lives, so we will endure your insults, but have a care."

"Be quiet all of you, or I will silence your tongues myself!" Zynaryxx said. "You forget who the enemy is. Save your anger for Her and the Dark Lord. If She were here, She would be delighted to see this kind of camaraderie among Her enemies. We need to rejoin Bill and Cobran at the Falcon and get some rest before we assault the nether regions of the Castle. So put aside your petty quarrels and your doubts about each other's integrity and intentions. We have no time for such foolishness."

The mage spun on his heels and strode into the darkness, using his staff to light the way. The passageway in which the group rested was left in darkness.

Olaf said, "The faerie's words make sense to me. Earlier today, you helped me face myself and my fears. I know nothing about whatever feud exists between yourselves and this ninja, but I know this: We will need to put aside our pride and cooperate, or we will fail." Turning, he left the two felpurs and the ninja in the darkness.

"The mook and the mage speak the truth," the elf maid said. "I don't apologize, but perhaps I should put off hasty judgments until I see whether you prove me wrong."

The two felpurs said nothing, rising to join the rest of their companions.

A short time later, they found Bill and Cobran waiting warily in a cavern passageway, their swords drawn.

"You found them!" Bill shouted.

Zynaryxx said, "Just in time. We barely managed to get to them before the Warriors found them."

Once Zorth recounted their experiences at the Martyr and their escape from Aleka, Bill said. "Well, she has received a just reward for betraying you. The Warriors have arrested her and taken her to their dungeons. They believe she aided your escape by slaying their soldiers. I suspect that her punishment will more than fit her crime."

"We needn't concern ourselves with Aleka," Zynaryxx said. "I'm more interested in this entrance into the castle. Olaf, how do we find it and where will it take us."

Olaf described a passageway near the Martyr leading into the very caverns the companions now occupied. Zynaryxx pulled out his map of the labyrinth, tracing out Olaf's route.

"It takes us too close to the main barracks of the warriors," the mage said. "It leads to a corridor between the dungeons and the upstairs barracks."

Zorth and the mook seemed crestfallen at the dismissal of their secret passageway.

"If we free your brother, we can use it for his escape," Zynaryxx said. "I fear, though, that it won't aid us in confronting the Lady. She lies beyond the barracks, and it is foolhardy to venture through them. I'm afraid my own plan offers our best hope to surprise Her. Let us rest and refresh ourselves before we begin."

Inside the castle's dungeons, Captain Grizzle stood impassively as two Inquisitors pressed a flaming brand against the bottom of Aleka's feet. She screamed, rattling the chains that suspended her from the dungeon's ceiling. She'd stopped cursing her tormentors hours ago, exhausted by the relentless agony inflicted upon her.

The Inquisitor passed a hand across her scorched foot, soothing the pain, healing the burning sores. "Aleka, you do not need to endure this misery," the Inquisitor said gently.

"Help us to help you. Renounce your treason. Tell us where your fellow conspirators have fled."

"I'm no traitor," Aleka said. "They murdered Blackie. If I knew where they were, I'd kill them myself."

The Inquisitors shrugged as they looked at the Captain. "We think she's telling the truth," the Inquisitor said. "You have the wrong person here."

"What do you mean, the wrong person?" Grizzle snapped.

"She's not part of the resistance," the mook said. "Her story never deviates. All she knows is the names of the felpurs, Zorth and Quatar. She says she was trying to capture the rebels, not aid them, but a psionic drove them insane and made your men attack her."

"That's ridiculous," Grizzle snapped. "She's beguiled you."

The mook said stiffly, "We know our job. Our methods do not fail. We heal the nerve endings we have injured to ensure that each time we cause pain, the subject feels it as intensely as the first time. We've tried to trip her up—but you don't have a rebel here."

The Captain paced around the interrogation chamber. He drove his fist into the helpless woman's stomach. "So you want me to believe that you are loyal," he sneered.

Aleka whimpered, gasping for breath from the blow.

"Why then did the felpur come to you?" he asked. "Why would they seek the aid of someone so loyal to the Crown?"

"They sought their brother," she said brokenly. "They thought we might know his whereabouts, because...he'd visited the Martyr."

"He had?" the Captain asked.

"Blackie said he had. Said he'd talked to Olaf. So...they spoke to Olaf."

"What did he tell them?"

"I don't know," she said. "Blackie came with your men and took them all away. I didn't have time to find out. It didn't seem important. I thought it was more important to find out if they were the ones the Crown sought."

Grizzle looked closely into the woman's frightened eyes. He slapped her, shouting, "Did they talk long?"

The sudden blow startled Aleka. Her brow furrowed as if her life depended on her answer, which it did.

"They wanted the information. They offered us gold. They talked a long time with the mook. I couldn't hear them, but the mook must have known something about their brother."

"A third felpur," the Captain said, lost in thought. "Where could this other felpur be that they would come so close to the castle, searching for him?"

"Captain," the Inquisitor said. "A felpur was captured inside the castle a while ago."

Grizzle's interest lit with this news. "Does he live?"

"I don't know," the Inquisitor said. "I'll find who conducted the interrogation and get the report of his confession. You might speak to the jailers, to see if he's still alive."

Grizzle left the torture chamber glad that he hadn't told the Regent he'd captured one of the rebels who had ambushed his troops. He might be hanging in Aleka's place if the Regent had discovered his mistake. He could still avoid punishment for his failure if this felpur prisoner could shed any light on the other two felpur.

He sent for the head jailer.

Chapter Thirteen

A ghoul wrapped in a decaying black shroud greeted Captain Grizzle. As the specter floated before him, Grizzle shuddered.

"You disturb our feasting?" the ghoul asked in a menacing tone. Its voice seemed to come from afar.

"Beware, phantasm," the captain snarled. "I'm on the Regent's business. You'll help me with what I need or answer to Her for your insolence." He looked closely into the shadow cast by the shroud but couldn't detect any features.

The shade shrank back at the warning. Captain Grizzle shuddered again as he considered the power that frightened even this ghoul of darkness.

"I meant nothing," it said. "How may I help the Regent, my Captain?"

"A felpur was given into your keeping sometime ago by the Inquisitors. I must question him immediately," the captain said. "Bring him to the interrogation chambers."

The shade hung suspended, unmoving. "Do it now, shade," Captain Grizzle ordered.

"You don't often go into our dungeons, do you?" the specter asked.

"I don't see what that has to do with my errand or your instructions. Bring me the prisoner, or must I advise the Regent that you've allowed him to escape?"

"Escape?" the ghoul uttered a weird chortling sound,

much like a chuckle but devoid of any joy. "No, my captain, those entrusted to us do not escape. Far from it. A number of soldiers in the Regent's service, many of them like me, require...how shall I say this?...a different sustenance than a barracks kitchen provides."

"I'm not here to discuss your rations or dietary requirements," Grizzle said. "Send for my prisoner."

"Ah, Captain, that is my point," the ghoul said. "What you call prisoners, we consider our supplies, if you will, a source of, uh, nourishment."

The ghoul waited for Grizzle to "digest" this morsel of information before continuing. "I can't be certain whether this prisoner you wish is still in our care or whether he's already served another, uh, higher purpose."

"You mean you may have eaten him?" Grizzle stammered.

"Not me," the ghoul said. "I dine on–"

"Don't tell me," Grizzle said hastily. "I don't care to know. But your fellows in the dungeon...eat prisoners?"

The creature stood motionless, its shoulders slouched in despair.

"I must report this immediately," Grizzle said, temporarily disoriented. "She'll want a detailed report. You'd better come along to explain." He recovered himself. "No, wait. I need the prisoner, this felpur–now!"

"How am I to know?" the shade stammered. "They're supposed to tell us when they have further need of them. Then, we keep those separate."

"You have to do better than that," Grizzle said. "Are you quite sure that you've...eaten this felpur?"

"I'm not sure whether he's been served or not."

"Then, why are you wasting my time?" Grizzle bellowed.

"Go down and find out. Move, shade! Or be prepared to report to Her!"

Without a word, the specter faded.

Captain Grizzle couldn't restrain the shudder that crossed his spine. He had suspected that something was happening to the prisoners his soldiers abandoned to the care of the dungeon masters. He knew the kind of creatures She'd enlisted, but the thought of using prisoners as kitchen rations repulsed him. Envisioning the dungeon's endless row of cells as some strange pantry filled him with a sense of fear and loathing. He pushed the vision from his mind.

A soldier approached. "My captain," the warrior said, "Our efforts to find the rebels have failed. About twenty-five troopers searching the streets as you ordered were attacked by superior forces and slaughtered."

Grizzle's eyes narrowed. "How many rebels were there?"

"We don't know," the soldier said. "No one survived the attack. The rebels have a powerful mage among them. He incinerated several men with fireballs. We suspect Olaf, the psionic, was with them, as well, because some of the troopers' minds were shattered. We have no defense against such attacks. The soldiers pulled out of Darktown to protect the castle."

"You mean you've hidden in the castle," Captain Grizzle snarled. "Filthy cowards! A ragtag band of rebels bloody your noses, and you run frightened like rats into the nearest crevice. The Arch Regent's army! You make me want to puke."

"We didn't know what else to do," said the warrior, stepping back from Grizzle's fury. "It was the second major attack in one day. We've already lost close to forty soldiers.

No one has ever attacked our troops before."

"You didn't know what else to do?" the captain mimicked the soldier. "You've lost forty comrades. I'll tell you what you do—what you've been trained to do! Fight! Crush this rebellion! You find these killers, and you destroy them. You don't run away the first time someone raises their hand against you."

"It's the work of this League of the Crimson Crescent," the soldier said. "They say the League has troops of its own waiting throughout the city, ready to pounce on us."

"The League. You speak as if it were some mystical force. Have you no wits? Do you not recognize the power you serve? You talk of a tiny faerie even you could crush in your bare hand. And a drunken psionic! As if their paltry powers could stand for a moment against the Regent's. Behind the walls of this castle dwell creatures whose powers come from the very force of the darkness that so frightens you."

"We felt we should protect the Arch Regent."

"You mean hide behind her skirts! You disgust me. You belong to an army. Armies go to war. They fight battles. They die. That's your job, to go out and take those streets back or die in the attempt. Now go. I want five hundred soldiers on the streets within the hour, or I'll personally run you through with my sword."

Grizzle watched the soldier scurry toward the barracks. "I'm trying to hold this city with cowardly bully boys that run away at the first sign of real trouble," he said to himself. He knew that the Arch Regent's anger would have no bounds if She discovered his troops had run and hidden. She would be enraged when She learned that another platoon had been killed by the rebels.

He pondered his choices. He didn't savor the idea of winding up a special course in the jailer's dungeon. Perhaps the jailer's incompetence could save him. Considering the Regent's mood, if he presented this correctly to Her, She would be so angry with the jailer that She might not even notice his errors. She might content herself with punishing the shade.

As he turned to tell the Regent that a prisoner with vital information had been eaten by Her servants, the shade reappeared. "He's here! He was being saved for a very special feast."

"Enough!" Grizzle said. "I'll await him in the interrogation room. Have him brought to me there."

The captain left hurriedly. When he entered the room, he instructed the Inquisitors to remove Aleka from her chains. Shortly, three goblins brought in a felpur. The three looked unhappy at leaving him chained him to the ceiling. One cackled, "Don't spoil the meat!" as they left.

Grizzle shook his head. "Do you have a name, felpur?" Grizzle asked.

"Portnal," the felpur said. "Among the Seven tribes, I am known as Portnal. I am a ranger."

The Inquisitor handed Grizzle a paper. "This is from his interrogation," he said.

"So you broke into the castle," the captain said. "That's quite unusual even for a felpur. Would you care to tell me why?"

"I hoped to learn the secret of this city."

"The secret?" the captain asked, amusement in his voice. "What secret is so vital that you would break into a castle that most creatures avoid like the plague? What secret lured you here?"

"The secret of Trillius," the felpur said. "A twisted mystery hides behind this city. People come here from across the known world. They come for the entertainments, the gambling, the vices, the exotic lures that serve as bait for the bored, the rich, and the foolish. Every day, travelers journey from near and far to sample its delights. Thousands of nameless, faceless people of all known races make the pilgrimage to this place. I have always wondered why the Regent allows Trillius to exist. It seems to contradict a tyrant's need to control the populace."

"She simply provides the people with a place to amuse themselves," the captain said. "It lessens their worries, provides them with distractions. You make it sound like something far more sinister."

"More sinister?" the felpur laughed. "Much like the gossamer threads of the spider that reflect the light to attract the fly, the beauty of Trillius disguises the ugly brooding secret within. Even you must wonder what happens to these visitors. Thousands arrive each day, many of whom never return to their homelands. They spend their money, sample the delights, and then disappear. Surely you've noticed."

"My responsibility is to keep order," the captain said. "We are not nursemaids to lost citizens."

"People disappear from the streets. Travelers visit Darktown and never return. That's why the people bar their doors at night. Something deadly stalks their streets. I wanted to find out where the missing end up. I felt the answer to that mystery was within this castle. Now that I've found the answer, I realize how foolish I've been."

"Enlighten me: What is the answer to this riddle?" the Captain said, bored by the line of questioning.

"The people of the city are being taken into the lower levels of the castle," the felpur said. "In these dungeons, they become the food source for the creatures the Regent brings into this world from the Nether regions. Demon spawn dine on living creatures. Wraiths, ghouls, monsters, trolls, goblins, werebeasts, gorgons, zombies, gargoyles—these undead are being assembled in legions below us. Not all of them eat flesh. Some suck the life force from their victims, dining on the spirit of those they kill. Now, I'm destined to become a meal for these morbid creatures."

"I'm not interested in your opinions of the Regent's recruits," Grizzle said. "The people of Trillius and the surrounding kingdoms are Her subjects. She can do with them as She chooses. It's not my place to judge Her. I'm a soldier. She identifies Her enemies, and I destroy them. You can help me in that respect."

"You don't care?" Portnal asked. "It doesn't matter to you? Don't you realize that She's assembling an army of hellspawn, and it's only a matter of time before they need more than just the travelers who come to Trillius to feed upon. They'll need the city's inhabitants. Then, they'll need the surrounding country folk to quell their ravenous hunger."

"My troops and I are at the Regent's command—whatever She commands," the captain said. "We have conquered the territories for Her, and we have held them for Her."

"Your troops?" the felpur laughed. "Do you think She'll need you when She commands an army of undead? You and your warriors will follow me into the stewpots. A time will come when you will remember my words, and you will wish you had heeded them."

The captain suppressed another shudder, recalling the

specter. "I've heard enough of your nightmares. Tell me of Zorth and Quatar."

"My brother and sister?" Portnal said.

"Of course," the captain said.

"What about them?" Portnal asked. "Don't tell me they have come to Trillius! The fools! They must have come to find me."

"Apparently, they have run into your friend Olaf," Grizzle said.

"By the clans, that drunken fool? He could..." The words died on his lips.

"What?" Grizzle said.

"I don't know," the felpur said. "I haven't seen them in a month."

The captain's eyes glittered in thought. "You think they'll come here looking for you," he said. "That's what you fear. I see it in your eyes. Here I am sending men chasing throughout the streets of the city searching for them, when eventually they'll come to me."

Portnal wildly looked around the room. "Why are you searching for them?" the felpur asked. "What do two felpurs from the country mean to you?"

"Much and nothing," the captain said. "They've been a nuisance to the Crown, they've murdered my troops, they've meddled in affairs beyond their ken. They have friends with whom my liege wishes to meet. You will help me catch them. You will draw them to me so that I and my troops can close on them like steel jaws."

Captain Grizzle signaled for the shade. "I return him to your personal supervision," the captain said. "Find a place where he can be kept, where you can mount a large guard nearby. His friends will come for him soon. They must not be taken lightly. They have killed large numbers of trained troops. A murderous mage and a deadly psionic are among them. Tell your friends below that it's time they earned their meals around here. They won't be dining on helpless prisoners, but heartier meat that can bite back. Prepare a reception they can't survive. I'll return to review your plans."

Without waiting for an acknowledgment, Captain Grizzle headed for the barracks. He now knew what to do. He was at war, facing an enemy force of unknown size.

Grizzle already felt more comfortable. He was no secret police chief who sent spies skulking into the shadows, no administrator maintaining order on the streets. He was a warrior, a commander. He would give this city a taste of what it was like to displease the crown. They would feel the same lash he'd used so well in the provinces. This League of the Crimson Crescent, like a celibacy cult, was doomed.

He smiled as he headed toward the heart of the castle to report to the Regent. Her anger over the deaths of the soldiers would dissipate when She learned Her enemies were about to walk into a trap. He would ask Her advice on how best to crush them once they had taken the bait. She would enjoy that, especially when She learned the faerie mage over which She had been so incensed might well be among them.

Meanwhile, he would tell Her they needed to begin reprisals against the populace to quell the revolt and to ensure no one harbored the rebels. The city needed to be reminded of the Crown's power and savage fury. That would drive any thoughts of this League of the Crimson Crescent from their minds. They needed to see the sword unsheathed, so they could see the reflection of Her power glinting from its bloody edge.

After the companions had rested, Zynaryxx directed Nagano to go inside the Falcon and ask Orwynn for food. The tavernkeeper seemed excited as he carried out refreshments.

"Soldiers visited us earlier," he said. "While they questioned us, a warrior came and told them that a troop of twenty–five had been found murdered. He claimed the League of the Crimson Crescent had hundreds of armed troops prowling the streets, attacking unwary Crown warriors. He summoned them back to the Castle to prepare against a major attack. You should have seen them scurry out of here, jumping at every shadow."

"We killed a few troopers," Zynaryxx said. "If only we did have an army to challenge them on the streets. However, their own fears may serve us as a shadow army just as well."

"The Regent's army seems to be suffering from a morale problem," Bill observed. "They don't stand up too well when someone strikes back. Zynaryxx, it's time for this League of the Crimson Crescent to strike."

"How?" the tavernkeeper asked.

"You must call a meeting of these conspirators of yours," Bill said. "The streets are clear. The Regent's troops have gone back to the castle."

"They won't like it," Orwynn predicted.

"Too bad for them," Zynaryxx said. "So many of them have become nothing more than armchair revolutionists. They've forgotten how to fight. We must set a fire under them." He paced back and forth, lost in thought. "How many do you think we can get to a meeting within the next two hours?" he asked Orwynn.

"Two hours?"

"How many can we reach?"

"They won't come," Orwynn worried. "Many of them have businesses to run, jobs. You can't expect them to just drop everything, because you've called a meeting."

"Don't be ridiculous," the mage said. "Have you been out on the street today? It's empty. The stores are empty, too. The city is hiding indoors, because the people know it's only a matter of time before the Crown grabs anyone found on the streets. No one wants to be out. I can't think of a better time to find most of our members home or at work. They'll be nervous and looking for any information about the commotion. They'll come, Orwynn, don't you worry about that."

The innkeeper sighed, unconvinced.

"Tell them we'll meet in the usual place, the old temple," the mage said, "In two hours."

"We won't reach them in time," Orwynn said dourly. "We'll never get to them all. Of those we do reach, many will be too scared to come."

Zynaryxx grinned. "Frankly, I hope you're right," the mage said. "I really don't want to listen to the frightened ones. Those who stay hidden won't be missed. The members of the League who do show up will be the ones willing to take a risk and strike a blow against the Crown. That's what we need to make this plan work. Now, round up your messengers, then meet us there. Take Yorth and Pasham. They deserve a chance to be part of this."

Orwynn hurried out to find runners to send messages to the League's membership.

"Is this wise?" Olaf asked after the tavernkeeper and the two humans had left. "What if someone catches one of your messengers?"

"Relax," the mage said. "The messengers will know nothing about the message they carry. When the league members receive it, they'll know we're meeting at the temple. They'll deduce the time of the meeting by the token's shape. Anyone else who sees it will simply assume it's a gambling marker."

An hour later, Zynaryxx gathered the companions. "My friends, you say you want to accompany Bill and me into the castle. We intend to leave immediately after a meeting of the League. Going into the castle is dangerous, far more dangerous than you can imagine. If any of you have changed your minds, tell me now."

Zorth broke the silence. "I can only speak for myself and my sister. If you'll have us, we'll join you."

The mage nodded. "Nagano?" Zynaryxx asked, looking at the ninja. "Are you still certain?"

"You need me," she said. "Especially if they're coming." She glared at the felpurs.

"Cobran go with friends," the lizardman interrupted. "Friends need Cobran in dark places."

"I'm coming, too," Olaf said.

The mage stared into each of their faces. "Very well." He led the way into the underground tunnels. "When we meet with the League, let me do the talking."

A short time later, they arrived at an intersection in the caverns where Zynaryxx used his crescent key in the wall. A passageway opened, leading them along a twisting hallway that emptied into a large meeting room, lit by smoking torches.

At the temple's entrance, Morko greeted them, flanked by two gnomes whom Bill assumed were his father and his grandfather. "You shouldn't have called a meeting," Morko said nervously. "It's too dangerous right now. If the Regent's troops come out of the castle, we'll be trapped here. We should wait until these troubles pass."

"These troubles will never pass," Morko's frail, elderly grandfather snapped. "The reason we have these troubles is because too many people have waited too long."

"Well said, old friend. That's what this meeting is all about," Zynaryxx said. "It's time the League took action." He strode by Morko and to a stone altar on a dais, motioning Bill and the other companions to follow.

As they climbed the steps to the stage, Bill saw Pasham and Yorth beside Orwynn. He nodded to them. They seemed nervous in the crowd.

A restless quiet settled on the audience as the faerie took the stage. The crowd filled less than half the room; they numbered under two-hundred. Zynaryxx measured them as if reading their thoughts.

"My friends," his voice carried easily. "Thank you for leaving your homes today. I know you've exposed yourselves and your families to great danger by coming here. Our enemies are massed inside the castle, gathering to strike out against our city. Each moment the threat grows. Our adversary is angry. She's looked over Her ramparts and seen that the city that once feared Her has risen against Her."

"You all know what's occurred this past week," Zynaryxx said. "The rebellion has begun. The people of the city have started to rise from their years of fear and hesitation. They have struck against Her troops, cutting them down in the streets like grain mowed down by the farmer's scythe. The people of the city have shattered the myth of Her invincibility, fighting their way into the Guildlords' chambers to free Her prisoners right from underneath Her nose. They have destroyed Her soldiers, launched daring raids beneath the very walls of Her fortress. Before this rebellion, Her warriors have proven themselves to be nothing more than frightened thugs who hide themselves behind Her walls."

He looked at the uplifted faces of the League's membership. "You all know that what I say is true," the mage said. "You have seen the arrogance leave the faces of our oppressors. You have seen their backs as they've retreated into their castle. As they ran away, you saw the look of fear on their features every time they passed a dark alley.

"You know another truth. It has not been the League that has struck against our enemies. Look around you. The League of the Crimson Crescent has not fought a single fight in the streets of our city to help us win back our freedom. The League remained idle, cringing while others fought the battle we swore to wage. I have called you, our comrades, together today, because I believe it is time we gave our support to those who at this very moment risk their lives in our cause.

"Look around you," the mage said, his voice lowering. "Have any among you struck a blow for our freedom? No. Our League has remained in hiding, cowering in the shadows while others have acted. There are those who are content with that, who argue that we should shrink from this conflict, let others risk themselves in our behalf. I know the members of this League. I know each has sworn a blood oath to rid this land of the shadow covering it. Most of us have waited a long time for this moment. We have plotted and planned. We have waited for a day to dawn when this city of ours would join us.

"That day has come, but it's found us still hiding in the shadows. I say, the time for hiding has past. It is now time to redeem our oaths and stand up before those who have oppressed us. The time has come for us to look into our hearts. It is time for this League to strike."

An uneasy silence hung in the air. Zynaryxx's gaze remained calm and steady as he prepared to answer the doubters, to respond to the skeptics, and to ease the frightened.

An old dwarf rose uncertainly. "Is it wise to show ourselves? Look around this room, Zynaryxx. Two-hundred can't overthrow an army."

"Maldon, I do not expect the League to get together and march down the street to the castle's gate," the mage replied. "I suggest we strike at the Regent's forces each time they come outside. An arrow from the darkness into a roving patrol will heighten the fear that already tears apart Her troops. Small raids by small groups will unnerve them. Others have done it and succeeded. Can we do less?"

"Who are these others?" an elf asked from the back. "Everyone believes it's the League. We know it's not. They are everywhere, killing troops, rescuing prisoners—they've got the whole city talking."

"I don't know who they are," the mage lied, "But look what they've managed to do without any help from us. If we join them, imagine the fear of the troops when they discover they are safe nowhere in this city any longer."

"It doesn't seem prudent" a dracon said. "You know how the Regent is, Zynaryxx. She ordered a massacre on the streets just the other day. There will be reprisals if we act. Many good people will die."

"There will be reprisals even if we sit back," the mage answered. "Her troops have been slaughtered, Her authority challenged. She will not brook that kind of interference. Soon, Her troops will emerge from the castle looking for revenge. The slaughter will anger the people.

"The spark of rebellion has already been lit. We are the wind that can fan the flame into a cleansing fire to burn away the evil that has covered this city. If the people see us striking out, they will join us. Do not doubt that. They have already seen it can be done. We do not yet have enough force to assail Her gate, but we can make Her minions fear to walk among us."

"I think Zynaryxx makes sense," a hobbit said. "We've all known him a long time. He's always counseled caution when hotheads urged action. He always said it made no sense to foolishly throw away our lives in vain. If he's changed his mind, he's got good reason. Every time a soldier sticks his head down our streets, we ought to make him wonder whether he'll still have it when he pulls back."

"We know the city better than these hired ruffians!" a rawulf shouted. "We can blend into the shadows or slip into the tunnels. I'm tired of doing nothing while they strut around. We meet now and then and talk about revolution, but we never do anything. They took my oldest boy last year and none of you did anything, just told me our time would come. Well, the time has come, and some of you still hope it'll just pass us by."

"He's right," a felpur said. "All of us have seen friends and family hauled off to the Regent's dungeons. Never have we so much as raised a hand against it. Shall we turn our backs again until they come to get us?"

"Come they shall," shouted the hobbit. "This time, however, they'll learn fear."

"What of you, Zynaryxx?" the dracon asked. "What hope do you offer if we agree to this."

"My friends, as much as I trust you, no one can keep our secrets hidden from the Inquisition for long. That's why I won't ask any of you to outline your plans. Choose your companions and strike where and how you think is best. Reach beyond our own membership and recruit others you trust. Harry our enemies. If only half of us strike blows, it will seem as if the entire city is alive with rebels."

"What will you do while we risk our lives?" the dracon pressed.

"My friends and I are going into the castle to confront the Arch Regent," the mage said.

Chapter Fourteen

"Are you mad?" the dracon asked Zynaryxx.

Bill felt the aftershock of the mage's announcement like a ripple in his blood.

"The streets are clear of troops," Zynaryxx answered the dracon. "They're hiding inside the castle, but they'll soon emerge, in force. If you use these few hours to prepare, each in your own way, then when Her troops come, you can strike. Hit them from the shadows, not in military confrontations but individually, attacking a few troops at a time. As you divert them, my companions and I will enter the castle. The more troops you can lure out to quash your attacks, the fewer we'll have to face inside.

"Send the word out to those who aren't here but share our dream. Tell them to strike whenever and wherever they can, at any agents of the Crown."

"You really intend to face Her?" the dracon asked.

"There is no alternative. To reach Her, though, we're counting on you to empty the castle of as many of her servants as possible. Make it seem you're everywhere. She won't suffer such insolence."

"Her troops are too afraid to leave the castle."

"Only for the moment," the mage insisted. "Any time now, the forces lurking inside those walls will strike far more terror in Her soldiers than whatever threat posed on the streets.

"Friends, use this short respite to tell the city the time is now. Remind those absentee members who have not yet joined us of their oaths. Tell them the One is among us, poised to vanquish She who we've sworn to overthrow. The day foretold has dawned. If we hope to see the light of a new day breaking through this long night of darkness, we must strike with all the power we command."

"The One is among us?" the dracon asked.

"I will not speak further of him, because the risk of detection or betrayal is too great," the mage said. "Let this suffice: We of the League of the Crimson Crescent no longer battle alone to overthrow the evil that besets us. Attacks by the One have already shaken the city. Even now he walks among us. I and my companions go to join him on this journey that was long ago foreordained. The League must now play the role prophesied for it. You must distract Her attention from us. You must force Her to empty Her castle. You must give us the chance to slip past Her defenses."

Rising, the mage raised his staff. Its tip exploded in an eerie light. "We go to our destiny!" the mage shouted. "You must buy us the time we need, even if it costs you your lives."

Without looking back, he and Bill, followed by their companions, strode from the stage into the tunnels.

Yorth and Pasham jumped to their feet to follow, but Orwynn blocked their path. "We must follow Bill," Yorth said. "He walks into danger. He'll need us."

"We are at a crossroads where all paths lead to danger," the tavernkeeper said. "Bill needs you to fight the Regent's troops outside the castle, so that fewer will be inside waiting for him."

Orwynn walked to the altar, taking the mage's place. The crowd stirred uneasily. "You've heard Zynaryxx," the tavernkeeper said. "Unless I hear objections, I call this meeting to a close."

"What are we supposed to do?" Maldon the dwarf, asked. "Do you expect us to attack the Regent's troops?"

"Have you heard nothing?" Yorth interrupted. "That's what the mage just finished telling you."

The dwarf stared at the freed slave in surprise. "I don't think I like his tone," Maldon said. "I've never missed a meeting of the League, and I don't recall this man being inducted, nor do I appreciate his tone to a senior member. I believe all races are brothers, and that men deserve the same respect extended to anyone else, but face it, men don't own property. They have very little to lose."

"Little to lose?" Yorth shouted. "What do you know of losing?" He peeled his shirt off, showing the whip marks on his back. "I've lost blood, both my parents; my sisters were taken when they were still children. You speak of property— I speak of lives!

"You think that if you hide, the Regent's troops will spare you. You're a fool. When the soldiers come out of the castle, they won't come looking for those who killed their friends. They'll aim at those who can't strike back. Hide, and you can be that much certain to feel their vengeance."

"He's right, Maldon," Orwynn said. "Whether anyone here likes it or not, wants it or not, the time for hiding is over. The Regent's troops will seek vengeance on the entire city."

"So, you want us to throw away everything we have

worked for. You want us to risk the lives of our children and loved ones. Is this what you ask?" the dwarf said.

"I ask nothing," Orwynn said. "Your children's lives are already at risk. Look around this hall. You have people here who have joined us, because one day the Regent's troops knocked at their doors and hauled away their loved ones—for nothing. Everyone in this room knows it could happen to any of us, any time. That's why most of us are here. What comfort will our property or our businesses provide if those we love are gone?"

Maldon sank back into his seat, contemplating the tavernkeeper's words.

"I don't see any further reason to continue this meeting," Orwynn said. "Some of you will refuse to fight no matter what anyone says or does. We've held meetings for years, talking bravely about revolution, swearing oaths, and skulking in the shadows. The time for words has passed. The time for action has come. Those of you who already know what you intend to do should leave. Those of you who are looking for others to join you on raids should meet near the altar. I would caution you to keep your specific plans to yourselves. The fewer who know, the fewer can betray you."

As the meeting broke up, Orwynn could see the membership breaking into excited groups who met briefly before rushing from the room. Others stood alone, frowning, worried. They looked around, not meeting anyone's eyes before leaving. Some shook their heads, Maldon the dwarf among them.

Orwynn shrugged. Zynaryxx had predicted that some would find they preferred shadowy meetings to deeds. The tavernkeeper suspected, however, that before the next week ended, even those who now intended to sit out the revolution would find themselves dragged into it, anyway.

Near the altar, Yorth and Pasham vigorously recruited groups. "We need to hit the slave pens off the market square," Yorth said. "We only had two–hundred here tonight. That's not a revolution. We need recruits, and there's no better place to get them than among those who've felt the lash. If we give the slaves some hope, we can rally thousands to our cause."

"I don't know if it's wise," a dracon interrupted. "A lot of people own slaves. We'll need their support at some point. We don't want to drive them to the other side."

"If they own slaves, they've already chosen their side," Yorth responded hotly.

"I can understand your feelings," the dracon said. "I'm simply being realistic. Revolutions need popular support if they are to endure."

"From the way you talk, we may need to follow this revolution with another one to achieve our aims," Orwynn interrupted. Ignoring the dracon's glare, the tavernkeeper raised his voice to ensure that everyone heard him. "I think Yorth is right," he said. "Right now, our goal should be to dramatically increase our numbers as quickly as possible while sowing as much confusion as possible. An attack on the slave quarters will achieve this. Those of you who want to accompany Yorth and me, come along. Those of you with your own plans can remain behind."

Orwynn turned his back on the dracon and headed for the door, not looking back to see how many followed. The tavernkeeper had decided that those who wanted to spend more time debating would debate any plans offered. He wanted League members who sought action. He stopped abruptly when Morko, Morko's grandfather, and father blocked his way.

"We would like to join you," the elderly gnome said. "We would like to show you our appreciation for all you have done for us over the years."

"It is you who have helped me," Orwynn said. "Your offer touches my heart, but I don't like the idea of leading you into danger."

"Orwynn is right, Grandfather," Morko said. "You've taken enough risks for the League and for others over the years. It's time for others to do their part. Come with us, and we will take you home where you'll be safe."

"Safe!" the gnome spat, tottering on unsteady feet. "Don't speak to me of safe. I'm old, but I can still wield a blade. How many of my friends have died at the hands of the Regent's troops? I can't recall all the insults we've endured. I won't have it said that my family went unavenged, or that we hid while others risked everything."

Orwynn glanced behind him. Eight others had joined Yorth and Pasham. "There's no time to argue this," Orwynn said gently. "When I return, I will find a way to ensure that such a noble spirit as your own has an opportunity to help us in our cause."

As Orwynn turned to go, the elderly gnome grabbed his arm. "If you will not allow me to accompany you, then take Morko, my grandson. He will exact my revenge for me in my family's name," the gnome said.

"Me, grandfather?" the younger gnome asked in surprise.

"Of course," his grandfather said. "You are young and strong. Your arm can strike for mine."

"Who then will protect you, grandfather?" Morko said

nervously. "The streets may already be filled with the Regent's troops." Sweat formed on the young gnome's brow.

"He's quite right," the tavernkeeper said. "I wouldn't hear of leaving you alone."

"My son can take me home," the elderly gnome said. "My grandson will accompany you." The gnome's grip tightened as he pulled Orwynn closer to him. "When you faced the prospect of losing your tavern, I helped you, my friend. I've never asked for anything in return. I ask this now."

Releasing his grip, he and his son turned away, leaving Morko aghast. "Come along then, Morko," Orwynn said, hurrying out of the room.

Knowing his grandfather and father watched him, Morko straightened his shoulders and hurried to catch up to Orwynn's group in the maze of tunnels.

Outside the warm buttery light of the torch–lit hall, Yorth asked the tavernkeeper in a whisper, "Is it wise to bring Morko?"

"Probably not. If we're lucky, he'll sneak off before we get there. I couldn't refuse his grandfather, though."

"I don't like it," Yorth said, fingering his blade. "The gnome smells of fear. His heart isn't with us."

"Leave him to me, Yorth," Pasham interrupted. "I'll be responsible for him."

After a lengthy walk through the maze, Orwynn halted the dozen members of the group. "Do you have a plan, Yorth?"

"Since Bill freed us, Pasham and I realized that freeing the slaves in the pens would not be very difficult or even all that dangerous," Yorth said. "They really don't guard the slaves. Most of the slaves are too frightened and broken to even think of trying to escape. If we're lucky, we shouldn't meet with much resistance." Quickly, he outlined his plan.

When they neared the slave market, Pasham led Morko and four others, while Yorth and the rest went in a different direction.

Pasham pressed his hand against the young gnome's shoulder and whispered as he took him aside. "If you don't want to do this, you can go. No one will say anything to your grandfather," he said.

"I can't run away," the gnome said. "I could never look at my father and grandfather again."

Pasham nodded. "If you decide to come with us, understand that there will be no place to turn back once we start," the former slave said. "If you change your mind at the last moment and do anything to endanger us, I will have to cut your throat."

The young gnome looked up at the quiet human in surprise. "What are you saying, Pasham?"

"I want us to understand each other. I have friends inside these pens. I'm scared too, possibly more than you. But Just Bill depends on me, as does Yorth, and those in the pens have no other hope if I fail," Pasham said.

"You would kill me?"

"I am not a warrior, Morko. I grew up as a domestic servant, waiting on others, obeying their whims. Today, I can help others the way Bill helped me. I can give others the freedom that I enjoy. I can give them hope, a chance for a better life. Morko, I like you, but I can't let you jeopardize this."

The young gnome breathed deeply. "I get so frightened."

The former slave nodded. "I understand fear, Morko.

Before Just Bill freed me, it was my constant companion. My masters would slap me, kick me, and sometimes beat me for the pleasure of it. I lived with fear."

"So, why are you doing this?" the gnome asked. "You're free now. You could leave the city, and they would never find you. Why take these chances?"

"Because I plan to stay free," Pasham said. "Because I don't ever want to live in fear again. I don't ever want to worry that someone will call me slave again. I can stand to be afraid a little longer, because I know that what I'm doing today will help ensure that I will never have to be afraid again."

The young gnome nodded his head in understanding. "Just tell me what I have to do."

Motioning to the others, Pasham gathered his band and pointed to the rough wooden palisades surrounding the slave quarters.

"We must pry open the back gate to the slave pens. It is locked, but I don't believe it's locked too securely or guarded," he said. "Beyond it, we will find a hallway lined by doors. The slaves are behind those doors. Our job is to free the slaves. Yorth and his men will start a diversion at the front gate that should keep the guards busy. If we find any guards, we must kill them quietly. I will go to the armory to see if I can get weapons for the slaves we free."

Silently, they scurried across the courtyard to the back gate. Near the front entrance, Yorth crawled through the dust, carefully watching the one guard lolling next to the gate. Despite all the hysteria about slave rebellions, Yorth suspected that those entrusted with guarding the slaves would not change their methods. They, more than anyone else, knew the general docility of the slave population. Far from the rebellious troublemakers feared by the population of Trillius, most slaves were too frightened to disobey, much less rebel. Those who displayed any trace of defiance were quickly taken for instruction and readjustment at the end of a lash. Those who still resisted tended to disappear late at night.

Yorth shuddered, recalling the number of times he had seen friends dragged off to the castle. He'd been freed before his masters could send him to join them.

Remembering Bill's dangerous mission into that same castle, Yorth quieted his nerves as he inched within a few feet of the daydreaming guard.

Bill's decision to leave him behind had hurt. Leading this mission would demonstrate his ability.

Just talk of a slave rebellion had left Trillius' citizens badly frightened. Yorth wanted to see what an actual slave rebellion would cause.

He carefully watched the guard in front of him, timing the regularity of his breathing. At just the right moment, Yorth silently launched himself at the guard. His knife cut off the startled scream that might have alerted the others.

He paused to listen for sounds from behind the gate. He signaled Orwynn as he pushed it open. Behind him, Orwynn and the others raced toward the gate to join him.

At the other end of the slave pens, Pasham's team had moved quickly, prying open the unguarded gate and quickly breaking open the doors to individual pens. Each room contained about ten slaves who eyed their liberators with suspicion and fear. Uncertain what to make of the grim freedom fighters, they obeyed them, puzzled to see a human in command.

"They don't seem very happy to be freed," Morko whispered to Pasham.

"They don't know what the word means yet," the former slave said. "If we left them alone, most would go back into their cages. Bill taught me that you can't give a man freedom; he has to earn it to know its value."

Turning away from the gnome, Pasham crept along the hallway. He moved quickly, wary of discovery. He turned a corner and drew back, realizing that one lone guard blocked his path to the armory.

Pasham struggled to control his breathing, which in the silent corridor sounded loud to his own ears. Behind him, his team systematically emptied the cells and herded the occupants to the back gate. If his team took them outside, it would be only a matter of minutes before they were discovered, and without weapons, the escaped slaves wouldn't last long.

As Pasham prepared to rush the guard, he felt a presence behind him. He spun, his knife darting out, when he realized it was only Morko.

Pasham saw the fear in the gnome's eyes. He motioned for silence, pantomiming that a guard waited just beyond the corner. He pulled Morko closer to whisper, "When I go after the guard, wait a few seconds, then come after me."

Pasham took a deep breath, forcing his hand to stop trembling. Without looking back at the gnome, he turned the corner and walked quietly toward the guard.

In the flickering torch light of the hallway, the guard appeared not to notice him as he advanced toward the armory, though he was awake, obviously alerted by the sounds of cell doors opening and the rustle of feet.

Nervously, the guard turned to see Pasham advancing. "What are you doing out of your cell?"

"Master! Master!" Pasham said breathlessly. "You must come with me."

"What is it?" the guard said.

"A master is hurt. He went into a cellblock after a slave woman he fancied, and she hurt him."

The guard relaxed. "So, that's what all the noise is about. A little fun in the cellblocks. Well, I hope he's been hurt badly, because the Guildlords don't like that."

The guard left his post and had begun walking alongside Pasham when Morko burst around the corner. "What's this?" the guard shouted.

Morko stopped, startled at the guard's voice. His eyes grew large and he turned, running away.

"Come back here, gnome," the guard ordered, just as Pasham drove his knife into the guard's throat. Yanking the knife, Pasham's blade carved a wide swath through the guard's neck.

The guard collapsed, dying. "Good work, Morko," Pasham said.

Glancing past the corner, Pasham saw that Morko was still running down the corridor, unheeding in his fear.

Pasham ran after him briefly, but met a group of slaves. He shrugged. He would catch up to the gnome later and tell him he had nothing to be ashamed of. Morko had distracted the guard. It had worked out. "Come with me," he said, leading them back to the armory.

Once they had broken into the armory, Pasham began arming the slaves. There were not enough weapons for all of them, but soon he had two-hundred slaves carrying swords, maces, knives, and clubs. A few who claimed to know about archery were given bows and arrows.

"That gnome ran out the back," a slave told Pasham.

The former slave sighed. "He doesn't even know his grandfather would be proud of him."

Pasham told the unarmed slaves to continue opening the cell doors and to bring the newly freed slaves with them.

As they neared the front gate, Pasham could hear the sound of clashing weapons. Apparently, Yorth's team had run into severe resistance once they'd captured the front gate.

Yorth, Orwynn, and one other League member held the gate against about a dozen guards. With a roar, Pasham and his army of freed slaves attacked.

Heading toward the castle in the underground labyrinth, Bill noticed that the cavern passageways led them downward on a steep slope. Foul odors assailed their nostrils. The walls glowed a contaminated green, as if infested with an unclean disease.

"Where is this place?" Bill asked.

"We've moved off the main corridors," the mage said. "We don't need to set off any more alarms than necessary."

Zorth said, "These fetid odors emanate from the direction we're heading." As they turned a corner, they ran into a wall. "Did you make a wrong turn? I'll gladly leave this tunnel."

Zynaryxx stood unmoving as he studied the wall.

"Ah, of course, your key," the felpur said.

The mage shrugged. "The Crescent key will not work here." Zynaryxx said. "I believe this wall is a more recent addition to these subterranean passages."

"What lies beyond it?" Quatar asked.

"Better to figure out how this wall was placed in our path, and by whom," the mage said. "The substance used to build it is unlike any of the other walls." He tapped it with his staff, chanting words in unintelligible tongues. When nothing happened, he stepped back, stymied.

The ninja moved to his side, examining the wall closely. "I don't see any indentations or crevices."

"No door?" Cobran asked impatiently. "Cobran make door." With a shout, he lunged at the wall, attacking the surface with his ax, carving chunks from it. As the others watched, his strokes drove deeper and deeper into the barrier, slashing slabs from the obstacle.

"My good Cobran, you can't tunnel through it," the mage said. "We don't have enough the time."

The lizardman ignored the mage's words and continued chopping into the slab. He grunted in surprise as his ax broke through, revealing a moist gooey surface on the other side of the wall.

With unflagging energy, the lizardman quickly cut out a hole large enough for the companions to wriggle through. He dove through first, somersaulting to his feet, his ax and sword raised and ready.

"Cobran no like this place," he said from the other side. "Floor slimy."

Seeing no reaction from the mage, Bill shrugged his shoulders and climbed through the hole. When he clambered out to join Cobran, he found himself drawing his sword.

"I can't see anything in here, Zynaryxx. Hurry with that light of yours!"

In the light from the mage's staff, Bill saw a grayish muck oozing from the walls. "Are you sure this is the right way?"

"Yes," the faerie said, "though I haven't been this way in many years, and I remember it as being much larger. This once served as a vast underground storehouse for the castle, where the king kept provisions enough to feed the populace in time of need. It seems much smaller now. This slime seems to come from the very walls."

Within minutes, the rest of the travelers had made their way through. Uncertainly, they followed behind the mage. Bill and Cobran took up positions on either side of Zynaryxx, their weapons unsheathed.

"I don't like this place," Bill said. "See the walls. They're beginning to move." In the glare of the staff's light, they could see a pulsing movement in the walls, small undulations that grew in intensity.

The goo seemed to tremble, quivering as vibrations built in the chamber. In the distance, a faint steady beating began in a steady rhythm.

"The ooze is rising," Zorth said nervously.

Looking at his feet, Bill saw it was inching higher, and thickening, making each footstep a chore. It seemed to throb, too, in a tempo that built around them.

"You have defiled me!" a voice thundered.

Bill looked wildly around him, but he could not place the source of the sound.

"Trespassers! Have you no idea what you have done?" the voice demanded.

"Show yourself," Nagano shouted. "Do you fear us?"

A bass chuckle echoed through the chamber. The floor and walls reverberated with its sound.

"Do I fear you?" Its laugh deepened. "You dishonor me as no one has ever before done. You sully me, leaving your insect–like tread to stain and taint me. You ask me to show myself, yet I surround you. I do believe you know not what you have done." A higher pitched cackle of glee replaced the deeper chuckle.

"What does he mean?" Quatar asked.

Cobran plucked up the faerie and handed him to Zorth. "Carry little friend."

"You do not know, do you?" the voice shouted. The ooze had risen to a foot deep, slowing them. It pulsed until small waves formed and lapped at their calves, while the laughter echoed on.

"You make this so easy for me," the voice said. "I would have preferred to tear you limb from limb, to taste the flesh of your broken bodies."

"Brave words for someone afraid to even show himself," Nagano shouted. "Come out, and I will show you what broken bodies really mean."

"Ah, yes, I'm sure you would try, my morsels," the voice said. "Facing you would amuse me, but through your own actions you've made that impossible. Now I must content myself with simply digesting you."

Slowly the horror of their situation registered. "This ooze is beginning to burn my legs," Bill whispered.

"By Yalor's flame, we're inside the belly of some giant beast!" Zorth said.

"It's trying to digest us," Olaf said.

Waves of slime poured faster into the chamber as the walls fluttered. A rumbling sound came from all around them. "It's the strangest feeling," the voice said. "I feel as if I have feasted."

"I knew this chamber was much bigger," Zynaryxx said.

"A lot of good that does us," Zorth shouted. "I'm so happy you feel vindicated. Meanwhile, my legs are on fire from this creature's gastric juices!"

"Perhaps that's what this creature needs," the mage said, amiably. Concentrating, he passed his hands through the air. Balls of fire burst in flames against the chamber's walls. Again. And again. The inferno set the ooze afire. Smoke billowed, choking the companions with acrid fumes.

"Oh, good, instead of being digested, we'll choke to death," Zorth said.

"Quiet fool," Zynaryxx commanded. "Watch the walls." The sides of the chamber heaved. In the distance, the thunderous sound of coughing erupted. "I think his meal may not have agreed with him," the mage said.

The chamber pitched, knocking them off their feet as the ooze flowed toward the sound, tumbling them in a wave of engulfing slime. The wave broke, and they poured out amid a waterfall of putrid sludge onto a stone floor.

Gasping for air, Bill wiped the muck from his face and mouth. His companions were strewn across the floor. Behind him, a monstrous mouth gaped open, choking in its own viscous fluid.

Bill pulled his friends to their feet, picking up the faerie, who seemed nearly drowned in the deep ooze covering part of the floor.

Zynaryxx's eyes fluttered open, his fingers clawed away the liquid. Spitting it out, the mage looked back, watching the smoke pouring from the creature's mouth.

"He can't extinguish those flames," the faerie said. "I fear his appetite may never recover." As if nothing had happened, the mage motioned at Bill to retrieve his staff.

Bill pulled it from the ooze and handed it to Zynaryxx, who walked unconcerned through the chamber. The companions stood unsteadily, staggered forward. "What if it comes after us?" Bill asked.

"I don't believe there's much chance of that happening," he responded. "I fear his appetite has quite consumed him."

Looking back, Bill saw the flames had broken to the surface of the writhing creature. Fiery coughing wracked the vast bulk of the burning carcass. "What was it?" Bill asked.

"Some sort of subterranean leviathan. I've never seen one so large before or with any degree of intelligence. Usually their appetite is insatiable. The Regent must have placed it here to guard this entranceway. Its hunger would make it the perfect sentry. But now, we have the advantage of surprise over whatever waits beyond this chamber."

"What if...?" Bill began.

"We can talk after we've rinsed off this burning slime," Zynaryxx said. "See that waterfall at the end of the chasm? I don't know about you, but I'll welcome a shower."

"What is this?" Zorth asked as he dove into the pool beneath the falls.

"The former king tapped an underground river," Zynaryxx explained. "This storage area served as a way to protect the populace in case of catastrophe. It'll serve us now. We can wash off this burning slime." The companions ran to it, some stumbling toward it.

"Aren't you afraid we'll be discovered?" Bill asked.

"No," the mage said. "A creature like the one behind us distinguishes neither friend nor foe. Anything that dares to enter is simply a meal to feed its unquenchable hunger. No servants of the Regent come here except those condemned."

"We have been lucky in our first encounter with the Regent's minions," the mage said as they gathered themselves. "Know that our next ordeal may pose far more dangerous hazards. We must be certain that any creatures we discover do not have the opportunity to alert others, or our journey will have been for naught." They followed as he led them to an area where the cavern narrowed.

"I do not know what perils lie beyond, but this way once served as a special passageway to King Liam's study. He would go there to meditate when his mind was troubled," the mage said. "It contains a secret staircase that provided a private way to his chambers."

"How will this lead us to my brother?" Zorth asked.

"It offers a way to the dungeon that allows us to avoid the upstairs barracks," the mage said. "The king's ancestors designed it so they could pass through most of the structure unnoticed. It comes out close to this storage area for convenient access to the tunnels."

"It didn't save King Liam," Bill observed.

"He wasn't the kind of man to flee when his people were in danger," Zynaryxx said, signaling for quiet. The band headed down the passageway. Cobran and Bill, their weapons drawn, led the way, with Nagano walking alongside them. Zynaryxx, Olaf, Quatar and Zorth followed close behind, warily watching the shadows cast by the mage's staff.

Chapter Fifteen

A signal from Zynaryxx stopped the companions near an indentation in the passageway along which they crept. The mage studied the wall before pulling out his key to open a doorway Bill knew he couldn't have found.

Fur–covered bodies leapt out at them so suddenly they knocked Bill to the ground before he realized they were under attack. A hissing and flash of teeth at his throat shocked him into resistance. His sword flashed, impaling a giant rat creature. Cobran, too, stood his ground, his sword and ax flailing at the dog–sized rats. At Nagano's feet one lay with its neck broken by the ninja's knee. A blow from her fist felled another.

The distraction served its purpose. A blast of power from the room slammed the group, crashing all but Bill into the wall behind. Zynaryxx, Quatar, and Zorth lay stunned.

A wizened old gnome stood framed in the doorway, his hands fingering a beaded chain as he muttered incantations. From behind him advanced four armored knights, swords drawn.

"Crush the invaders," the gnome intoned, his fingers passing rhythmically over the sparkling string of jewels. "Shackle them, tie them."

Bill had raised his sword the instant he'd felt the force slam him. While Cobran and Nagano were knocked backwards, their weapons jarred from their hands and their arms apparently bound to their sides by invisible manacles, Bill managed to keep his sword in hand. A spark crackled off its blade as it fended off the spell. Bill stared as its blue glow shone like a beacon in the darkened room. It must have the ability to ward off magical attacks.

Olaf's arms hugged his sides as if tied in place. He strained against the invisible bonds. His jaw clenched in concentration. A gust of mental energy darted toward the gnome wizard, jolting the beads from his hands. The sorcerer looked up in surprise at the mook. The gnome's mouth opened as if to say something, then closed again.

When the beads hit the ground, both Cobran and Nagano could move again. While Bill charged the knights crowding toward the doorway, Cobran scooped his ax from the floor and hurtled it over Bill's shoulder into the leading knight's head. The warrior's helmet cracked, revealing a skull. The armored skeleton staggered, giving Bill an opening to hack the skull from the body.

Nagano leapt past Bill, slamming her body into a second knight, who lost its footing and fell clattering to the floor. A dagger materialized from the ninja's sleeve. She drove it through the mask with enough force to crack the bone beneath.

Cobran brushed past Bill, wielding his sword like the sweeping blades of a windmill. Effortlessly, the gladiator parried a thrust from an undead warrior, forcing the thing back. Bill plunged his blade into the creature, his glowing steel piercing the armor.

The fourth knight took advantage of the confusion to charge past them through the doorway toward their stricken companions. Bill could see Zorth had begun to waken as the skeleton knight raised its sword.

The felpur priest's eyes widened as his gaze fixed on the undead warrior.

"By Yalor's flame, return to the paths of the dead that spawned you," Zorth shouted. "I, his servant, command it!"

Before Cobran or Bill could stop the knight, it exploded, bone fragments ripping through the metal. A pile of dust served as the only mark of its place.

"What did you do?" Bill asked, amazed by the sight.

Zorth struggled to his feet, shaking his head. "I am a priest of Yalor," the felpur said. "I have been taught incantations to destroy creatures of the darkness. I must admit that never before today have I ever had occasion to see if they worked."

The companions helped Quatar and Zynaryxx to their feet. They seemed dazed from the sorcerous attack but quickly recovered from its effects.

"That was far too close for my taste," the ninja said. "Twice now we've met the enemy, and twice we've slipped death's embrace by only the narrowest margin. Deeper into the castle, the Arch Regent's protectors become even more powerful than those lying at our feet. My instincts led me correctly when I joined forces with you, yet even this powerful mage was knocked unconscious by this last attack. The outcome could have been fateful for us if not for a few lucky chances."

"You think it was luck?" Zynaryxx asked, his voice mild. "You point out that I was disabled as if that is some amazing feat. Did you think you could just stride through the castle, while I cleared the way with magic bolts jumping from my fingertips?

"My friends, you've done well," the mage said as they entered the chamber and closed the door to the passage. "Bill's sword apparently affords him some protection from occult assaults. Zorth's priestly gifts provide us with a weapon against the undead. Olaf can disable and slay other of our adversaries. Weapons in the hands of skilled fighters can slay still others. But none of us alone can defeat all of them. If we hope to win the day, we must combine our skills against this lair of wickedness."

At the back of the room, the mage examined the wall panels, looking for some unseen latch to open the doorway to the stairwell.

The ninja joined him, her fingers tracing the decorative carvings. "I think it's here. In my line of work, we specialize in methods of entering and leaving places without being noticed. This is superb craftsmanship." Her fingers probed a button embedded in the woodcarvings, and an unseen door popped open, revealing a staircase. "There's very little dust on these steps," she observed. "They don't see much use. We should take extra caution."

"How do you propose we get to my brother?" Zorth asked.

"Right now, we are on the same level as the dungeon prison, which is on the opposite side of the castle," Zynaryxx said. "We must go up above it, near the main castle chamber, on a path that avoids the barracks. There is a passageway there that should allow us to enter the dungeon without being detected."

"As undetected as we have been so far?" Zorth asked. "If this is what it's like to be undetected, I shudder to think about being discovered."

"You would do more than shudder," Zynaryxx snapped. "If the Arch Regent discovers us and marshals Her forces against us, I doubt even our combined abilities can withstand the onslaught. Stealth, secrecy, and surprise remain our most effective weapons."

At the first stairway landing, the mage stopped and pressed close to a doorway. "Quiet," he commanded. "If we hold any chance of rescuing your brother, we need to make it through here. This door leads to a passageway that will take us to the king's audience chamber. We can access a channel from there that leads into the dungeons and allows us to stay clear of the barracks and the main entrance into the jail. Both will be heavily guarded. We must remain absolutely quiet and draw no attention to ourselves."

"Better if I go ahead," Nagano said to the mage. "Meaning no disrespect, I possess the greatest skill in evading detection. Let me scout the way in case any sentinels have been posted." The elf slipped silently out the door, her black ninja garb blending into the darkness, her footsteps silent on the paving stones.

The companions waited silently as the seconds crawled into minutes. Down the hallway, beyond their sight, they heard a sharp intake of breath, suddenly cut off. Not long afterwards, Nagano returned, wiping blood from her dagger.

She signaled them to follow her. At the first corner, they saw a body stretched across the ground, its head dangling. The ninja motioned to Cobran to pick it up. Nearby, a second sentry lay crumpled, its neck slit from ear to ear, like a second mouth. Cobran effortlessly lifted it over his shoulder, as well, as they followed the ninja down the corridor.

When they neared the entrance, they heard sounds of heavy boots marching in cadence beyond. The mage quickly motioned them into a small alcove. By the time the troops turned the corner, the companions had escaped from sight.

The mage motioned Cobran to leave the bodies in the alcove. Zynaryxx opened the door to the dungeon's stairwell. "This was used for prisoners found guilty in the king's court," Zynaryxx said. "I didn't think it would be guarded, because they would never expect anyone could gain entrance to it without being discovered.

"When we go below, we risk detection," Zynaryxx said. "Even worse, we have no way of knowing where they are holding Portnal, if he still lives. You recall the size of the storeroom where the leviathan dwelled? The dungeon is much, much larger and is honeycombed with cells. The Arch Regent enlarged it shortly after She took up residence in the castle. Over the years, Her minions have continued delving deeper."

"He could be anywhere in there," Nagano said.

"I'm afraid so."

"And we face a good chance of being seen."

"I'm afraid it's true."

"So, why are we going? The Arch Regent is our target."

"Because he's my brother!" Zorth hissed.

"Even I can understand that you'd want to rescue someone you loved from the torments of such a place. If it were my mother, I would feel the same way. But we may not find him down there; he may already be dead. We could sacrifice everything for nothing."

"There is a way," Olaf interrupted. "for us to find out if he's alive and where he is."

"How?" Nagano asked.

"If we can capture a jailer, I can mind—probe him to find out. I helped get Portnal into this mess. I came here to help destroy the Arch Regent, but I also came here to help Portnal escape. If there's any chance he's alive, I must try to help him, even if I have only the two felpurs to go with me."

"We go together," Bill said. "We'll capture a jailer, find out if he's alive and where he is. Portnal must have come here for a reason, one so important that he risked his life by entering this place. Finding him may help us more than we may know."

The ninja shook her head, unhappy but resigned. "Then I'll go first again. That gives us our best chance of finding a captive without being discovered."

Silently, they followed the ninja down the steep spiral staircase. At the bottom, they found a heavy iron door blocking their way. Nagano quickly picked the lock and slowly opened it. She knelt on one knee and peered around the door's edge as an orc kicked it open, sword drawn.

"Who are you, skulking in the dark?" it asked.

Cobran's fist crashed into the orc's jaw, silencing it. Bill caught it as it fell. "We have a jailer. Does he need to be conscious for this mind–probe to work?"

"No." Olaf bent over the helpless orc. He placed his hand over the creature's forehead, gripping tightly as he concentrated on the still form. He remained motionless for minutes before he rose.

"Portnal lives," he said. "At least I think so. This creature pays no attention to names. He's aware of a felpur, though. Apparently he's seen him recently, for some reason. He's on this level. The orc saw him being dragged to a cell under heavy guard only hours ago. It must have been an especially heavy guard, because the orc seemed quite frightened by it."

"Do you know how to get there?" Bill asked.

"I think I can find my way," Olaf said. "For some reason, not many guards are on this level. I pushed the creature very hard for the locations of any sentry points, but there aren't any."

"I doubt they expect anyone could get here," Zynaryxx said. "As paranoid as they are in this castle, they would never think that anyone could come this way. They must have most of their guards posted at the main entrance into the dungeon."

"It seems too easy," Nagano said.

"A moment ago, it was too dangerous," Zorth said. "For once the stars have smiled upon our journey. Let us be glad of that."

Cautiously, they began to follow the mook down the corridor, past rows of cells, each of which contained prisoners. "Open them," Bill said to Nagano.

"You must be kidding," the ninja said. "We'll have the entire castle on us."

"We can't leave them here," Bill said.

"Don't be a sentimental fool," the ninja said. "If we waste time freeing these people and the guards discover us or them, the whole of the castle's forces will descend upon us."

"Open the locks," Bill repeated.

"We have a mission," the ninja said stubbornly. "We've come to get the Arch Regent. I was against coming down here in the first place. You can't seriously want to risk the entire kingdom's fate just to satisfy an emotional whim."

"Call it what you want," Bill said evenly. "If we free these unfortunates and give them a chance, however small, to escape, at least we know we've accomplished something."

The ninja folded her arms across her chest, shaking her

head. "I won't do it," she said. "I won't ruin the one chance we have on some dramatic charitable gesture."

"Don't be ridiculous!" Zynaryxx snapped. Bill started to argue, but the mage cut him off.

"Nagano, you're the one who is being ridiculous," the faerie said. "If we are to have any chance at all, we need to distract the Regent's forces away from us and in as many other directions as we can. Freeing the prisoners can create countless diversions for us. The more troops chasing after them leaves fewer for us to face when we confront Her. So open those cages but make sure those poor wretches stay quiet and stay put until we're ready."

The elf started freeing the prisoners from their cells, showing them how to pick the locks to free the others, signaling all to remain quiet. Soon, close to one–hundred prisoners jammed the corridor, whispering in hushed tones.

"I'd given up hope," a wizened dwarf told Bill. "I owe you my life."

"Then keep quiet," Zynaryxx ordered. "That's all we ask. If you want to see your homes or loved ones again, hold your tongues until we decide how to get out of here."

"I believe Portnal's down that corridor," Olaf said. "I saw in that orc's mind that he's in a large chamber at the end of that corridor."

Zynaryxx ordered the prisoners to wait for them.

"The guards may discover us," the dwarf whispered. "We can't wait here. You have no idea what we've been through and what we've seen. We must escape while we have the chance."

Nagano snorted in disgust. "I told you we should have left them in their cages," she said. "Look at them. We risk our lives to rescue them, and no sooner do we get them out than they decide to betray us."

"They won't betray anyone," Bill said quietly. "They'll wait here for our return. There are over one–hundred of them. If a guard or even several discovers them, they'll know what to do.

"We'll be back for you after we've found the prisoner we came to free," Bill said, turning his back on the dwarf and the prisoners, motioning his companions to follow.

The companions followed Bill down the corridor. The prisoners followed them with their eyes, but stayed where they were. A few stationed themselves near entrances and intersections in the corridor, but they made no effort to flee. At the end of the hall, the companions found a large chamber filled with new cells. Zorth and Quatar darted ahead, dashing down the hallway, searching the cells for their brother.

The cells contained a variety of fell creatures, their red, undead eyes flashing with bitterness and hatred as Bill and his friends searched for Portnal.

"You want me to free them, too?" Nagano said.

"I wouldn't," Bill said. "Their malice would goad them to attack even someone who tried to help them."

"I find it baffling that these simple cages can contain them," Zynaryxx said.

Hearing a startled shout from Zorth, they hurried after the felpur, finding them in a separate corridor at the end of the chamber. They had discovered Portnal in a lone cell.

"Tell your friends they must flee," Portnal said.

"After we get you out of here," Zorth said, motioning Nagano toward the locked gate.

"Get out of here," Portnal pleaded while the ninja snapped open the door. "The captain knows you're coming. This is a trap."

Behind them, they heard the sound of cell doors creaking open, all along the passageway. A metal grate from above opened, revealing a dracon warrior officer whose bellow of laughter echoed through the chamber.

"Welcome, welcome," Captain Grizzle laughed. "So, I finally meet the League of the Crimson Crescent. Forgive my laughter, but I really expected something more impressive than a rag–tag band like yourselves.

"For days, you've had the kingdom in an uproar with talk of revolution. You're like a disease, spreading contagion wherever you go. Some of our city's fairest citizens have risen in revolt, following your example."

The captain looked them over again, shaking his head in disbelief. "Your example has ignited a very unwise subversion," the Captain said. "Luckily, it is still in its initial stages, small pockets of mutiny burning intensely but confined to marginal areas. My troops can still extinguish this blaze, though some citizens have been emboldened to attack my warriors. A few of my troops are actually frightened to go out on the streets, if you can imagine. If you only knew how many I've sent out to search for you.

"And you come to me. Just as I knew you would. You slip by all of the castle's guards, work your way through our elaborate defenses, and blindly stumble into my little trap. Once your followers learn that I have crushed you, they'll lose heart and this uprising will fail. You've saved me a great deal of work.

"How ever can I thank you?" the Captain asked.

"You can die quietly," Zynaryxx said. "That would more than suffice."

"Ah, yes, the mystery mage with whom the Arch Regent is so upset and obsessed," Captain Grizzle said. "You have no idea how much consternation you have caused everyone in the castle. Where is he? She keeps asking. Find him! However, She won't tell us why you haunt Her so intensely. What is this strange bond between the two of you?"

"Come down here, and I'll whisper it in your ear," Zynaryxx said.

"Oh no! I might get more than a few words," the captain laughed. "Though you can't blame me for being interested. If I didn't know better, I'd say She's acting like a smitten school girl."

"I'm sure your mistress would be interested to learn that the Arch Regent has become the subject of idle gossip by servants," Zynaryxx said.

"Perhaps She would," the captain said. "You do have the opportunity to tell Her yourself. She left me instructions to spare you if you leave this riffraff."

The companions watched the mage intently.

"Come now," the captain said. "You have no time for dramatics, false pride, and foolish loyalty. Your friends are dead. Oh, they may still breathe at this moment, but soon those creatures you passed down the hall will feast on their bodies—even on their souls. You saw them. You might even have recognized some of them."

"I can see She has told you very little about me," Zynaryxx said. "For I know those creatures and their powers. I know them as well as She, much to my shame."

"They are Her personal guard," the Captain said. "More

await below."

"He's telling the truth," Portnal said breathlessly. "The Arch Regent has been recruiting them, bringing them from other dimensions, promising them the flesh and blood and spirits of the living races. That's why She has kept Trillius all these years. It serves as a vast trap, drawing all the intelligent races to its delights and vices. When travelers disappear, no one notices. She started with humans. Then, She began using Trillius as Her web, spinning traps that brought thousands of victims to Her. They come to the city, lured by Her siren song of wealth, flesh, drugs, alcohol, and more sinister delights. After the Guilds have fleeced them, She takes Her tribute in gold and flesh to feed the abominations in the lower depths of this castle. Her efforts to bring in ever more of these undead have made it impossible to satisfy their appetites. They will soon go forth into the city to take what they must to survive. After they've sated themselves on Trillius, they'll cover the kingdom and surrounding lands like a great darkness."

"Your knowledge will die with you," the captain said. "I have spent my life in battle, yet I, too, fear these creatures. Look now and see your doom."

From around the corner, the fell creatures advanced—twenty fell warriors, their swords as black as pitch. Four rock golems stood among them, advancing with stone sledges, their strange, lifeless eyes the color and luster of fine, old polished pewter. Four netherscourges closely followed, scimitars raised. Two wraithkings floated above, escorted by six undead nightguards. At the rear, four abyss dwellers skulked in the shadows, avoiding the light.

Bill couldn't have named the creatures advancing on them,

but the shadowed faces and grinning skulls offered no hope.

"I have no more time to waste, mage," the captain said. "Decide. My mistress offers you life. If you refuse and have not the wit to save it, these creatures will take it for themselves. I care not how you choose."

As Zynaryxx was about to answer, the ninja interrupted. "Faithless old fool," Nagano said bitterly. "You lead us to our deaths and abandon us."

The mage ignored her, pushing aside his companions as he walked forward. The advancing creatures parted to make a path for him. "I have lived long enough to know when I am outmatched," he said, his head bowed. "We have gambled, and now I must play the roll of the dice that fate has ordained."

Chapter Sixteen

"Hear my answer, Lady of Darkness!" Zynaryxx raised his head, his voice booming through the chamber. Stretching out his staff, he bellowed in an ancient tongue that shook the stone ceiling. He raised an open palm and slapped the air, sending a lightning flash at the undead host. The bolt struck two netherscourges, and their shrouds burst into flames. As they writhed, slabs of rock fell from the ceiling, crushing three abyss dwellers.

"So be it!" Captain Grizzle slammed the panel shut.

The wraithkings signaled, sending their legion against the companions like a wave. As the fell warriors advanced, Bill observed Olaf focusing his mind. His psyche punched out like a solid force, knocking twelve of the undercreatures to the floor.

As the stricken warriors climbed unsteadily to their feet, it seemed to Bill that the irises of their eyes spun like wheels. Though their weapons trembled in unsure hands, they turned on their companions with howls of manic fury.

Zorth shouted Yalor's name and chanted an incantation. The six undead night guards pulsated. A flash of blinding white light enveloped them.

When Bill's sight returned, the creatures were gone. Cobran, followed by Bill, Quatar, and Portnal, charged the rock golems, dodging through the fell warriors locked in combat with their own fellows.

The wraithkings raised their hands and worked their mouths in silent supplication to the dark gods. A wall of force smashed through the companions, knocking them to the floor, strewing them alongside fell warriors and golems. An abyss dweller leaped on Cobran, while the netherscourges advanced toward Olaf and Zorth.

The abyss dweller resembled a land crawling octopus. It wrapped its tentacles around the lizardman, squeezing as its suckers ripped Cobran's scaly flesh. A mammoth beak at its center plunged into his shoulder, ripping through the flesh, sucking his blood.

Cobran flexed his back and arm muscles, trying to free himself, but the grip around him only tightened in response. With superhuman strength, he pulled his knees underneath him and rose to his feet, swaying dizzily as the creature's viselike grip squeezed the air from his lungs.

The abyss dweller's beak moved to Cobran's chest, over his heart, and prepared to burrow between the lizardman's ribs. Cobran flung himself to the stone floor, trying to crush the creature. It bashed against the paving stone unfazed, clamping its tentacles more solidly around Cobran, squeezing the air from his lungs. Cobran's mouth opened, but he could draw no breath. He watched helplessly as the obscenity drove its sharpened beak toward his heart.

Bill's blade flashed, severing first the beak, then the creature's body from the tentacles. The tentacles slowly shriveled, releasing their grasp as shuddering gasps wracked Cobran's body.

While checking to see if the lizardman would survive, Bill didn't see the golem's rock sledge swinging toward his head. Nonetheless, His sword darted into its path, splintering the stone as it drove into the golem's chest. A heavy shard of the broken stone struck Bill a glancing blow. He fell unconscious.

Zorth watched the netherscourge advance toward him. As he called Yalor's name, the shade grinned maliciously, whispering a silent curse. The incantation struck the felpur in the throat, silencing him as the ghoul advanced with an obsidian dagger it pulled from under its shroud. Zorth stepped back, his mouth moving soundlessly. The netherscourge swung his knife. The felpur drew his sword barely in time to block it.

Separated from the rest, Olaf battled the other creature who drove him back against the wall. Olaf's forehead wrinkled in furious concentration. Zorth could see the air between the mook and the creature disturbed by the force of his psychic blasts. The scourge only grinned. Casually, it drove a fist into Olaf's stomach, knocking the wind out of him. With its other hand, it grabbed the fur on the mook's head, grasping it tightly as it slapped him back and forth.

Stepping behind the dazed mook, the scourge pulled Olaf's head back, exposing the psionic's throat and sinking its teeth into the old mook's neck.

Zorth's own adversary advanced toward him, flashing its obsidian blade. He lifted his own sword over his head and threw it with all his strength, praying as he watched it spin end–over–end until it pierced the scourge about to open Olaf's throat and drink his blood.

Weaponless, Zorth dodged the knife stroke, while Olaf's adversary crumpled to the floor. Zorth switched his attention to his own scourge, reaching to block the blade with his arm. He felt the stone–cutting edge bite into his wrist. It felt like fire. His arm fell to his side, limp.

The scourge stepped back, its teeth dripping blood in a satanic grin as it watched the look of horror crossing Zorth's face. "Yes," hissed the creature. "You feel my bite. My blood now flows through your veins."

The fire raced up past Zorth's elbow, heading higher up his arm as his heart pumped it inexorably through his body.

"Relax, priest," the creature said. "Soon you will be mine. You will have no strength to resist me. I will feed upon your blood, and devour your very soul."

Zorth felt his knees buckle as he fell kneeling to the floor.

The netherscourge said, "In another place and time, I would be amused to have you serve me in the eternal darkness, but today I am hungry. Your selfless decision to save your friend tells me your soul will make a meal such as none I have enjoyed before."

The fire raging in Zorth's veins reached his shoulder. Zorth placed his other hand there and mouthed a silent prayer.

"You pray to Yalor," the scourge gloated. "Perhaps you call on Yalor's healing powers to cure you of the deadly venom now coursing through your bloodstream. Yalor cannot hear you, though, can he? Your healing powers have failed. You can only submit to me!"

The scourge moved closer, opening its mouth as it bent over the felpur's neck. It jerked his head up and screamed just as Nagano's dagger pierced its eye.

It struggled to its feet as the ninja leapt, slamming its head back with a swift kick. She ripped the shroud from the beast and drove her fist through its rib cage. When her hand pulled back, it held a beating heart. Crumpling to the floor, the nightscourge shrieked once and died.

The obsidian knife lay next to Zorth. Nagano watched him try to speak. "Drink this," she said, pulling a flask from her belt. "You've been poisoned."

Zorth felt the flask against his lips. Hot liquid slid down his throat. It burned.

"I don't know if it's in time," the ninja said. "You saved the mook, leaving your own life in danger. I've said many a harsh word to you. I misjudged you." She turned away.

The warriors driven insane by Olaf's mental blast attacked their remaining comrades. Four still stood, locked in combat with three rock golems. Quatar and Portnal fought with them, slashing the troll–like creatures and dodging their sledges, standing between them and their fallen companions. Cobran and Bill lay only a few feet away from the Golem's advance. Nagano ran to join them, frightened by a far grimmer tableau at the other side of the chamber.

Zynaryxx stood alone before the two wraithkings. An aura surrounded each of them, deflecting bolts of energy that flashed back and forth between them.

The mage was tiny compared to his adversaries. His staff, outstretched in his hand, glowed with a bright white light. The radiance surrounding him looked like a painting of some elder king battling nether gods.

The wraithkings rained bolts of fire, lightning, and ice on the faerie. Most never penetrated Zynaryxx's magical shield. Those that did crash through the barrier shredded it and knocked the faerie to the ground. Battering aside the remains of his protective screen, the wraithkings advanced on him, baring their teeth in hideous smiles.

As he lay on his back watching the wraithkings advance, the mage saw his own death mirrored in the reflection of their undead eyes. The creatures leered as they approached, drawing dark weapons.

"We will feast on you, faerie mage," one gloated.

The mage shouted an incantation that echoed through the chamber. The room rumbled as the words of power resonated from the walls. Above the tiny figure, the very air seemed to open, revealing a passage to a different plane. In the dimness, flames and darkness battled over an unearthly landscape. From across the room, Bill glimpsed the path to hell, littered with broken creatures, peopled by satanic figures. A creature clothed in flame howled as it tore through the ephemeral gate, blazing as the air exploded around it. Even Zynaryxx shielded his eyes.

With an unearthly shriek of hunger, fear, and hate, it glared at the mage, its malevolence at bay but barely so. The faerie shouted a hoarse word that cowed the creature, forcing it to face the wraithkings, stunned like all the others by the spectacle summoned to their midst. Roaring, the flame creature leapt at the wraithkings, its fiery claws ripping through their protective auras.

Zynaryxx shouted again, dropping his staff and leaping to his feet. From the tips of his fingers flashes of energy cut through the air, smashing into the wraithkings. The fiery creature pounced on them, consuming them in an inferno of fire.

When the wraithkings fell, the rock golems shrieked and turned to escape. Portnal, Quatar, and Nagano cut them down.

The felpur and the ninja went to Bill, helping him rise. Blood ran down his face from the shard of rock that had gashed his forehead. He staggered unsteadily, his eyes finally focusing.

He helped Cobran rise. The lizardman gingerly touched his ribs, his shoulder still bleeding heavily.

Olaf stumbled toward them. "I tried my best," the mook said, "but I was helpless before that ghoul. I struck him with all the power my mind could command, and he only grinned. Thank Thea that Zorth acted when he did."

Zynaryxx looked shaken by his ordeal. "I was outmatched. I once vowed I would never again open a doorway to summon a dark lordling to this plane. Like a coward, when I saw death approaching me, his hands outstretched, I broke my oath."

"There is no shame in victory," Nagano said. "You saved your friends from death and won us another chance. Putting evil to good use is not wrong."

They gathered around Zorth, who remained sprawled across the floor. Nagano seemed to read his feline face like a page of a book, deliberately, line by line. "He threw his sword at a netherscourge that was about to kill Olaf. He saved the mook, but suffered a poisonous stroke from the creature. I gave him an antidote, but I don't know if it was in time."

Quatar bent over her brother, feeling his forehead and pressing her ear against his chest. "It appears that you did," the monk said. "I am not as skilled in these matters as my brother, but I perceive that the dark poison has robbed him of much of his strength and will."

Quatar rubbed her brother's arm, whispering words of healing. Zorth's eyes fluttered as she called him back. He tried to speak, but failed.

"The scourges silenced him," Zynaryxx said. "No wonder he fell to them. His spells died in his throat." The mage handed Quatar a small vial.

"Give him this," the mage said. "It should help him regain his voice. If we are lucky, he may help the other wounded and himself."

Zorth reacted quickly to the potion. He muttered hoarse spells that soon helped Cobran and Bill's wounds.

"The Regent's troops will soon appear to gloat over our deaths," Zynaryxx said. "We must move quickly if we are to escape them and find the Regent."

"Quatar, take Portnal and go back the way we came," the mage said. "You must get word to Orwynn and the rest of the League about the Regent's evil conspiracy. If the people of the city discover this secret, they will join the League in rising against Her."

"I can't leave you," Quatar said.

"We don't have time to argue," Zynaryxx said. "Portnal can't go alone. He doesn't know the way. The prisoners are waiting outside to storm the dungeon's gates. That should empty the barracks and create enough diversion for us to find the Regent."

"It's not fair," the monk said.

"Don't be ridiculous," Zynaryxx said. "You saw how close we were to defeat just moments ago. We need to rouse the people enough to convince them to storm the castle. The Regent knows we're here. If we don't get word to Orwynn to send us reinforcements, She'll devote Her entire force to us. We cannot survive that kind of devastating attack. You and your brother are our only hope.

"If you stay, we all die," the mage said. "If you go, you might bring enough help so we can survive."

The felpur's shoulders slumped.

"Olaf, you and Zorth need to realize that your powers do

not work against every creature we'll face in this castle," Zynaryxx said. "We were nearly killed in that encounter, because we allowed ourselves to be split up, fighting separately, instead of together. We must fight as a team if we are to have any chance for victory."

They left the chamber and soon found themselves amid the liberated prisoners. "We heard a battle," the dwarf said. "We considered going to you."

"Then decided to remain here where it was safe," Nagano said. "Your gratitude never ceases to amaze me."

The dwarf pulled a sword from under his cloak. "We had orders to remain here in case any of you escaped our trap."

The companions saw that each prisoner had pulled a weapon from underneath their clothes.

"Our captain ordered us to wait here in these cells for you," the dwarf said. "He didn't think you'd open them. It was all we could do to keep from laughing when you did. Frankly, none of us expected to see any of you come out alive from the trap he had set. But the captain always prepares for any possibility."

"Does he now?" Zynaryxx said. "Did he prepare for this?" With a wave of his hand, fire balls rained down the middle of the prisoners blocking the hallway. Most dove to the side to escape the flames.

"Follow me," the mage shouted, dashing past them. Drawing his sword, Cobran slashed his way through the startled crowd, flanked by Bill, the two of them widening a passage through the wall of flesh. The flames and the flash of steel cut through them easily. Many ducked back into the cells to avoid the assault.

The mage pointed down the corridor. "Quatar, Portnal,

you know what you must do," the mage ordered. "Go, while we buy some time."

"I shall stay," Portnal said.

"You'll do as you're told." Quatar grabbed his wrist and jerked him down the hallway. "Zynaryxx risked his life to save you. If now he says he needs us to go for help, we'll go for help—or I'll crack your stubborn skull."

Portnal stared at his sister in surprise, earning himself another yank. Shrugging his shoulders in resignation, he followed his litter sister to the spiral staircase the companions had used to enter the dungeon. Behind them, they heard the clash of steel on steel.

"This way," Quatar commanded, leading Portnal up the stairs. "Don't make a sound," she said, gasping for breath when they reached the top. "There's an alcove just outside here. We must take great care when we enter the corridor, because guards may be nearby."

As they entered the alcove, the ranger stooped to examine the two as yet undiscovered bodies Cobran had dumped there after Nagano killed them.

"What are you doing?" the monk hissed.

"I need a sword," the ranger said. "It's bad enough being dragged around this castle. I've had enough of this place. I won't go any farther unarmed, though. I won't let them take me again."

Drawing a sword from a fallen guard, he examined the blade. "It'll have to do for now," he said. He leaned down again and pulled a short knife from the guard's belt.

"We're not going to be able to fight our way out of here," the monk whispered. "If we're discovered and they sound the alarm, we're doomed."

"I know that," Portnal said.

Together, they crept from the alcove into the corridor, staying close to the wall.

"Herzo!" a voice shouted from behind them. "If you're asleep again, they'll have your hide."

The two felpurs pressed closer to the wall, their fingers tightening around the hilts of their blades as the voice neared.

Bill, Cobran, and Nagano faced the warriors who had been posing as prisoners, while the two felpurs ran for the exit. The Captain's guard seemed uncertain. They evidently had not expected anyone to escape the trap. They had seen the creatures assigned the task of killing Zynaryxx and his friends. Fear caused them to hesitate, anxious about what the companions might do to them.

The dwarf and eight warriors pushed their way to the front to confront them. "Don't just stand here gaping! You know your orders. Kill them. If we allow them to escape, the captain will feed us to Her monsters."

As the dwarf stepped forward, Zynaryxx signaled Olaf, who struck the dwarf and his advancing force with a mental blast. They stumbled, their steps faltering as the psionic's wave assaulted them. Howling with insane fury, they turned and leaped on their own men, pushing them back.

"Follow me," Zynaryxx ordered. "Once they subdue their fellows, they'll be after us. We must lead them away from Quatar and Portnal's trail." The mage ran past the doorway the two felpurs had used, making sure that the warriors could see them taking a different corridor. "This will take us up into the castle's main audience chamber," he said.

Behind them Bill heard the sound of clanging steel, punctuated by demented laughter. "That treacherous dwarf has earned us a head start," Zynaryxx said.

At the top of the stairs, they ran headlong through the hallway and into the audience room. "There's a trap door in the floor," he said, startled by the sight that greeted him.

The room looked more like a vast underground cavern than a royal audience room. The ceiling was covered with stalactites reaching toward the floor. Sharp stalagmites stuck up from the floor like a forest of spears.

"What evil bewitchment is this?" Zorth asked.

"It matters not," the mage said. "The Regent must have been experimenting. One of her enchantments has melted the stone ceiling and created this. Inspect the floor. We must find a way out of here."

The companions spread out, searching. "We'll never find it," Zorth said. "They'll be on us at any moment."

"Perhaps," Zynaryxx said. Turning to the lizardman, he pointed to the center of the room. "Look there."

Cobran walked gingerly through the field of stone knives rising from the floor.

He tripped, cut his hand on one, and angrily smashed it with the shaft of his sword. It broke loose from the floor.

"Of course," Zynaryxx said. "When the molten stone fell from the ceiling, it did not fuse with the cold floor. We can find the hatchway. Just knock the stalagmites aside. If the door isn't underneath, put them back up so the guards won't trace our path."

Cobran fell to with a will, using his ax to topple stalagmites like wheat before a newly sharpened scythe. The others joined him, tipping them over with abandon but carefully putting them back in place.

Nagano spied an outline on the floor. "I found it."

"None too soon," the mage said. "I hear them coming."

After Nagano cleared the way, Cobran pulled the heavy stone slab free, while the rest made sure the stalagmites looked undisturbed.

"Quickly, everyone inside," the mage said.

They clamored into a musty passage that led to a room thick with dust.

"Maybe they've forgotten about this room," Zynaryxx said. "It served me well many years ago. The true king and I would sometimes enjoy a leisurely repast here when we sought to escape the tiresome routines of court life. I suggest we rest here until the pursuit dies off. They'll have alerted the entire castle by now. If we blunder forth haphazardly, we'll just walk into one of their patrols. With any luck, they'll think we've taken our imprisoned comrade and fled the castle."

"What of Quatar and Portnal?" Zorth asked. "What chance do they have?"

"It depends," the mage said, stifling a yawn. "Their chances are excellent if no one has discovered the bodies we left behind. If someone finds the guards we killed, then our friends could be captured. However, even if they discover the bodies, I doubt they'll look in the storehouse for fear of the leviathan. If they can reach that room, they'll be safe."

"What if they've been captured?"

"Then, we'll have to rescue them again," Nagano said.

The companions stretched out to rest in the crowded chamber, keeping their weapons close—except for the ninja, who couldn't seem to relax and kept looking at the mage.

"Well, do you have something to say or do you intend to keep the rest of us from sleeping with all that squirming?" the faerie said irritably. "For someone with all that training in silence and stealth you keep telling us about, you seem to have great difficulty keeping still."

"I can't sleep," she said. "In all my life, I seldom have had to apologize. Today, I apologized to Zorth for my insults. When I saw him throw away his weapon to save Olaf, leaving him with nothing with which to protect himself, I realized that I had misjudged him."

"And now you can't sleep, because making an apology upsets your entire life plan, which is based on distrust."

"No," the ninja said. "I can't sleep, because I find that I owe you an apology, as well. I called you an old fool and accused you of betraying us when I thought you intended to go to the Regent. As I looked across that chamber, I saw death approaching. I knew then that if they offered me a way to live, even if it meant betraying you, I would take it. I am ashamed. In the face of death, I found I was a coward. And so I lashed out at you."

"You are no coward," the mage said gruffly. "You fought against heavy odds. We all did. If we can put our differences aside and fight together, trusting in each other, we may have a surprise for Her."

"Now go to sleep." The mage pulled his cloak more tightly around himself.

Nagano gazed at him, unwavering.

Zynaryxx sat up again. "What is it?" the faerie demanded. "I have forgiven you your rash remarks. Now let us sleep."

The ninja looked uncomfortable. "I hoped you might tell us why the Regent offered to save you."

"You don't trust me?" the faerie said. "I must explain myself to you?"

"When I laid on the floor of Orwynn's tavern with a knife at my throat, you kept them from slaying me. I have always trusted you. I just hoped that you trusted us enough to tell us this strange tale of why the Arch Regent puts such value on your life. Why would She offer you, Her sworn enemy, his life? How does She know you? Why do you mean so much to Her? Why were you so upset when you summoned that dark creature to battle those wraithkings? What is this oath you swore never to command the Nether creatures?"

"You don't want to know much, do you?" the mage said sourly. "And the rest of you are just as bad, pretending to sleep while you eavesdrop."

"Peace," Bill said, breaking the silence. "I do believe that the powerful Zynaryxx, leader of a feared underground cabal, destroyer of armies of the undead, is embarrassed."

"Pah," the mage spat. "I just don't like snoops prying into matters that have no bearing on our present mission. What you ask about lies buried in the past."

Chapter Seventeen

"You don't trust us, do you?" Nagano said.

The question hung in the air. The mage looked around the room, annoyed. "You're being ridiculous, all of you," he said. "A pox on you, then. If you must know, the Regent and I were once engaged to be married."

He looked defiant, almost daring them to say something. "I now suppose you want to know even more," he said sourly. "I thought I had recruited a stout band of fearless warriors and what do I find—busybodies and gossips. Well, if you must know, then I'll tell you a story of a young fool who fell in love.

"We were ambitious, our dreams knew no bounds. We studied the ancient secrets and found both ourselves adept at learning the mysteries of earth, wind, air, and fire. Our teachers marveled at our skills. That wasn't enough. We were vain, we wished to know more. My own taste for knowledge couldn't be sated.

"We were entranced with the idea of bringing creatures from the dark plains to perform our bidding. Our teachers refused to teach us this lore, warning us that it was forbidden. We laughed at them, calling them fools. We boasted that, while taming the dark creatures might be too much for them, it was certainly not beyond our skills. My love and I traveled the world, searching, gathering lore long buried. We learned that creatures called onto this plane were unable to attack those who enlisted them in their service. We felt safe in our daring. The more skillful we grew, the more we wished to know. At least, I wished to know more.

"She liked having the dark creatures at Her command. Simply knowing held no interest for Her. To Her, the knowledge meant only more power. As we grew more adept, She grew less and less willing to send Her servants back to the pits that had spawned them. She would keep them on this plane, questioning them about the darker powers they served. She constantly asked how we could use our skills to summon their lords to this plane to serve us.

"I paid no heed to such ideas. I couldn't bring myself to believe that someone I loved could seriously be interested in such dark fantasies. The hellspawn played on Her desire, describing the powers they could bestow upon Her if She summoned their lords to Her service. All She needed was to feed their hunger for blood and souls, and the world would be Her dominion.

"She used my desire and my youthful arrogance to convince me to help Her summon their prince to this plane. When I'd learned all I wanted from him and was ready to send him back, She refused. I discovered that without Her help, I could not command him. Enraged, I tried to slay him, but I could not match his strength. She ordered him to spare my life. She tried to lure me with promises that we would rule the world together. I refused. I told Her that these creatures of treachery and darkness would betray Her once they had ensnared Her. She laughed. The monster told Her that She did not need me if She could summon his master, a creature even more powerful than he.

"He told her of the innocents She would need to slaughter to bring him forth. I sickened when I realized She intended to go forward with such a mad enterprise. Finally, I saw Her for what She really was. I left Her and went into the world alone.

"She continued Her studies and eventually succeeded in summoning the creature's master. We call it the king, the Unnamed One. As I predicted, he betrayed Her. But he cannot kill Her. He rules the kingdom but allows Her this city as Her own domain.

"I did not know Her plan until today when we spoke to Portnal, although I should have guessed it. She has spent Her time building an army of dark creatures that She can command to slay the dark king and his minions. Then, She will rule, even if all the living must be sacrificed to feed their dark hunger.

"The blood of all those slain in Her name stains my hands. I've devoted my life to learning how I can undo the damage I've done. I've traveled the world seeking knowledge to find out how to slay the dark king. That is how I learned of the One.

"I recruited the League of the Crimson Crescent. I spent years searching for the One. I've devoted my life to expunge the harm of foolishness my vanity has caused. I probably should have told all of you before, but I was ashamed. Who would admit that his former fiancée coerced with the dark lord, intent on mounting the throne of hell. Who would choose to admit that they lost the woman they loved to such creatures or that they have sworn a vow to destroy Her?"

Zynaryxx bowed his head, his eyes lowered, his shoulders slumped, exhausted from the telling.

"You can't blame yourself," Bill said softly.

"Did you not listen?" the mage said. "I brought these creatures here. If not for the part I played, death would not be walking the kingdom. It was my foolishness. My folly. I am to blame. She was the loveliest woman of my race. I wanted to give Her the world. Little did I know the manner in which She would choose to take it."

"I think I hear hurt pride and vanity talking just as loudly as remorse," Bill said, ignoring the anger that flashed in the mage's eyes.

Bill continued, "Evil would enter this world without your aid. We're lucky it happened the way it did. Otherwise, we wouldn't have you on our side to send it back."

Zynaryxx looked at Bill, shaking his head in amusement. "You speak kindly to lighten the heart of an old fool," he said. "Thank you. Vanity prevented me from telling you what you had the right to know, since you have accompanied me on this quest that is rightfully mine alone. I've carried this secret for a long time."

"It is often said that the weight of a secret shared is halved," said Zorth. "I'll rest easier now that the riddle has been answered."

The mage asked, "Are there any other secrets in my life you care to pry from me?"

"No," Bill said laughing. "You can't blame us for asking about your love life. You never cease to amaze me."

The companions slept soundly until morning when the trap door above them ripped open with a fiery explosion. Shards of rock showered them.

From above, they heard a light, cheerful, feminine voice. "Zynaryxx, Zynaryxx," the voice chided. "Why do you hide in this dreary hole when you know that I have summoned you? My servants were ordered to bring you to me yesterday, but they told me some foolish tale that you would rather die than rejoin your beloved. When I sent them to drag you to me by your beard, they told me that you had escaped and fled the castle. Can you imagine that?

"I knew that you could never leave here without seeing me one last time, but I also remembered how fond you are of your little surprises. I knew you were here somewhere, waiting to see me at a time of your own choosing. I just couldn't wait. You know how impatient I get."

"I'm honored that you should go to all this trouble," the mage replied. "After all the time we've spent apart, there really was no need to rush."

"I should be annoyed with you for making me stay up all night searching for you." Bill found her voice unexpectedly melodic. "My servants didn't look here, in this forgotten little room. When I started thinking about you, I remembered how you came here when you wanted to slip away from the fuss of the court. You have no idea how much trouble it was to clear this room of rock so we could unearth your little hiding place."

"I am flattered that you can still remember those days," the mage said. "For someone who has so many more important matters pressing on your mind, I'm surprised that you have time to even think of that distant past."

"Ah, Zynaryxx," the Regent cooed. "If truth be known, I often muse about those old days, especially as I grow so close to achieving all we dreamt of when we were young."

"We, my lady?" the mage said. "Your memory tricks you if you think I ever yearned to destroy the innocent and trample the free. I never wanted to rule, in light or darkness.

Your dreams are waking nightmares visited upon the land I love. As you say, I intended to see you before I left this place, not to talk of days gone by or to watch you gloat over the lives you've ruined, but to offer you a final chance to atone for the evil you've done."

"Evil?" the Regent repeated. "You speak to me of evil as if you had the right to judge my works. You presume much. Yet, I shall not allow your insolence and bad manners to ruin our reunion. For you have brought me the gift I crave, the present I have long sought. It is a gift beyond reckoning, and one I greatly desire. I can't stay angry with someone who made it possible for me to achieve the dreams you dare to call nightmares."

"A gift, my lady?" the mage asked, puzzled. "What gift have I brought you, other than the opportunity to renounce your evil?"

"You don't know, do you?" she said. "Why, you've labored in my service, planning, plotting, seeking out for me just the tools I need to achieve my fondest desires. Just as when we were young you helped me gain the knowledge to rule, you have served me ever since, good Zynaryxx."

"I?" the mage sputtered. "How have I served you?"

The Arch Regent laughed, a clear sparkling girlish giggle. "Oh, my beloved, I am saddened to think that your once great mind has deteriorated over the years," she said. "If only I could keep you, perhaps as a jester to amuse me when affairs of state grow too tiresome. All this time, you've ignorantly sought in my behalf, fought to unearth for me that which I couldn't find myself. Now, when you should receive your reward, I can only destroy you. The same qualities that made you so valuable pose dangers to me if I let you live."

"You speak in riddles," Zynaryxx said testily. "I'm tired of these word games. My friends and I labor to rid the world of your works, not to be mocked."

"Oh, Zynaryxx, I fear I have wounded your pride," she said in her melodic voice. "I see that you have not lost any of your vanity. Can't you see the humor in knowing that all these years you've devoted to destroying were nothing more than a way of serving me? It must be a great blow to be revealed as a pawn, a puppet whose strings have been in my keeping. Come out from this hidey hole and face me if you want to learn how you've done nothing more than pay the penance I assigned for your betrayal."

"Come out!" she said, her voice rising in tones of command. "I don't care to see you dragged from there. Maintain what little pride you still hold and face me freely. I would like to see the expression on your face when you present me the precious gift I sent you out into the world to find for me."

"We're not going out there?" Zorth asked. "You don't seriously plan to walk into the arms of the enemy?"

"I see few other choices," Zynaryxx said. "We have no means of escape. If we refuse, She can destroy us while we hide in here, or She can entomb us. We'd better confront Her. On open ground, we may have a chance. Besides, Her overconfidence may be misplaced. We have shown that we are not so powerless as She seems to think."

"I vote with Zynaryxx," Bill said. "Being buried alive in this pit doesn't appeal to me. If we've learned nothing else, we've at least learned that when all seems blackest, we should trust each other."

They nodded.

"I'll go first," Nagano said. "I've traveled far to see the face of the one I've come to kill." The ninja moved swiftly to the entrance way, climbing out into the vast audience chamber. Cobran followed closely behind, his ax and sword ready.

As the companions climbed out, a vast black creature confronted them, its piercing red eyes glowing in hatred. On its shoulder, a dainty faerie robed in gold and tiny flawless jewels sat watching them in amusement.

Beside her stood Captain Grizzle, backed by fifty soldiers. Nearby stood two demon lords, resplendent in ebony armor, their swords bathed in fire. They held the leashes of four hellhounds. Four rockdwarfs stood on the fringes with a half dozen greater scourges, two phantom princes, and the walking skeletal remains of eight warriors.

The Arch Regent laughed at the look of fear that crossed the ninja's face. "So, you thought that you could slay me?" The Regent's melodious voice held a bright sting of mockery. "See now the host that guards me and know the bitter meaning of black despair. I should reward you for guarding this gift the mage has brought me, but knowing that I'll soon rule all the people in this world and others will have to suffice."

Cobran stared at the Regent's guards, a snarl curling his lizardlike features.

"I see the gladiator is too stupid to even realize that his crude strength and skills will avail him naught against my protectors," the Regent said. "If I hadn't grown so impatient, it might amuse me to let him test his prowess. Time grows short, however. Bring the human to me, Zynaryxx. I wish to see him."

Bill, followed by Zorth and Olaf, came out of the chamber. Zynaryxx brought up the rear. Bill felt as if they'd stepped into the funnel of a tornado.

"Yes, you have finally come to me as I knew you would," the Regent gloated. "You are a fitting present indeed. Know this, Zynaryxx, if it eases your heart, I will always be grateful to you for spending your life making my dreams of domination possible."

"What are you prattling about?" the mage snapped. "Have you spent so much time with ghouls and demons that you've forgotten how to address the living? We haven't fought our way to this place to amuse you. Your years of isolation have addled your mind. As your plans shatter, your mind turns on itself, preventing you from seeing that your ambitions are checked and your days numbered."

The Regent tinkled with laughter. "You amuse me so." She stifled her mirth. "I'm disappointed, though, that the once keen mind of Zynaryxx can't recognize when he's been outfoxed. Does your pride still prevent you from realizing that this human you have brought to me is the present I have sought?"

"Twice now you have spoken of me as if I were merely one of your servants," Bill said angrily. "I have come to destroy you, then your master."

"Of course you have," the Regent said in Her most patronizing tone. "Well said. Now, keep quiet so we can see if your teacher's wits have returned enough for him to guess the answer to the riddle that has so upset him.

"Have you not guessed, Zynaryxx?"

She shook Her head. "Let me help you, so that before you die you can comprehend how your life has been devoted to helping me achieve the very goals you once mocked."

Seeing no response from the mage, She smiled. "Have you never asked yourself how this human came here?" She asked. "Do you still honestly believe that he came here as an answer to your prayers?"

"We found him in the mountains," Zorth said. "He comes from some strange place far away. He came to the city hoping to find someone who could help him return to his home."

"He has found that someone. You know, mage, you didn't summon him to this plane. You have neither the skill nor the knowledge. No, but you should have guessed that this human was part of a far higher and greater design than any that you could comprehend. He has been summoned by me to this place to guarantee me the realization of my lifetime dream."

"The One?" Zynaryxx angrily shouted. "Don't banter with me, queen of foulness. I've watched him. He'll die before he serves you. If you hope to divide us by planting suspicions of our loyalties to one another, you waste our time."

"I waste your time? What do you know of time? I've traveled across eternity searching for this man. The Unnamed One can be slain only by a man wielding the sword this one holds. It was I who found that sword. It was I who placed it in that cave. I who summoned this man into our world. And I will rule when he vanquishes my betrayer.

"Did you think I would be content to rule this city when kingdoms await? That I could abide that creature set up as king when it was I who brought him here? You still can't grasp the enormity of your own foolishness, can you, mage? Did you believe I wasn't aware of your efforts? I knew you could never rest, knowing He ruled these lands. I knew you would find the secret to sending Him back. That's why I allowed you to serve me. He watches me too closely for me to have taken those risks.

"After I learned of your discovery about the One, I started searching for this human. I brought him to that cave and left him to his own devices as a test. I told my servants nothing, ordering them only to find and destroy him, because I knew that if he couldn't survive them, I'd be a fool to employ him on my mission. When I learned that you, my beloved, had joined him, I was overjoyed. Under your tutelage, he would learn everything he needed to vanquish my foe. Your success in reaching me shows that he really is the tool I need to achieve my dreams."

"I've come here to kill you," Bill said evenly. "If your slaves kill me, then your dreams of power die with me."

"Such bravery. I chose well. Your courage cheers my heart, man. Before you act rashly, however, consider a moment your own desires. If you slay me, do you not slay the only hope you have to return to your own world? Ask your friend if you have any hope other than me? Look at his face. It is written there. If you don't serve me, you're destined to wander this unfriendly world."

"I could slay you before I slay this dark king."

"You don't listen, do you?" she said. "I summoned you here to this world to serve me. You may not kill me. It is forbidden. You may hate me with all your heart, but if I were to lay down before you helpless, your hand couldn't strike. Hasn't the mage explained that those who summon creatures across the planes are protected from them? Ask him. Zynaryxx does many things, but he doesn't lie."

Bill looked at the faerie beside him and saw the truth of the Regent's words written across his face. Bill's shoulders slumped as the consequences of the Regent's words hit him with their full impact. "So, I'm simply another creature summoned to serve you?" he said.

"You talk as if it were something sad," the Regent laughed gaily. "You should be celebrating to learn that you were called to serve me. If I die, you'll never return to your home. Only I possess the power to transport you between the realms. If you refuse me, my servants will slay you.

"I don't know what your tutor thought when he brought you on this fool's errand, but now he's recognized the creature I ride. It is the same one whose powers vanquished him once before, long ago. I saved Zynaryxx from his wrath then, but I will not act so kindly if you refuse to serve me now. This creature serves me, not the dark lord, and its powers have grown over the years, as have mine.

"The sword you wield is mighty enough to protect you from the dark king, but it can't save you from the powers I've assembled. I have a simple offer for you. March with the host I have gathered here and in my dungeons below to challenge the might of the king. Slay him, and I'll spare your comrades and return you to your home. Defy me and die."

Seeing the indecision in Bill's face, the Regent pressed her advantage. "Zynaryxx is helpless. He's but a mere chess piece in the contest between the two ruling powers of this world. If you wish to save the fool and these creatures you call your friends, you must choose now, for I grow weary."

Bill saw the mage watching him closely. "Bill, throughout our adventures you've always kept faith with me. If She has the power to return you to your home, I won't mislead you by claiming I can match the offer. Nor can I say how, if we survive, I'll seek that knowledge with you.

"You must now make this choice for yourself. Don't let Her offers about us beguile you into thinking She'll spare us once She achieves Her desires, however. Treachery has always been Her one enduring trait. As for this fell creature on whose shoulder She rides, I expect it's grown in power. Gladly would I test myself against Her hordes before I would do Her bidding."

An ogre had entered the audience chamber while Zynaryxx was speaking. It signaled Captain Grizzle. As the two huddled in conference, the captain cast fearful glances toward the Regent. Hesitantly, he began to follow the ogre to the door.

Bill stared closely into the eyes of the Regent, who was distracted by the ogre's consultation with Her captain. "I will not serve you, Regent," Bill said. "I haven't come this far to let the tyrannies I've seen go unavenged. If I must die, I at least will die as a man, trying to rid this world of you and your works."

The Regent ignored him. "Have you been dismissed from my presence?" She said to Grizzle.

"My lady, I did not wish to disturb you," the captain stammered. "I could see that you were busy and had no time for petty matters beneath your concern. I thought to handle them myself while you devote yourself to affairs of state."

"Didn't you hear my life threatened, Captain?" the regent said softly. "Let me help you toward the light of remembrance: You and your troops exist to guard me. After hearing this man repeatedly threaten me, however, you try to scurry from the room."

"Never, my lady," the captain said. "Gladly would I give my life for you. I thought only to handle a matter of some urgency, to ensure that you were not disturbed."

"What is this matter so beneath my concern, yet so important that it calls away the captain of my guard? Know you not that I have been quite aware of your failures of late? Tell me of this latest failure that you wish to hide from me."

"Perhaps, my lady, we could speak privately," the captain said uncomfortably. "I do not believe you would have such as these listening to our discussions."

The Regent dismissed the comrades with an imperious wave of her tiny hand. "It matters not what they hear. Their choices are clear, whether they like them or not. Give me your report. My patience runs out."

"I really think you would prefer to hear it without them," Grizzle said. "It would be better to discuss this matter upon my return."

"So, now you choose when I should hear the reports I request? Be warned, captain, for someone whose record is as stained as yours, this is not the time to try my patience."

"I'll only be gone a moment," he said.

"You will not be gone at all." She nodded to the eight skeletal remains. "Slay him."

Revulsion for her malice burst through Bill like pus from some secret internal abscess.

"My lady!" Captain Grizzle shouted as the undead warriors advanced toward him, their swords gleaming. "The castle gate has been stormed by the people. I sought only to go to its defense. My soldier tells me that it will soon fall unless aid reaches it in time."

"The city rebels?" the Regent asked, stunned by the revelation. She motioned to the skeletons to halt. "They dare to challenge my wrath? They dare to enter my very home? You assured me that you had broken the spirit of this insurrection. Now, I find it threatens me personally. You described this as a petty matter."

The Captain stepped back, drawing his sword before the undead warriors. "I didn't want them to know. Your warriors have been frightened by these rumors of this League of the Crimson Crescent. For the past few days they have been subjected to increasing attacks wherever they have gone in the city. The increasing ferocity and frequency of these attacks have quite unnerved them.

"This morning we received word that the Guild Lords have joined the rebels. The community apparently learned that you intend to feed them to your pets beneath the castle. I had hoped to speak to you of this, but you commanded me to be silent and to help unearth these rebels." He pointed at the companions. "I feared that if they heard this, it might give them hope. They might refuse your alliance if they knew the city had risen in revolt."

"Fool! It's your own hysteria that's infected them. The dark legion I've assembled will overrun this rag–tag band easily. Kill him," she repeated to the skeletal warriors.

"My lady, what of the reinforcements needed at the gate?" Grizzle asked as he backed away from the killers advancing on him. "Have you not listened to what I've said? Who will see to the castle's defense if I am killed?"

"I will. I see my mistake in trusting your incompetence. This guard will scatter the rebels."

"I'm afraid we can't permit that," Zynaryxx said.

"You!" the Regent sputtered. "You dare to speak in such an insolent manner to me?"

"Ah, yes, my lady, I dare. All those years when you claim I was serving your ends, I was also plotting your destruction. The League of the Crimson Crescent has been called forth. It has raised the city, broken the curtain of fear, and given the people hope that they can destroy the shackles that have bound them. The felpurs we freed from your dungeon have told the people the fate in store for them if you succeed. The frightened citizens of Trillius have finally decided they'd rather die fighting for their freedom than wait in fear to be served as delicacies to your dark minions. I must insist that you and your personal guard remain here."

"You must insist? You think your League can stand before my army of undead? Old fool, even the creatures you see here are far beyond your powers. You must realize they can sweep you and your friends aside like dried leaves before the wind. The creatures I've gathered below howl for the blood of these traitors who dare threaten my fortress. The citizens of Trillius shall rue the day they chose to join with your League of the Crimson Crescent. This day will be marked in their blood in the calendars of the world."

The Regent drew herself up, cupping her fingers to her lips. A sound exploded from her throat, thundered through the chambers of the fortress, and echoed in the dark dungeons below.

"Arise, my slaves," she thundered, the sound of Her voice reverberating through the hallways of the castle. "Your day has dawned, creatures of darkness. Come forth! Vanquish those who would oppose you. Eat their flesh and drink their blood. Consume their spirits. Mastery of this world awaits you. Come forth from the bowels of this, my home. Slay those who would oppose me. Feed your ravenous hungers. Seek and destroy the living. I, your rightful queen, command you and summon you. Go forth. The days of feasting have begun."

From below, as the sound of her deadly words ceased echoing through the layers of stone of the citadel, the companions could hear the fearsome shrieks of ghoulish celebration. A deep drumming began, and ghostly horns trumpeted the assembling host.

"You hear them?" the Regent laughed. "They rise. Long have I struggled to keep them below, forcing them to subsist on the limited rations I could provide them from those I took from the city. Always, they cried for more, their dark hungers unsated by the frugal nourishment my servants brought them. Today, I unleash them. Think of that, Zynaryxx! Think hard on the horrors you have brought upon the city today. As they feed on your insurrectionists, think on the folly of your actions. For you have hastened the day. You have robbed the people of what little time they might have had left. You have provoked me and visited my wrath upon them. Think upon it and despair, for your vanity and foolishness has served only to rob the people of this city of their lives."

The rumblings from below emphasized her words. Bill visualized the creatures assembling to march to the castle's defense. He shuddered as the eerie drum rolls and trumpet calls quickened as the dark host prepared to sally forth against the rebels at the castle's gates.

He'd seen the powers of the Regent's undead servants. He knew the host below, once unleashed, would easily overrun the forces attacking the castle. Once the dark creatures occupied the streets, no force in the world could stand before their hunger.

The Regent's eyes fastened on Zynaryxx who stood unbowed. His eyes showed no fear or doubt.

"Don't you grasp what you've unleashed?" She said. "Do you still believe that you have the strength or the power to stand before my dread host? The city is doomed. Its people will not live beyond the sunset. After my forces have vanquished my enemies, they will feast in a banquet that you in your darkest nightmare could not conceive. Kneel before me, mage. If you and your friends wish to be spared, if only for a while, swear your allegiance now. Swear now upon whatever you value, or I will take your lives!"

The Regent looked closely at the mage, who only smiled.

"Have you lost your mind?" she screamed. "All that you treasure shall die this day. Your hopes are nothing but fantasies. This man, who you hoped would slay me, is nothing more than my servant, summoned to slay my enemy. Your vaunted rebellion is but a diversion that I crush without the slightest exertion. Yet still you defy me? Still you stand there smirking like some school child withholding a secret from its master? Do you not realize that you and your friends have lost?"

Zynaryxx said, "I smile, because I anticipated you reaction. My dear, you have always been as predictable as you were beautiful, striking out in anger whenever anyone dares to oppose your will. Do you believe we came here to challenge you alone? I will confess we have gambled our lives, but did you truly believe I would come here without some hope?"

"You have put your hope in a revolution doomed to failure," the Regent said. "My army will soon fall upon your feeble rebellion, rending the very flesh from their bones. They will scatter them. You have not the power nor the strength to destroy me."

"You are quite correct," the mage said. "I don't. I never did. I knew when I decided to face you inside your own stronghold that we alone do not hold the power to destroy you."

These words fell on Bill like fists, like iron sledgehammers.

"You admit you are doomed?" the regent cackled. "Perhaps you have come to your senses."

"I do not speak of my doom, my lady," the mage said. "It is you who will fall this day. For I did not come here to die or to serve you. Nor did I come here to watch you gloat over the destroyed remains of this city like some foul carrion beast. When I came here, I gambled on more than myself or my friends. I bet on more than this rebellion I plotted. I wagered on your one trait that I knew had endured through the long years of our separation. You yourself would give me the one ally I needed to destroy you."

"I grow tired of your nonsense," the Regent said, signaling her guard. "Destroy the old fool."

The mage leaped aside as a bolt of fire streamed from the creature on which the Regent rode. A golden aura surrounded the faerie as his hands swept through the air. It encircled Bill and his companions with a magical shield.

A silver aura enveloped the Regent and Her dread beast. She howled in laughter. "Do you truly believe that you can pierce our shield? Do you not know that no protection can long withstand our fury?" the Regent asked. "Alone, either one of us could destroy you. Together, no one on this world can stand before us."

"No one?" Zynaryxx asked, his eyes sparkling. "There was a time when that was true. You forget, however, that there is one power on this plane that even you fear. You know it better than anyone. You brought it here, and you betrayed it—as you betrayed our rightful king, our people, and our love. Now, know its wrath!"

Chapter Eighteen

The Regent registered surprise as Zynaryxx intoned a dark chant in a hoarse and guttural language that caused Her servants to cringe. "I name The Unnamed One; I summon He that you hath betrayed, He that you would supplant, He that you would destroy."

The Regent wailed fearfully, "You don't have the power to summon Him."

"Not across the planes of existence. But you've already done that for me. You brought Him to this plane. I'm only summoning Him to this room where He can see His betrayer."

A dark cloud appeared, flickering, growing in brooding intensity. A sullen voice thundered through the chamber as a shape took form within the blackened sphere.

"Who dares to call me forth?" it bellowed. "Who dares to disturb me?"

"I call you," the mage shouted. "I have summoned you here. I have dared."

"Then dare to die!" the black force said.

"Is that a fitting reward for one who seeks to reveal the treachery of a servant?" the mage shouted into the whirling black vortex that had appeared in the sphere. "Look you upon your Regent. Look into the black heart of this creature. She rides astride that which would aid Her in taking your life. Look upon them and see the treachery, see the legion of hellspawn they have brought forth to challenge your rule!"

As the vortex turned to the Regent and Her creature, the fell beast shook her from its great shoulder, knocking her to the floor. The creature fell to its knees, babbling in a loathsome tongue.

The Regent picked Herself up and tried to recover Her composure as Her servant confessed Her treason before the dark lord.

"It is as you say, little one," the vortex intoned.

A blast of black fire spewed from the vortex, consuming the creature, which writhed in its flames. Standing, the creature staggered as the black inferno devoured it.

Turning, the vortex faced the Regent. "What have you to say, traitor?" the dark lord thundered.

"I brought you to this plane," the Regent shouted defiantly. "Without me, you could never have crossed into this world. You cannot destroy me. It is forbidden."

"She speaks the truth," the vortex said. "My hand is stayed against this creature."

"I knew that when I summoned you," Zynaryxx said. "She is protected from your wrath. But shatter the shield that surrounds Her, and I will punish Her treachery in your stead. I'll perform this one service for you if you will command the dark host She has conjured onto this plane in Her service. Send the black army She's gathered back into the darkness that spawned it, for they have given oaths to Her to help slay you. Punish the traitors at your leisure, so that all may know the fate awaiting those who would challenge your rule. This one service we can do for each other, then the truce between us will end."

"You dare?" the Regent said to Zynaryxx.

"Much will I dare!" the vortex roared as a dark bolt

slammed into the Regent's silver shield. A thunder clap shattered the air as the room rumbled from the assault, the walls quaking in its aftermath. The shield split like a glass bubble bursting, fragments showering the room. The blow propelled the Regent through the air and into the wall.

"Kill them!" She wailed as She fell in a heap to the floor. "Destroy them."

"You threaten me?" the vortex asked. "You would command these lesser creatures to attack their lord and master? I knew your vanity was vast. I saw that when I first discovered you bringing my servants to this plane. I enticed you, through them, to bring me here. In your girlish vanity you thought to command me, a power beyond your reckoning. Now you think to send them against their own true master?"

Black beams burst from the darkened sphere, smashing into the Regent's servants, knocking them aside like ants smitten by a fist. "I knew of your treacherous thoughts," the vortex said. "But your cunning has grown through the years. Somehow, you have hidden from me the undead legion you have assembled below. I now see my mistake. I shall send them to my dominion to serve me, their rightful master."

A blast of power exploded from the vortex, reverberating through the hallways. Shrieks of fear echoed from below as the drumming ceased and the trumpets stilled.

"It is done, tiny mage," the vortex said. "I have fulfilled my end of the bargain. Her host is gone. They have left this plane forever. I shall torment them at my leisure. They shall serve as an eternal reminder of the fate awaiting all who would dare to oppose my will. That fate awaits you, unless you fulfill your promise to me."

The mage nodded toward Bill, motioning at the dark lord,

as his hands passed through the air. A lightning bolt leaped at the Regent, knocking her back against the wall, leaving her dazed and confused.

Her servants appeared bewildered and weakened from the dark lord's assault. The bolt that smashed the Regent stunned them by revealing Her weakness. Their master had been easily buffeted by blows from someone She had long derided and mocked.

Zynaryxx used the respite to strike again and again, raining bolts of energy upon the regent and the two demon lords who sought to protect Her. The Regent's screams of agony tore through the chamber. The demon lords quailed before the onslaught, raising their hands uselessly to ward off the mage's magical fury.

The phantom princes watched in wonder and anguish as their dark queen's torment mounted. Regaining themselves, they shrieked as one and descended on the companions.

Captain Grizzle, fencing with the undead skeletons, stabbed one as it turned to watch its mistress' torment.

The two demon lords, seeing their Regent's plight, unleashed the four hellhounds on the companions, while they themselves cast spells at the mage. Zynaryxx's shield withstood the magical assault.

The dark lord's laugh sounded from inside the vortex. "You amuse me, mage. Her shrieks are like music, her misery cheers me. I would punish her just so if it were but mine to mete out."

Distracted by the woes of the Regent, the figure inside the dark vortex did not notice Bill creeping toward Him. Raising his sword, Bill struck the dark sphere, cutting a gash large enough to allow him to dive through. Leaping into the darkness, he was lost from view.

Zynaryxx shouted to his companions in the confusion. "Stand together," he pleaded. "Our strength is in our unity. We have confused and divided our enemies. Bill faces the dark lord alone, as his destiny demands. We must protect one another if we are to emerge alive."

Heeding the words, Cobran raised his ax and sword to repel the hellhounds leaping toward them. Nagano, who had been looking across the room at the Regent, shrugged her shoulders and braced herself beside the lizardman. Zorth and Olaf stood on either side of the mage, warily watching as their adversaries advanced toward them.

The phantom princes intoned a dark chant, sending waves of fire cascading against the golden shield the mage had created. Like waves against a stone wall, the flames lapped against it and harmlessly rolled away.

Zynaryxx briefly closed his eyes, then opened them, fixing his gaze upon the Regent and Her demon guard. Bolts of lightning flashed across the room, their roar thundering through the chamber, crackling as they fell upon his former lover. With Her magical shield broken, still dazed from the dark lord's assault and Zynaryxx's repeated attacks, She was defenseless from the blast.

She shrieked in pain, Her shimmering finery igniting into flames that covered Her and the demons.

Zorth chanted a curse at the greater scourges following closely behind the rockdwarfs and hellhounds racing toward the companions.

A blast of white fire engulfed the scourges, leaving only two still standing. Olaf closed his eyes, placed his fingers to his brow, and muttered a silent prayer to Thea that sent a wave of psionic force striking into the rockdwarfs. It crashed into them with silent power, but they ignored it, marching toward the companions with a cold fury.

Zorth struck out at the rockdwarfs, bathing them in the white fire of his incantation. They stepped through it, unsinged and unharmed.

"They have no minds or souls," the mage said. "Magic cannot slay them."

The two remaining greater scourges, screaming in fury, charged alongside the rockdwarfs as the hellhounds leaped at the party.

Cobran's sword flashed out at the charging hellhounds, spearing one of them in the throat. A second creature locked its massive teeth around the lizardman's leg, bowling him over. He willed himself to ignore the pain, while he drove his ax into a third creature's skull.

Nagano drove her fist into the eyebrow ridges of the fourth canine, kicking it in the throat three times before it staggered, its neck broken.

Olaf struck at the phantom princes, concentrating with intensity as his mind focused the psychic attack. His adversaries winced from the impact, hurt but unbowed. Speaking in guttural sounds, they struck back, their magical blows cracking the mage's shield.

Zynaryxx ignored the assault, striking again at the Regent and Her consorts, but the demon lords had recovered enough to raise a barrier of their own. Though the mage's magical blast pierced it, its force had been cut in half.

At that moment, the door to the chamber crashed open as Portnal and Quatar emerged, leading Morko, Pasham, Yorth, and Orwynn, followed by a host of heavily armed city dwellers.

The warriors following behind the scourges turned to face them, racing toward this new threat.

Captain Grizzle, who had slain three of the skeletal warriors during the confusion, found himself standing between Portnal and Quatar's force and the soldiers he had once commanded. "Join me, my troops, or we shall be but a snack for the Regent's monsters."

The warriors ignored him, charging past him toward the city dwellers.

The two sides clashed in a frenzied melee.

Zorth, seeing that their protective shield was waning, struck at the phantom princes with an enchantment. It slammed into them, stunning them, but failed to dissipate them.

As Nagano leapt at the hellhound that had overpowered Cobran, the two greater scourges brushed past and pounced on Olaf and Zorth. Behind them came the rock dwarfs.

Nagano repeatedly struck at the hellhound, while Cobran struck it with both his ax and his sword. Slowly, the great creature's jaw relaxed in death, releasing the lizardman's bloodied leg.

Cobran struggled onto his one good leg just as the rock dwarfs charged. His sword crashed into one, chipping fragments from its head. Nagano punched another, cracking its torso.

Zynaryxx could see that Olaf and Zorth were outmatched by their adversaries. Ignoring the phantom princes and the demon lords, he struck at the scourges, frying them in one fiery burst.

That break in his concentration was enough to allow the demon lords and phantom princes to strike back, hurling bolts through the weakness in his golden barrier.

The companions reeled from the assault.

The Regent staggered to her feet and struck, cracking the shield and sending the companions to the ground.

Forgotten in the frenzy of the battle, Bill found himself alone, facing the dark lord. The chamber he had entered contained no light, except for the soft glow emanating from his sword.

"What have we here? Who is this that sneaks into my presence?" the dark lord chuckled. "Has the mage offered me a snack to sate my hunger, sealing our pact in blood?"

"I have a snack for you, hellspawn," Bill said into the gloom. "But this meal won't enter your stomach through your mouth. I will cut through your entrails to save you the trouble of chewing."

In the darkness, he could hear it sniggering. "You joke, fool," the voice said. "For I have no mouth. I have no form, no body, no entrails to slice. Whoever sent you on this fool's errand told you little of what you face. I am Lord. I am the power and the force. No creature born of this world can harm me."

"But I'm no creature of this world," laughed Bill as he drove his sword into the shifting blackness.

"Don't be a fool," the voice said. "How came you to this place?"

"I was summoned from my world, brought here through the dimensions," Bill said. "I am a man, summoned here from another plane to send you back into the nothingness that bred you."

"A man?" the vortex choked.

"Some call me the One." Bill slashed with his sword.

A bolt of deeper blackness erupted out of the darkness, hurtling toward Bill. His sword flashed out, striking it, deflecting it, and send it back into the shadowy gloom.

"See my sword?" Bill asked. "Can you not see your death reflected in its steel? You know the prophecy. For thirty years you have attempted to enslave all men to prevent its fulfillment. How many lives have you ruined? How many have died? But you have failed. I have come here to punish you. I have come to help you reap the grim harvest of your treachery and deceit."

Around him, Bill could see the chamber shifting as the blackness swirled, creating dim shapes in the darkness. The twilight outlined figures that writhed at the sound of the vortex's words.

"Fool! You dare to threaten me?" the dark lord thundered. "You talk to me of punishment and revenge? You face me here in my own nest, because you know no better. Look around you and see the darkness, my darkness. I feed on it. Do you not see these dark shapes that cower at the sound of my voice? These are enemies that, like you, dared to stand against me. This is all that remains of their foolishness. I keep parts of their souls here to nourish me when my hunger grows. Some are half eaten. I keep them as reminders of those who once defied me. They quail at the sound of my voice, each of them holding onto this twilight life I allow them to maintain for my own amusement. When I tire of them, I sup on them, sucking the remaining life–force from them like the marrow of a bone."

Bill looked more closely into the dark shroud of the room. In the dimness, he could make out frightened faces in the dark shape, each of whose features were frozen in grimaces of stark terror.

"They too defied me," the dark lord said. "Like you, they mistook their vanity and conceit for power. Now, they writhe in eternal torment. Do you wish to join them?"

"Join them?" Bill asked. "No, I've come to free them and this world of your vile presence. I've come to send you back into the darkness that is your true home."

"So, you've come to slay me?" the voice echoed in the room. "Do you truly believe these myths you've been told, that your bright shiny sword can kill someone who has mastered both time and space? Do you really think that someone as powerful as I can be slain by something as pitiful and powerless as you?"

Bill heard a dry chuckle. "I admire your courage," the voice said. "It's seldom that I see it. Leave this room now, and I will spare you."

"You will spare me?" Bill shouted into the twilight. "You admire courage? I have seen how you treat those who show courage. I have seen it at your slave blocks. I've seen how you have divided the free peoples with your lies and threats. I know the fate that awaits this world if your wickedness goes unchecked. You offer to spare me? Tell me, king of blackness, king of treachery, do you think I would believe you would allow me to live because you admire me? I think you fear this sword I carry. And in your hope that I might leave, you offer me my life."

Bill's weapon exploded in light as the twilight constricted around him. As the illumination grew in intensity, driving the pitch black from him, Bill could see the dingy shadows congealing in a corner, cowering from the glare reflected from his sword.

Bill felt, rather than saw, beams of blackness exploding at him, but his sword slashed through the air, cleaving them apart. As if it had gained a will of its own, the shining blade hacked through the darkness, chopping it into pieces that fell to the floor in black chunks. The air around him crackled with a dark charge as his blade tore through the gloom that seemed on the edge of congealing into a mass.

"Do you tremble, dark lord?" Bill demanded as he approached through the ebony cloud. "Do you begin to feel the fear that you have inflicted?"

"Why do you come here, man of another plane?" the voice cried. "What is this place to you? What business do you have disturbing the natural order of things?"

"You call this the natural order?" Bill asked, advancing on the dark shape, prodding it with his steel point. "You who have no form nor substance. You, who wish to rule. You speak to me of my business when your very existence calls out for all living things to join together to extinguish your vileness from sight. I have seen the misery you have created. I have witnessed the suffering you have inflicted. Feel it yourself as you return to the darkness that begat you."

When Bill stabbed, the darkness imploded. The sphere spilled in on itself, converging into a ball before it exploded into a thousand fragments.

All that remained was Bill, standing in a corner of the audience chamber.

Seeing his companions beset, he charged the Regent and her demons, distracting them from their attack.

Hearing her shrieks of fear, the rock dwarfs turned and ran to aid Her. In the confusion, Zynaryxx, Zorth, and Olaf struck at the phantom princes. Howling, they collapsed and died.

Seeing Bill charge the Regent, Nagano sprinted after him, passing the rock dwarfs as she dashed toward her mother's killer. The demon lords struck at Bill, hurling sorcerous blasts at him.

His sword deflected them. Blocking his way, they drew their own weapons, stabbing at him to fend him off.

Bill's sword crashed against one of the demon lord's weapons, splintering it. Ducking a thrust, Bill parried another and plunged his weapon into its midsection. Light exploded inside the beast as the sword pierced him. Pulling it out, Bill blocked a blow. He spun from the creature and raised his sword against the Regent.

As he strove to slash Her, She laughed.

"You did not listen to me, man," the Regent said. "It is as I said. I am your master. I summoned you here, and you can't harm me."

"But I can, witch queen," Nagano shouted as she ran past Bill, vaulting over the fallen creature.

Zynaryxx, joined by Olaf and Zorth, struck at the Regent with their spells, dazing Her from their combined blows. As Bill turned to duel with the demon lord, the ninja pounced on the tiny faerie, stabbing the Arch Regent with her blade.

Stunned by the attack on the Regent, the demon lord faltered, allowing Bill to pierce its chest with his sword. Bill turned to face the rock dwarfs lumbering toward him.

Nagano rose as she watched the Regent writhe in torment from the mortal wound.

"Beloved?" the Regent called out to Zynaryxx. "Will you not come to me now?"

"Your true beloved, the dark lord, already awaits you, my love," Zynaryxx said. "After all your labors, I would not now come between you."

She sighed. "If I must go to him, then you shall join me—for eternity," she snarled, raising her hands to cast a deadly enchantment, Her bewitchment dying with Her.

Bill spun, slashing Her head from Her shoulders.

The rock dwarfs staggered, then froze. With Her death, the last skeleton warrior crumpled before Captain Grizzle, who breathed a sigh of relief as Portnal stepped in front of his former tormentor and stabbed him. The rest of the castle warriors threw down their arms in defeat.

Bill looked around the room as the sound of steel clashing on steel ceased. "Is it over?" he asked the mage. "Have we won?"

Zynaryxx walked over to stand beside the fallen figure of the only woman he had ever loved. Reaching for Her tiny hand, he held it gently, feeling its stillness as he studied Her features.

"I'm afraid it is," he said, kissing Her cool fingers.

The companions gathered around the mage, staring at Bill. "You struck Her," Nagano said. "How could you kill Her if you were summoned by Her as she claimed?"

"I don't know," Bill said.

"It's clear enough to me," Zynaryxx said. "She lied. If She had truly summoned you, when She died, you would have disappeared along with Her other creatures. She said it to convince you to fight alongside Her host. Always, She was a treacherous wench. She would have used you to vanquish Her foe, but when you claimed your reward, She would have only laughed and killed you."

"Then how did I get here?" Bill asked.

"I promised you that we would discover that," the mage said. "First, we have a kingdom to free."

Chapter Nineteen

"Now what do I do?" Bill asked as he reached for a tankard of ale. "I still have no way to go home."

"You are home," Zynaryxx replied, leaning over to scoop more from his own tankard. "You have a place with us. You are among friends. You're a hero to the people you've freed. Here, you have a place of honor."

Bill looked around the Falcon. It didn't seem as though four weeks had passed since the victory in Regent's castle. Humans sat wherever they wished, sprinkled among the tables of rawulfs, hobbits, dwarfs, dracons, and others.

At a nearby table, a man recounted his role in what had become known as the Great Revolution. "When I led my friends out of the slave pens, all I had was the sword I'd taken from the jailer I strangled." He took a deep swig from his tankard for emphasis.

"I thought it was a knife," a dracon table interrupted.

"It was a sword," he insisted. "I used my bare hands on the jailer."

"I thought the League set the slaves free at the market?" a hobbit said.

"They played a role, certainly," the man said. "But if that jailer had given a warning, the entire raid might have failed. And if I hadn't made it possible for the slaves to escape, well, I don't even want to think what might have happened to the entire revolution.

"Think about it. When all those slaves got loose, it put the whole city in an uproar. The guards streamed out of the castle to hunt us down. But they found a nasty surprise waiting when they came out of that fortress.

"We knew what fate awaited any of us who might have been recaptured. Once we got out, we had no choice. Every warrior had received orders to kill us on sight.

"Let me tell you, once I discovered how easy that jailer died, I realized I'd spent years cowering for nothing. I took a few of the lads and went prowling. Others followed our example, too. The warriors soon discovered it was none too healthy for them to snoop in the shadows and alleys."

"I'll grant you, the humans played a part," the dracon responded. "But you had nothing to lose but your lives. Those who carried the crimson crescent put their homes and livelihoods on the line, along with their lives."

"Were you a member of the League?" the human asked.

"It's not something one talks about," the dracon said, reaching for his tankard. "Let's just say the revolution didn't just happen. It took years of planning."

"I never saw you at a meeting of the League," the hobbit said.

The dracon paused in mid–sip, eyeing the hobbit.

"That shouldn't be too surprising," the dracon responded. "The League had many members whose responsibilities prevented them from attending meetings. It was important to keep the identities of some members secret even from others in the League."

"We had to be careful about traitors," the dracon said, his voice dropping for emphasis. "Even today, I'm not at liberty to talk about what those responsibilities entailed.

"I could be like certain others," he said, glancing in the hobbit's direction, "Who boast about their membership, but I feel it's more important that those who made the Revolution happen know my own small role in bringing freedom to humans like yourself."

The human nodded, raising his glass to the dracon.

"Bring my friend here a drink," he said to the waiter.

"It never ceases to amaze me," Zynaryxx whispered to Bill, "how many League members we must have had and just didn't know it. It seems I can't go anywhere without finding members."

"And isn't it surprising," Bill added. "how many members you had who never attended a meeting. But they all assure me that, when the word went out, they were in the forefront of those striking a blow for freedom."

"I think it's revolting," Zorth said. "Everybody in this city claims they were a member of the League in one capacity of another. You ought to publish a list. Then there'd be some red faces and a lot of explaining to be done by some people."

He looked over at the dracon for emphasis.

Zynaryxx chuckled.

"Oh, Zorth," the mage laughed. "You take all this far too seriously. I prefer that everyone think that everyone was a member of the League."

"I don't understand that at all," Nagano said. "I agree with Zorth. These impostors and pretenders cheapen the League and the achievements of the real members who fought for their lives and ours, so we could make it through the castle. It makes me sick to listen to all these liars who hid under their beds, while a few others made our efforts possible."

"You miss the point," the mage said. "The more people we have claiming to be members of the League, the more we have who publicly subscribe to the principles on which the League is founded. I hope everyone in Trillius gets a free drink from someone for their imagined exploits. The more people we have bragging about how they personally freed the humans, the more we have condemning the old regime."

"The ones who worry me," Zynaryxx said, lowering his voice. "Are the quieter ones, the ones who talk as if the old regime had the right idea but only made a few errors in judgment. They condemn the excesses, but praise the stability and the order that the Arch Regent represented."

"Some stability," Olaf sniffed. "If the Regent's host had poured out of the castle, thirsting for their blood and hungering for their very souls for nourishment, they'd have an entirely different viewpoint."

"They dismiss that as a lie spread by the League to justify the revolution," the faerie said. "That's why the League does nothing to discourage anyone who claims a role in the Revolution. I'll take any converts I can get, no matter how late they may be in coming."

"You talk as if the Revolution was only hanging on by a thread," Zorth said. "Go anywhere you want in the city, the people are still celebrating the victory."

"That's quite true," the mage said. "Right now, we enjoy widespread support from the populace. The good people of this city see it as their revolution, which is something I do all within my power to encourage. The more people we have taking credit for the revolution, the more committed supporters we have."

Orwynn brought another tray of tankards of ale to the

table. The tavernkeeper smiled as he pulled up a seat. "I never thought I'd see the day when I could sit with my customers without fear of someone informing the authorities that a human was consorting with his betters."

"You are one of the authorities now," Bill laughed.

"Ridiculous," Orwynn snorted. "This nonsense about me serving on the new council—what are they thinking? A month ago the Guildlords pretended they'd never even heard of Darktown. Now they're falling all over one another trying to find someone to represent this part of the city."

"It makes perfect sense," Zynaryxx replied. "The people of Trillius are none too happy with the Guildlords right now. They can't forget that the Guildlords served as the Arch Regent's handmaidens. The Guildlords need someone like you, a genuine hero of the revolution, a real leader of the League of the Crimson Crescent to lend them the legitimacy they need to retain some of their power."

"Hero! Leader!" Orwynn snapped. "Foolishness! That's what I say. Bill should have accepted the crown when they offered it to him. I understand them selecting you, Zynaryxx, as their advisor, but what do I know of affairs of state?"

"You're the one who rallied the people to attack the castle," the faerie responded. "Just in the nick of time, I might add. You're the one who led the League into action. You really are a hero to the people of this city."

"It should have been Bill," Orwynn grumbled. "I have a tavern to run."

"Don't be silly," Bill said. "I don't know anything about this city. They made the right choices. Besides, with the reforms you two have proposed, the Guildlords must be wondering why they ever asked you to join them."

"I consider the referendums quite mild," Zynaryxx said.

"I would have liked to have seen their faces when you proposed banning some of their more lucrative businesses," Bill grinned.

"Just the more deadly ones," the mage replied. "The Guildlords told us they wanted the city to prosper as a place for visitors to come, relax, and spend their money. I just reminded them that it's not good business when visitors disappear."

"Especially when you threatened to inform the city that some of them had secretly turned visitors over to the Arch Regent to feed her troops," Orwynn said. "If you had revealed that bit of news, it would have launched another revolution—against the Guildlords."

"A little blackmail?" Nagano asked.

"Such an indelicate term," Zynaryxx smiled. "I prefer to call it enlightened negotiation. They want to stay in business, I need some stability in Trillius while we figure out what to do next. They lost their slave business—they've lost quite a few of their businesses. But the ones who stayed have found it's in their own best interests to go along with us in exchange for our silence on a few matters of their past indiscretions."

"Indiscretions!" Zorth snapped. "My litter brother nearly lost his life to those living nightmares they were feeding. The honorable solution would have been to execute the lot of them."

"In a perfect world, we might have considered it," the mage sighed. "But instituting a reign of terror right after a revolution would serve no one's interests. We could put the slaveholders on trial, but with so many people involved with the old regime in one way or the other, we would find ourselves badly outnumbered. This way isn't quite as righteous or as tidy, but it's practical."

"Practical! Hah!" Zorth sniffed. "It is dishonorable to consort with these black-hearted rogues, much less to allow them to keep their ill-gotten booty."

"My good Zorth," Zynaryxx responded amiably. "I don't disagree with anything you say, but you miss the point. It wasn't just a handful of people who acquired ill-gotten booty. Thirty years of it corrupted far more people than you can even imagine. It's easy for us to sit in judgment today. We can look at what they did and judge it to be cowardly. But you must remember that many of these people were not so much evil themselves as they were struggling to cope with the evil that dominated their lives. It corrupted everyone and everything it touched. It crushed any who attempted to stand up to it. People made accommodations with the Regent and the black lord She served simply to survive."

"Better to die than to serve such evil," Zorth said.

"Yes, you're right," Zynaryxx said. "Those of us who felt that way can take comfort in knowing that we removed a cancer from our midst. But, our goal now must be to create the conditions for a just society, even if we must endure some injustice to make that possible."

"I don't know how you can accept that idea," Zorth said. "I don't understand politics. How can you make those kinds of compromises?"

"If we start prosecuting everyone who compromised or made an accommodation during that period, we'd be forced to put three-quarters of the city's population on trial. It's just not practical, let alone possible. When an entire society has been corrupted, you must examine why. They had no hope. The regime succeeded in stamping out any belief they may have had of ever being rescued. In their despair, they compromised to survive. Today, many of them know what they did was wrong, but they rationalize it. Everybody did it, they say. They had families to think about. They would have been killed if they had objected. There are thousands of reasons."

"And you accept all of this?" Zorth asked.

"I don't accept any of it," the mage said. "Neither do they. Deep down, they see through their own veil of justification. They are far more harsh in their judgments of themselves than we could ever be. Their friends and neighbors know their part in it. And they all have to live with what they did and didn't do. For that reason—this collective sense of guilt—this revolution will work. No one is as righteous as the re-formed sinner.

"That's why I like seeing so many of them claiming to have played such pivotal roles in the League and in the Revolution," he said. "We will receive no support stronger than from those who feel they have to prove their allegiance to our cause."

"I think you're all just trying to change the subject," Bill said.

"You aren't still talking about leaving us?" Orwynn asked. "Zynaryxx, can't you talk any sense into him. We need him here."

"I've told him that. I've told him that his place is here with us now. But I gave him my word that once we had freed this city, I would do all I could to help him return to his home. I don't intend to go back on my word to someone to whom we all owe so much.

"I just haven't figured out how to keep my vow," the mage said. "I don't know how to send him. What's worse, I don't know where to send him. This place he describes is unlike any place I've ever heard of."

"Friend Bill," Zorth said. "Among the elders of my people are some who might have knowledge that could help you. My clan stands ready to repay our debt to you. The Seven Tribes will help with your search."

"Why do you wish to return there?" Nagano asked. "I can't go back to my home. Zynaryxx convinced the Assassins' Guild to lift the bounty they had placed on my head for not fulfilling the terms of the contract the Regent had placed on you. But in exchange for my life, I've been banished from the Guild."

"They didn't have much choice," Orwynn laughed. "They realized that if the people discovered they had been trying to kill the One, the man who had freed them from the dark lord, the entire city would put a contract out on the Assassins' Guild. Besides, you wouldn't want to go back to your old line of work."

"It was an honorable calling," the ninja said stiffly.

"No doubt, I'm sure," Orwynn replied hastily. "I meant no offense."

"Orwynn just meant that an assassin leads a lonely life," Bill said. "You once told me yourself that before you joined us, you had no close friends. You said that in the Guild you were expected to keep to yourself. After all we've been through together, I can't see you going back to that kind of solitary life."

"Why not?" the ninja snapped. "You seem to be in an

awfully big hurry to leave us."

"I'm not in a hurry," he said.

"Well, what do you call it? You talk about all we've been through together in the same breath as you talk about going back to this nightmarish place you describe. What do you have waiting for you there that's so much more important to you than the friends you've made here?"

"You've helped to build a new world here," Zynaryxx said. "Look around this room. You've made this possible. We haven't swept away all the prejudices and intolerance that built up over 30 years, but we've made a bold start. We haven't yet freed the entire kingdom, but we've set a revolution in motion. We've lit the spark and fanned the flame of liberty. Certainly, that's just as noble as anything you could accomplish in your homeland."

"It's more than I could ever accomplish there," Bill said. "At home, I never accomplished much of anything."

"I doubt that, friend Bill," Zorth said. "As long as I've known you, you have always been modest to a fault. In this land of yours, I have no doubt we would hear of your heroics."

"Hardly," he said. "Back home, I doubt anyone has even noticed I've been gone."

"Then why not stay here?" "Orwynn asked. "Here, you are needed. Here, you can help to ensure that all of your work has not been in vain."

"I hadn't really thought of it that way," Bill said thoughtfully. "I just always thought that going back was something I was supposed to do."

"Do they have need of your sword?" Zorth asked.

Bill laughed, imagining the reaction he'd provoke carrying his sword down a busy street. "At home, I wouldn't be allowed to carry my sword. I guess I'd just have to hang it over my fireplace."

"Forgive me," the mook said. "It sounds like a barbarous place, unfit for a hero."

Bill's hand strayed to the hilt of his sword. As his fingers curled around it, he felt that sensation coursing up his arm, a feeling of rightness as he clenched it.

Could he hang what had become a trusted friend above a mantle? Could he resume his life, pick up where he'd left off, cook TV dinners in a bachelor pad, watch television on weekday nights?

"If you found a way to send me home, I'd probably spend the rest of my life searching for that cave," Bill said as much to himself as to the circle of friends around him.

He looked at the faces of his friends and at the friendly faces seated at other tables across the tavern. He felt more at home already.

Other Proteus Books Now Available from Prima!

The 7th Guest: A Novel $21.95
   Matthew J. Costello and
   Craig Shaw Gardner

Hell: A Cyberpunk Thriller—A Novel $5.99
   Chet Williamson

The Pandora Directive: A Tex Murphy Novel $5.99
   Aaron Conners

Star Crusader: A Novel $5.99
   Bruce Balfour

About the Author

Wizardry: The League of the Crimson Crescent may be the first work of fiction by *James E. Reagan*, the managing editor of the *Ogdensburg Journal and Advance News*, but his twenty-year writing career has ranged from true crime writing to award winning investigative reporting.

Born in Syracuse, New York, Reagan grew up in Ogdensburg, New York, a small town on the banks of the St. Lawrence River, bordering Canada.